N

CMCC
DODD

GOWDY
JOHNSON

'I think maybe you were right, Gilan,' she spluttered out. 'I've made a mistake. I should go home.'

'You're changing your mind?' he said, incredulous. 'After all that effort you put into persuading me to bring you along? Why?'

She flinched slightly. How could she tell him? How could she tell him that being this close to him sent her whole body into a flutter of excitement, of anticipation?

'I...er...well...' She shrugged her shoulders. 'I thought it was better if we carried on... that's all.'

'That's not it. You were the one who suggested we find shelter,' he pointed out.

She pursed her lips and sighed. 'If you must know, I'm not in the habit of doing things like this. Sleeping in a cave with a man I hardly know.'

He smiled, teeth flashing white in the gloom. 'Oh, don't worry,' he said. 'I'll keep well away. You're safe from me.'

Turning away from her, he returned to his horse, unbuckling the saddlebags. The lie scorched through his conscience—a flare of brilliant light.

AUTHOR NOTE

My story of Matilda and Gilan originated in a medieval tale of two sisters—wealthy heiresses in their own right, who were ultimately manoeuvred out of their fortune by the powerful men surrounding them. This was a fact of life for most medieval women: to have their lives controlled by their fathers or their husbands.

I wanted my heroine to fight against these male constraints: to be a strong, feisty woman who breaks with convention and attempts to forge her own path. Despite her wayward behaviour and his own initial reluctance, Gilan, a knight who has travelled to England with the exiled Henry of Bolingbroke, is the man who helps her. She achieves her goal—and wins a handsome knight at the same time!

INNOCENT'S CHAMPION

Meriel Fuller

First published in Great Britain 2014
by Mills & Boon, an imprint of Harlequin (UK) Limited,
Large Print edition 2015
Harlequin (UK) Limited, Eton House, 18-24 Paradise Road,
Richmond, Surrey TW9 1SR

© 2014 Meriel Fuller

ISBN: 978-0-263-25540-9

Meriel Fuller lives in a quiet corner of rural Devon, England, with her husband and two children. Her early career was in advertising, with a bit of creative writing on the side. Now, with a family to look after, writing has become her passion... A keen interest in literature, the arts and history, particularly the early medieval period, makes writing historical novels a pleasure. The Devon countryside, a landscape rich in medieval sites, holds many clues to the past and has made her research a special treat.

Previous novels by the same author:

CONQUEST BRIDE
THE DAMSEL'S DEFIANCE
THE WARRIOR'S PRINCESS BRIDE
CAPTURED BY THE WARRIOR
HER BATTLE-SCARRED KNIGHT
THE KNIGHT'S FUGITIVE LADY

Chapter One

Summer 1399—south-west England

'**W**hat *is* that? On the bottom of your gown? Actually, *my* gown.' Katherine's peevish tones emerged, shrill, from the shadowed interior of the covered litter. Striding alongside, Matilda slackened her brisk pace at the sound of her sister's voice, glancing down at the hem of her skirts. In the cloying heat of the afternoon, the heavily pleated silk bodice stuck to the skin around her chest and shoulders; the high neck, buttoned tightly around her throat to the pale curve of her chin, made her feel constricted, trapped. Her sister had insisted she wear the elaborate gown, with a light-blue cloak to match, indicating with turned-down mouth that none of Matilda's clothing were suitable for visiting the Shrine of Our Lady at Worlebury.

'Well?' Katherine addressed her shrewishly,

peering out from between the patterned curtains. 'Oh, God Lord, stop bouncing me so!' she snapped at the servants who each shouldered a wooden strut of the litter, one on each corner, endeavouring to carry their lady as carefully as possible along the rutted track. Katherine sank back into the padded cushions, her face grey-toned and wan, the rounded dome of her stomach protruding upwards into the gloom.

Matilda twisted one way, then the other, trying to spot the problem with the gown. The smooth blue silk of the skirts billowed out from below a jewelled belt set high on her narrow waist. One of the knights in the service of her brother-in-law, riding up front on a huge glossy destrier, smirked beneath his chain-mail hood, before he snapped his gaze smartly forwards once more. *Let him laugh,* thought Matilda. She was used to being told off by her older sister and paid little heed to it. Katherine was suffering greatly in this late stage of pregnancy and this heavy, torpid heat wasn't helping matters.

'It's nothing,' she called to Katherine. 'A lump of sticky burr, snagged on the hem.' Reaching down, she pulled at the clump of green trailing weed, throwing it to the side of the track. The dark chestnut silk of her hair, firmly pulled into two plaited rolls on either side of her neat head, gleamed in the sunlight filtering through the trees. A fine silver net covered her intricate hairstyle, secured with a narrow silver circlet.

'Come and sit in with me, Matilda, please.' A nervous desperation edged her sister's voice as she stuck her head out between the thick velvet curtains that afforded her some privacy within the litter. Her face looked puffy, skin covered with a waxy gleam that emphasised the violet shadows beneath her eyes. Matilda glanced at the sun's position, thick light pouring down through the beech trees lining the route. The fresh green leaves bobbed in the slight breeze, lifting occasionally to send brilliant shafts of illumination straight down to touch the hardened earth of the track. It hadn't rained for weeks.

'If I climb in, it will only slow us down, Katherine,' Matilda answered. One of the servants carrying the front of the litter mopped his face with his sleeve. 'We're almost at the river now. It's not far from there.' Guilt scythed through her as she saw the panic touch Katherine's worried blue eyes. 'Here, I'll walk closer, alongside you.' Matilda reached out and grasped her sister's hand, shocked by how cold and limp it felt. 'Are you quite well?' she said sharply.

The jewelled net covering Katherine's hair sparkled as she nodded slowly. 'I can feel the baby kicking inside me,' she whispered. 'That's a good sign, isn't it?'

'It is,' Matilda replied, with more conviction than she felt. The cold sweat from Katherine's fingers soaked her palm. From the haunted look in her eyes, Matilda knew her sister was remembering that awful time before. And the time before that.

'Do you think our prayers will work? Do you think I've done enough?'

Matilda nodded, throwing her sister a quick reassuring smile. She certainly hoped so. She wasn't sure Katherine could endure another fruitless labour, another baby born that failed to live, to breathe. John, Katherine's husband, had insisted they visit the shrine as often as possible, providing them with a litter, servants and two household knights as escort. He was determined that this pregnancy would be successful. He needed an heir. A male heir.

Worry trickled through her; she kicked at a loose stone beneath her leather boot, sending it spinning into the long grass at the side of the track. Although Katherine was four years older, and a married woman, Matilda often felt as if she were the more mature sibling, looking out for her sister, protecting her. All day she had watched Katherine, crouched awkwardly on the hard, iron-coloured stone of the chapel, muttering her prayers, calling on the Virgin Mary to grant her a successful labour, tears running down her perfect, beautiful face. Matilda had had to help her to her feet, almost dragging her away from the carved wooden effigy; it was as if Katherine wanted to stay there for ever, as if the longer she stayed, the more chance she would have of a successful labour.

Matilda reached out and touched Katherine's shoulder, a gesture of support. The raised embroidery of her sister's gown rubbed against her fingertips. 'Your baby will be born soon and he will be fine. You must stop fretting, Katherine...'

'What will John do to me if...?'

'You mustn't think like that.' Matilda gripped Katherine's fingers tightly. She must say the things that Katherine wanted to hear, even if she didn't believe them herself. 'John loves you...'

'I need to stop...now.' Katherine's voice had taken on a new urgency, her eyes flicking up, searching Matilda's face for understanding. She hunched forwards over her swollen stomach. 'Earlier...I had too much to drink.'

Matilda signalled to the servants to lower the litter, then grabbed Katherine's upper arm to haul her out. 'No, stay here,' she ordered the men, who, relieved of the heavy weight on their shoulders, stretched out their arms to alleviate the soreness in their tired muscles.

'My lady…?' One of the knights dismounted. 'I should come with you…' he offered dubiously, his gaze sliding quickly over Katherine's stomach bulging out beneath the waistband of her gown.

Honestly, these men, thought Matilda, noting the young soldier's reddening features. They treated pregnancy as if it were a disease! Something to be ashamed of, despite the fact it was the most natural thing in the world. She knew that the growing baby increased the amount of times Katherine needed to visit the garderobe, and when there was no garderobe available…well, the shelter of the trees and shrubs would have to do.

Leaning into the litter, Matilda seized her bow, shouldering the quiver full of arrows. She caught the glancing grin of a servant as he eyed the curved wood of her weapon. Let them think what they like, she thought irritably. It never hurt for a lady to know how to defend herself, especially one with her own precarious domestic arrangements.

'No need, we'll not be long. We'll go over that little bridge, into that ruin behind the trees.' Matilda pointed out a low-lying packhorse bridge spanning the river's swift flow and the tumbled stones of a collapsed tower. She tucked her arm through Katherine's and the two sisters walked together with a laboured, ambling pace through the soft, swaying grasses of the riverside.

Their progress up the steep cobbled surface of the bridge was slow; Katherine's face reddened, sheened with sweat. 'This heat, this heat affects me so,' she gasped, as she reached the apex of the bridge. Pausing, she bent forwards, pressing one hand against the rickety parapet, her scalloped-edge sleeve falling in a graceful arc against the warm stone.

'Why not take your cloak off?' Matilda suggested, eyeing the rectangle of red silk-velvet that fell back from Katherine's shoulders. It matched her own cloak of light blue, fastened across the neck with a fine silver chain and secured with a pearl clasp on one shoulder.

Katherine shuddered, fixing her sister with a horrified glance. 'To be seen in public without a cloak? Are you out of your mind? Really, Matilda, you have no sense of propriety!'

Matilda shrugged her shoulders. 'I only thought it would make you cooler,' she replied. 'You shouldn't be travelling at all, at this stage of your pregnancy. I'm surprised that John—'

'It was he that insisted upon it!' Katherine interrupted. 'You know what he's like...'

Yes, thought Matilda. She knew what John was like. Arrogant and overbearing, with a short, irascible temper, he was unbearable at the best of times and ten times worse if things didn't go the way he wanted. On his marriage to Katherine, he had made no secret of his joy at inheriting one half of the Lilleshall fortune: the castle at Neen and its vast tracts of fertile pasture. Now, it seemed, this was not enough for him; he had begun to drop very large hints about how he should be controlling the other half, the manor and estates of Lilleshall itself, still in the possession of Matilda and Katherine's mother.

As Matilda steered her sister carefully down the other side of the bridge and into the shadowed privacy behind the toppled stones of the tower, Katherine clutched at her arm, her long fingers surprisingly strong. 'You will stay with me, Matilda? Until I give birth? I need you to be there with me at Neen...do you promise?'

'Katherine, you know I have to return to Lilleshall... I cannot promise that I will be there all the time.'

Lifting her skirts above the fallen stones to pick her way through the jumbled mass, Katherine pinned angry eyes on her sister. 'Only because our useless mother refuses to do what she's supposed to do!'

'Katherine, that's not fair! You know how she's been since Father died.' Matilda raised one hand to an errant curl of dark chestnut hair, tucking it back behind her ear. 'I have to go back, to make sure the estate is running properly. You know that.'

'Aye,' Katherine whispered, her lumpy figure lurching with a curious side-to-side motion across the moss-covered stones. 'I'm sorry, I know how our mother suffers. It's only that I'm so worried about this baby...'

'I will stay with you as much as I can.' Matilda patted her hand. But to her own ears, her voice sounded hollow. There was so much to do at Lilleshall at this time of year; although the crops had been planted and were growing well in this hot weather, she now had to turn her attention to the early harvests.

'Can they see me?' Bunching her skirts about her knees, Katherine made her way awkwardly into the undergrowth behind the tower, bristly thistles scratching at the delicate embroidery of her skirts. Butterflies fluttered lazily through the wild, verdant growth: the feathery purple grass heads, red sorrel gathered in scrappy clusters, the yellow-fringed hawkbit flower.

'Wait. Let me check.' Leaving her sister, Matilda placed one foot on a crumbling staircase that ran diagonally upwards across a section of wall, and peeked out at their escort. Two of the servants had taken the opportunity to sit on the dried earth, setting their tired backs against the framework of the litter. One chewed idly at a piece of long grass, drawing the freshness from the end of the stem. She caught a ribald chuckle from one of the knights, his head bent as he listened to the other, no doubt telling some bawdy tale.

'They can't see us.' Matilda laughed softly, tripping gracefully back down the steps. 'We're well hidden here.'

Squatting down, Katherine closed her eyes in relief.

Matilda helped her to her feet and Katherine adjusted her gown. 'How do I look?' Katherine asked once she had straightened up, her eyes narrowing across the bulk of her belly.

Matilda set her head on one side, a teasing smile lifting the corners of her mouth. 'How do you look? You're asking me?' she declared in mock horror. 'Since when do you trust my judgement on appearance?'

Katherine drifted one wan hand across her fore-head. 'Don't tease, Matilda. You know how John likes me to look my best. Is anything amiss?'

'You look perfect, as always,' Matilda reassured her. Her sister's sable hair maintained a neat, rigid parting, twisted into two identical knots either side of her head. All the buttons that secured the tight neck of her gown were in place, straight. Not a speck of dirt, leaves or travel dust stained the finely woven red material of Katherine's gown. It was a source of constant surprise to their mother that, despite being so physically similar, the two sisters could not have been more different in character and their approach to life. Where Katherine was neat, Matilda was messy, untidy. Where Katherine was demure, simpering, Matilda was argumenta-tive, stubborn.

A shout split the air: the outraged roar of a man.

Shocked by the harsh, guttural sound, Matilda grabbed Katherine's arm, listening intently.

Then came a sickening sound of splintering wood, of clashing metal. From the other side of the river, the knights cursed, rough voices raised in alarm.

'Oh, God!' Katherine sagged in Matilda's hold, her eyes wide and fearful. 'What's going on?'

Through the dry, heavy air came the distinctive

whirr of an arrow. Then another, travelling straight and true. Matilda knew the sound, was familiar with it. Icy fear slicked her heart.

'Wait here!' She skipped up the steps once more, cloak and gown trailing behind her, the lightweight silk dragging against the coarse-cut stone. From the vantage point at the top, leaves casting dappled shade across her pale, worried face, she watched in horror as one knight toppled sideways from his horse, gripping his shoulder in agony. Blood poured from between his fingers, soaking his sur-coat. Wheeling his horse around, the other knight drew his sword, flicking his eyes around, searching for their attackers. The servants, realising what was happening, started shouting and running around haphazardly, delving frantically in the litter for the one or two weapons they had brought to defend themselves.

'Matilda…? What is it?' Katherine was on her feet now, standing at the bottom of the steps, one arm bent protectively around her stomach.

'Ssh! Stay down!' A horrible weakness sapped the strength in Matilda's knees; her fingers drove into the shattered limestone of the tower, searching for purchase, for equilibrium. She spun away from the open space that had once been a window and flattened herself against the wall, heart thumping in her chest. 'The knights… They're being attacked!' she whispered urgently. 'Katherine, get away from here! You need to hide!'

'But you…?'

Matilda held up her bow. 'I will hold them off as long as possible. You must get away from here, Katherine. Now. Find somewhere safe.'

With a practised flick of the reins, Gilan, Comte de Cormeilles, slowed his gleaming destrier to a walk, urging the animal towards the group of knights gathered at the river's edge. Beneath the heavy metal breastplate, his skin prickled with sweat. He longed to rip it off. Steel plates dragged at his muscled arms; his fingers itched within his gauntlets. Pulling them off, he threw them to the ground, then lifted his hands to unstrap his helmet, resting it on the horse's neck. The quiet breeze sifted through his hair, lifting the bright, corn-coloured strands, cooling his hot scalp. His piercing, metallic gaze swept the area where they had stopped, eyes set deep within thick, black lashes.

'Fancy a swim?' Henry, Duke of Lancaster, strode towards him across the soggy, hoof-marked mud, his short, stocky body moving with an unexpected grace. Several knights had already divested themselves of their armour, the glinted steel discarded messily on the ground amidst the horses. Now they plunged into the fast-flowing river with shouts of glee, scooping up handfuls of clear, sparkling water and splashing each other, like children.

Gilan handed his helmet down to one of the soldiers. The burnished metal glowed in the afternoon sun. He frowned down at Henry. 'Are you certain we have time? There are still several hours of daylight left.'

Henry grinned. 'The men are tired, Gilan. Not everyone can keep going as long as you can. And by my judgement it will take only a couple of more days to reach our destination. Let's rest here tonight and move on in the morning.'

Gilan shrugged his shoulders, nodded. Whatever Henry's decision was, it made little difference to him. Eventually, he would have to go back to his parents' home, but he was happy to delay that return as long as possible. Unconsciously, he kneaded the muscles in his thigh, trying to ease the ache in the scarred tissue. He swung his leg over the horse's rump, dismounted.

'You push yourself too hard,' Henry said, clapping his friend on the back. 'Most of my men are not in as good a shape as you. I have to make sure you don't run them into the ground, so they are useless when it comes to finding King Richard.'

'As long as we keep our wits about us, Henry.' Gilan watched the knights in the water through narrowed silver eyes. 'This is hostile country, remember.'

'How can I forget?' Henry replied, the smile slipping from his face. He stuck one hand through the russet-gold strands of his hair. 'Banished to France by my own cousin, the king, just so he could grab at my fortune with his grubby little hands.'

'Which is why we are here.' Gilan grinned, white teeth flashing within his smile. 'To grab it back.' Gathering up his reins, he moved towards the water's edge, pushing aside the jostling, sweating horseflesh to gain access. His stallion's head nudged at his shoulder, keen to reach the water. Some of the knights had moved out into the middle of the river now, swimming properly in the stronger, deeper current, but others had climbed out, undergarments dripping around their knees, drying themselves on the large squares of linen extracted from their saddle-bags. Farther along the river, where the flow narrowed between higher banks to cut through the meadow, swallows flicked low, catching at the flying insects above the water.

The wet mud at the water's edge darkened the travel-stained leather of Gilan's calf-length boots, oozing up around the soles. Henry appeared at his side, barrel chest clad only in a white shirt, loose drawers flapping about his legs. 'Are you sure you don't want to come in?' he asked again.

Gilan shook his head. 'Later.' His arm jerked sharply down as the horse pulled against the reins, desperate to drink. A cluster of mosquitoes danced crazily above the water's surface and he slapped at his neck, irritably.

A hoarse scream rent the sticky air. Then another. The sound barged incongruously into the torpid languor of the afternoon.

Gilan dropped his reins immediately, lean, tanned fingers seizing the jewelled hilt of his sword, drawing it with a long, steely hiss. 'You, and you—' he jabbed his finger at a couple of knights standing by the river, still fully clothed '—come with me, now.'

Henry had already turned, was clambering back out of the water. 'No, you stay here,' Gilan growled at him. 'I am dispensable. You are not.'

Despite the significant weight of his breastplate, Gilan ran surprisingly quickly for a large man, the sturdy length of his legs pacing along the track with the strength and agility of a cat, his step fast and sure. Moving swiftly away from the sunlit bank where they had stopped, he and the two other knights followed the river upstream to the point where it ran into woodland: large beech trees trailed delicate branches into the water like brilliant hair braids, tickling the mirrored surface. With no time to seize his helmet, his thick golden hair shone out from the shadowed gloom beneath the trees, where the air pressed in choking layers, ominous, vaguely threatening.

Was it only a couple of months since he and Henry had forged their way through the frozen Lithuanian forests? Slashed back the impenetrable undergrowth where no horse could make progress, felled the brambles and the spent nettles, fixed in ice? Sometimes the snow had been so deep that their horses were forced to plough through man-made trenches, picking their way through towering walls of snow. He had relished that hardship, the impossible landscape that they had to work around, those icy, hostile conditions. They suited him, suited his current frame of mind after... He shook his head smartly, dispelling his thoughts. A wave of grief crested through him, but he clamped it down. Nay, he would not think of that now.

Crouching into the bank, Gilan rammed a broad, muscled shoulder into a bunch of glossy ferns growing high and indicated with a quick, decisive handsignal that his knights should do the same. Up ahead, he could see a covered litter set upon the ground, patterned curtains fluttering outwards in the warm air, like spent butterfly wings. A soldier lay sprawled in the dirt, his face white-grey, his hand pressed against his shoulder; despite his motionless appearance, Gilan could see his eyes were beginning to open. And beyond this fallen knight, other men were fighting, scuffling, hands at each other's throats, swords swinging, their grunting efforts rising hoarsely.

Springing away from the bank, Gilan jumped towards them, raising the sparkling blade of his sword before him with a roar, and hurled himself into the writhing, spitting mass. Grabbing one man round the neck, he pulled him out of the fray, kicking him in the back of the shins so that he buckled easily.

'Kneel. Hands on the back of your head where I can see them.' He signalled to one of his knights to keep guard, his voice guttural, harsh, barking orders.

'It was them, they attacked us!' the man was babbling, as he fell to his knees in the soft dirt.

An arrow whistled past Gilan, quiver feathers whispering against his ear. It stuck into the earth opposite him, the shaft bouncing violently with the force of the shot. Too close! He whirled angrily, searching for the archer. A shot like that could only have come from some distance, so someone was watching them from afar. His eyes swept along the river, through the sibilant trees and bulky trunks to a small stone bridge, a crumbling wall of loose stones blotched with orangey-yellow lichen.

And the glint of an arrowhead, peeking out from a high spot on the ruined tower.

His knights were bringing the fight to a close. Already three men were on the ground, hands bound behind their backs, heads bent, subdued. One more man to bring down and his situation appeared increasingly precarious. Gilan sank back into the shadows, using the substantial tree trunks as cover. His boots made no sound as he crept through the waist-high cow parsley, his legs brushing against the delicate, white-lace flowers. Crossing by the bridge was no good, being in full view of the tower. He would slink back along the path, cross the river at a lower point. The element of surprise had always served him well.

Chapter Two

Bracing her body against the thick stone, Matilda reached up to extract another arrow from the narrow bag on her back. Adrenaline rattled through her veins; her hands shook so much she was finding it difficult to shoot straight. Her trembling limbs skewed her aim. But every time she peered around the wall, there seemed to be more men down there! The gang's reinforcements had obviously arrived, armed with swords and short daggers, big and fearsome looking, some even wearing armour that they no doubt had filched from somewhere. For one tiny moment, she considered the possibility of running, of running and hiding with her sister. But the thought of cowering behind a tree trunk, waiting for the thugs to finally catch up with them, seemed a far worse situation than the one she was in right now, tackling the problem head-on. Fine, she might lose, but at least she had tried.

She had missed that last shot, but he wouldn't be so lucky next time, that huge ruffian who'd appeared from nowhere, with his wild thatch of blond hair. Drawing air deep into her lungs, Matilda fought to control her breathing, the reckless thump in her chest. How many times had she practised, how many times had she drawn back the gut string and sighted an arrow on the target since her brother, Thomas, had given her this bow? But her days and days of endless practising had not prepared her for the real thing. How could she have known that her heart would beat in panic; that her knees would weaken and quiver with nerves at the sight of their household knights falling to the ground; that her fingers would shake uncontrollably as she fitted the arrow up to the bowstring? Her own cowardice conspired against her. Gritting her teeth, she prayed that Katherine had found a good hiding place.

Lifting the bow, she set the arrow in a horizontal line from the edge of her ear, training the point down into the chaotic scene of fighting below, moving her shoulder fractionally to pinpoint an enemy target. The arrow shaft was warm against her cheek.

'You there! Stop!' The harsh command hit her

like a blow, a deep guttural voice slicing through the air.

In shock, she jolted forwards, the loosened arrow dropping, bouncing down across the tumble of stones to the deep water below. She whirled around, aghast, horrified. A man was running towards her, advancing swiftly. She staggered back in fright, her feet snagging in the bunched train of her gown, heels clipping the low edge of stone. Her bow clattered down on the rickety steps. In a vain attempt to balance herself, her slim arms flew out, like the wings of an angel, scrabbling futilely at the sides of the window to prevent herself falling.

'No!' Matilda wailed, a terrified, drawn-out howl, as her body tipped backwards, toes losing contact with the rubble-strewn step. She had the briefest impression of sunlit hair, diamond eyes, of a cloak billowing out from broad shoulders as the man sped up towards her.

She fell.

Gathered skirts rippled around her slender form as she flew gracefully through the air, her cloak spreading like a vast wing behind her, before she smacked the cold water below with a sharp, outraged cry. The bag of arrows loosened from her shoulder, drifted off in the current of water, downstream.

'Hell's teeth!' Gilan cursed, turning and running back out of the tower. Momentarily blinded by the sun, all he had seen was the blurry outline of a figure poised to shoot, and the shining glint of the arrow. Shouting up, he had assumed the archer to be a man. But when the figure turned and screamed with high-pitched girlishness, he had realised his mistake. The archer was a woman.

Guilt flooded through him; he squashed it down as he vaulted the collapsed boundary wall. Man or woman, it didn't change the fact that the archer had been determined to stick an arrow between his shoulder blades. Determined to kill him. He charged through the swaying grass at the edge of the river and waded in, eyes focused on the concentric circles of water where the maid had disappeared. Water soaked his boots, the dun-coloured wool of his chausses. Luckily, he chose not to wear plate armour on his legs, which would have weighed him down. Beneath the surface he could see blue cloth shimmering, swirling in the current, and the pale gleam of skin rising up. A neat head bobbed up in the warm, summer air, coughing and gasping, water sluicing across a sweet, heart-shaped face that shone like alabaster. Small hands flayed out, trying to float, to swim, before she sank again beneath the glittering water.

He propelled himself forwards, digging his arms down into the crystal-clear liquid, scooping his hands beneath the girl's armpits and hauling up the spitting, screeching mass of femininity. The sound clashed in his ears, an ear-splitting cater-wauling that made his brain ache. He winced as her screams crested over him, holding the maid's lissom weight at arm's length, wondering if she was ever going to stop. Coils of sable hair looped crazily on each side of her head, several silver pins threatening to dislodge; her dress and cloak clung to her like a second skin, emphasising the firm, delectable curve of her bosom, the narrow curve of her waist.

'Let…go…of me!' she spluttered, huge blue eyes scorched with fury. 'You barbarian!' She swung one bunched fist in his direction, her arm swinging woefully short of its intended destination. The gleam of his breastplate mocked her.

'Stop this!' he bellowed at her. The taut lines of his face were rigid, hard.

Hampered by great swathes of wet, sticky material, her arms flailed towards him, struck out at the tanned, handsome features, the grey-coloured eyes, as she wriggled violently, arching back against his hold.

'Stop right now!' he warned again, eyes darkening to smouldering pewter. 'Otherwise I will drop you.'

Blood roared in her ears, blotting out his words. *Oh, Lord, he's going to kill me,* Matilda thought, panic flooding her solar plexus. She had to get away from him! Thrashing about in his arms, churning her legs through the water as if she were running, she fought against the brute's imprisoning grip. Who knew what this strong-armed bully had in store for her? Rape, or a knife in her side? She had no intention of finding out.

She lunged forwards, fear giving her strength. Her sharp fingernails made contact with one hard cheekbone, slicing across his skin. A single line of blood appeared, oozing down the shadowed cleft of his cheek.

'Why, you little...' Stunned by the maid's temerity, unprepared for her attack, Gilan loosened his grip on the floundering, squirming woman.

He let her drop.

Watched as she sank below the surface once more, her screeching outrage silenced. So be it. Let the little spitfire learn her lesson the difficult way, he thought, arms crossed smugly across his breastplate. He would wait here until she ran out of breath, until she was forced to take in air. And he would be ready for her.

As the cool, limpid water closed over her head, Matilda held her breath, moving her arms in a wide arc in an attempt to swim away from him, underwater. But her extravagant gown, her cloak, with their yards and yards of fabric, dragged her down, the sodden material acting like lead weights on her legs, pulling at her feet, her hips, making any forward movement impossible. Her own clothes hobbled her. She wanted to weep at the sheer futility of her efforts.

Defeated, she drifted down, knees resting on the river's stony bottom, the tiny, brilliant pebbles poking sharply into her shins. How long would he wait? A peculiar heat burned the lining of her lungs, eroding her capacity to breathe; through the clear water she could see the man's legs encased in well-fitting chausses, brawny muscle roping his thighs, boots planted sturdily astride. He would grow bored soon, surely, and go away. The water flowed across her face and neck, soothing her skin, and her mind began to dance, strange flickering lights pulsing across the darkness of her inner mind.

'God's teeth!' Gilan cursed, swiftly realising that the maid had no intention of surfacing again. He reached for her, big thumbs gouging into the soft flesh of her armpits as he hauled her up from the depths. 'Do you truly want to drown?' he shouted at her, his strong fingers gripping beneath her shoulders. What was the maid playing at?

Her body was limp, head hanging forwards so that it drooped towards his chest, her soaking hair dripping water across his breastplate. Her silver circlet tilted crazily, the net that secured the coils of her hair hanging down like limp lace, stuck to her ashen cheeks. 'Oh, for Heaven's sake!' he exclaimed, sweeping one hand beneath her knees so the length of her body was shoved up high against his chest. The faintest smell of lavender rose to his nostrils, the delicate scent of her wet skin. Her head lolled back crazily against his shoulder, loosened hair straggling down across the pleated fall of his cloak.

Sloshing towards the bank, the generous arc of her hem sweeping through the shallows, he carried the maid easily. Despite the amount of water absorbed by her clothes, she weighed nothing, fragile in his arms. Kneeling down carefully, he tipped her onto the bank, where the grass grew long and lush. He bent his head to her mouth, catching the flimsy shift of air against his cheek. So the chit was alive, in spite of her best efforts to drown herself.

Black lashes fanned down over pale cheeks, thick lashes spiked with delicate drops of water, diamonds clinging to velvet feathers. Her face was a delicate oval, devoid of any colour. A small sigh escaped her lips; she moved her head restlessly against the hot grass. Beside them, crickets clicked and whirred.

'Come on,' he ordered briskly, cupping his hand around one narrow shoulder, shaking her gently. Faced with the barely conscious maid, he felt awkward, at a loss as to how to treat her. He spent most of his time in the company of other soldiers, pitting his wits against the elements and the enemy. It was a harsh life, unforgiving, but infinitely preferable to lounging around at the royal courts, flirting with the ladies and eating sweetmeats.

But now, one of those ladies lay prone at his feet, her small-boned frame pillowed in the lush, verdant grass. He hadn't the faintest idea what to do with her. She was of noble stock; her hair was elaborately styled and her clothes were of silk, intricately embroidered; expensive gemstones studded her jewelled belt. A couple of pearl buttons at her neck had come adrift; the gaping fabric exposed a frantic pulse beating against her throat: white skin, translucent, fragile. His eyes tracked down to her mouth, the beautiful full curve of her bottom lip, stained with a delicate rose colour. His senses jolted, a warm feeling curling across his midriff. He frowned.

'Wake up!' he said, louder this time. 'I'm not going to hurt you.' How had he even managed to become caught up in this mess? He should have ignored the shouts, turned his back on the situation. Henry would be along in a moment to see what was keeping him. He swallowed the thought that the maid was fortunate not to have been killed; if she hadn't fallen, he would have run her through with his sword, thinking her to be a man. She was lucky to be alive.

Her eyelids fluttered open; she observed him hazily for a moment. Her eyes were blue, enormous in her oval face, the lilac-blue of forget-me-nots. Limpid eyes, stunning.

Desire surged through him. Shocked, he sat back abruptly on his heels, tamping down the lurch of pleasure, annoyed with himself, annoyed at his body's response. With her hair dishevelled and her gown askew, the maid was a mess, with a shrewish tongue as well, if her reaction to him in the river was anything to go by. And yet his body had responded to her like a callow youth in the first flush of romance. He was at a loss to explain it.

Her gaze sharpened, turning to an expression of sheer terror, her pupils dilating in fright as she remembered where she was, who he was. She opened her mouth.

'No!' He held up his hands, palms flat. 'No, please don't scream. Not again. I told you I'm not going to hurt you!'

Spine pressed back into lumpy ground, Matilda focused on the stern lines of the man's face, the forbidding slash of his mouth, his tousled hair. He looked like a Viking of old, a barbarian who had waded in from the longships, raiding and ransacking everything in their path. An expanse of grey metal plate covered his huge chest; his arms were covered in flexible chain mail. Impenetrable eyes, the colour of rain-washed granite, bore into her.

Breath punched from her lungs in fear; she shook her head from side to side. 'No, I…don't…believe… you,' she managed to stutter out. The cold stickiness of her clothes seeped into her bones. 'You're going to kill me, aren't you?' Her voice rose, wobbling, on a wave of shrill hysteria.

To her surprise, the man lifted his chin and laughed. The sun caught the rich wheat colour of his hair, augmenting the vigorous strands to shining gold. 'Believe me, if I was going to kill you, I would have done it by now.'

Well, that was reassuring. Lying prone and limp beneath his intimidating perusal, Matilda glared at him, chewing at her bottom lip, unsure. She needed to sit up, stand up and face him, eye to eye, but right at this moment, a debilitating weakness sapped her strength, made her muscles floppy. What was the matter with her?

'What were you playing at, shooting at us like that?' Kneeling at her side, the man spoke with the cool, modulated tones of the nobility, and his clothes, despite being travel-worn, were of good quality.

'You attacked us!' she hissed, trying to stop her teeth from chattering. Pressing her hands back into the grass, she struggled into a seated position. It was a mistake. With this hulk of a man right next to her, his rough-hewn features and exquisitely carved mouth were on a level with her own, too close! She shifted her hips, straining her body backwards to create a bigger space between them. His nearness unsettled her. 'You attacked defenceless women, attacked our knights, our servants!'

'Not me, not us.' He shook his head, blond hair falling across his temple. The hood of his hauberk, which he wore beneath his breastplate, gathered in glittering metallic folds behind his head, emphasising the corded strength of his neck. 'We heard the screams and came running. You're fortunate that we did, otherwise something worse than falling in the river might have happened to you.' His piercing grey eyes swept the length of her shuddering body, from her glossy silken hair, past her neat waist, to her diminutive feet in soft leather slippers peeking out from beneath her gown.

Matilda flushed, heated colour flooding her cheeks beneath his diamond stare. His eyes were like silver coins. She tilted her chin downwards, setting her mouth in a fixed stubborn line. The insinuation was unmistakable and she hated him for it. 'It would never have come to that,' she stated, trying to inject some confidence into her voice, drawing her spine up straight. 'Someone would have stopped them, either our knights...or me.'

'You?' He tilted his head to one side, a small smile playing across his generous mouth. His tanned skin was flushed from the sun, emphasising the taut hollows beneath his high cheekbones. 'But you were floundering in the river.'

'Only because you made me fall!' Her voice rang out with accusation. 'You're on my gown,' she croaked out irritably, tugging at her skirts. 'Can you move, please?'

Gilan looked down at his knees planted firmly in the expanse of blue, very wet, velvet silk. He didn't move. 'Is that all you have to say for yourself? Most people would be thanking me, and my men, for what we did back there.'

'You nearly drowned me, or have you forgotten?' She folded her arms high across her chest, trying to keep her shivers hidden from his predatory gaze.

He quirked one eyebrow at her. 'Forgive me, my lady, but from the way you lurched back from my hold, I think you were trying to drown yourself.'

'I thought you were one of them,' she mumbled, plucking at a loose silver thread that had come adrift from the belt around her ribcage. Her fingernails were pale pink, like the polished interior of a shell.

'What were you thinking of, shooting like that? You had a perfect hiding place, why did you not keep quiet? Wait until those men had gone?'

Her blue eyes flashed up at him. 'Because I wanted to help. I could help. I can shoot as well as any man.' Hands pooled in her lap, Matilda laced her fingers together, trying to stop them trembling.

Gilan raised his eyebrows at her bold words, surprised. Why, he had never heard a woman speak thus, with such a sense of pride in her own ability. She was a good shot, too, he thought grudgingly, remembering the hiss of the arrow past his head. He narrowed his eyes suddenly, noting the telltale shake of her shoulders beneath the countless pleats of her bodice, the blueness around her lips.

'You're freezing,' he announced bluntly. 'Do you live hereabouts?' Rising swiftly to his feet, he stepped off her gown. Matilda pulled at it hurriedly, gathering the voluminous folds around her slim legs. Why did he not just go away? He made her feel vulnerable, exposed, as if her own efforts had all been in vain. He towered over her, big shoulders blocking out the sun, dark blue cloak swinging down to his knees, emblazoned with small golden fleur-de-lis.

Golden fleur-de-lis? Her heart flipped dangerously, warning her, a small pucker of skin pleating between her dark eyebrows. 'Do you ride with the king?'

He grinned down at her pale, worried face. 'No, the complete opposite. I ride with the man who intends to push him from the throne.'

'Henry of Lancaster,' she whispered.

'Correct.' Gilan nodded. Insects buzzed and whirred in the tall grass, the sound soporific in the pressing heat of the afternoon.

Matilda's heart lurched, fear scything through her. She would have to be careful. They would all have to be careful. Katherine and her husband were staunch supporters of King Richard, and by association with them, so was she. She was certain Henry of Lancaster would not take kindly to such a kinship, so the sooner she was away from this man, this formidable stranger, the better. She lifted one hand to her forehead and pushed distractedly at the silver net which seemed to drag lopsidedly over one ear.

'I said, do you live hereabouts?'

Really, he talked to her as if she were a dim-witted peasant! But with her flesh prickling uncomfortably with river water, and her mind fuddled by his overbearing presence, she was finding it difficult to concentrate. She breathed in deeply, trying to gain some control over her tattered senses. 'Yes, yes, we do. We were on our way home when we were attacked.'

'We?' He raised one dark blond eyebrow.

'My sister and I.' She clapped her fingers over her horrified mouth. 'Oh, Lord… Katherine!'

Gilan arched one thick blond eyebrow, the tanned skin around his eyes crinkling. 'There's another one of you?'

'I have to fetch her!' Bending her knees, Matilda struck both feet firmly against the ground, struggling against the wet, sticky material in an attempt to rise.

'Allow me.' His voice curled over her, a low,

seductive rumble. Leaning down, he seized her icy fingers in his bearlike grip, catapulting her upwards in one swift movement. There was nothing gentle about his offer of help: one moment she was sitting on the ground, legs outstretched before her, the next she was on her feet, teetering dangerously at his side. His fingers remained around her hand, steadying her.

'You can let go now,' she said, her voice prim. Anything to remove his compelling touch from her body. 'I'm fine.'

'You don't look fine.' He studied the shadowed patches beneath her eyes, noted the rapid pulse beneath the skin of her neck. 'You look like you're about to collapse in a heap.'

'Well, I'm not,' she snapped, wrestling her hand away from his hold. 'I'm stronger than I look.' She caught the supercilious raise of his eyebrows; he didn't believe her! 'I need to find my sister, that's all. I told her to hide when those men came and not to come out until I called her.'

'Call her, then.' His silver eyes scanned the tumbled-down tower, the lumps of stone covered with moss and lichen, the dense forest of trees behind, and he sighed. How long was this going to take?

Chapter Three

Matilda ran a slender finger between her neck and the high collar of her gown, trying to relieve the uncomfortable sensation of wet fabric against flesh: an unconscious movement. In the strong heat of the afternoon, her looped-up hair dried rapidly, curling tresses pulling against silver hairpins. She attempted to pat some of the pins back into place, to adjust the net that held her hair in place. She supposed she must look awful.

Lifting her chin, she called out to her sister. Her clear, bell-like tones cut across the torpid languor of the afternoon. 'Katherine!' she shouted, holding up her weighty skirts so she could manoeuvre over the stones. 'You can come out now, we're safe!' *Or safer than we were,* she thought, casting a hunted, sideways glance at the stranger. The knight rode with Henry, Duke of Lancaster, a man who had the potential to make their situation far worse.

'Do you think she might have run into the forest?' Gilan suggested. The maid's hair, silken and lustrous, sagged precariously. Hairpins stuck out at all angles from the plaited rolls on each side of her head. He wondered what her hair would look like when it was unpinned. Would those curling ends brush against the enticing swell of her hips?

Matilda twisted around to face him. 'She is incapable of running anywhere… Katherine is pregnant, you see.'

'Ah.'

She sensed the irritation running through his lean, muscled frame. He stood there with the stance of a fighter, legs planted firmly in the swishing grass, cloak spilling down over his shoulders, the dark blue fabric framing the burnished steel of his breastplate. Beneath the armour he wore a hooded tunic, a thin material that reached the middle of his thighs, split at the sides for ease of riding. Driven into a leather belt around his hips, the jewelled hilt of his sword flashed in the sun. The formidable power of his body was plain to see; she was in no doubt that he was a force to be reckoned with. She had to get rid of him before he realised they supported King Richard, before he had a chance to punish them for that loyalty.

Glancing across to the packhorse bridge, she saw

with relief that all the servants were safe, the gang of ruffians driven away. Even the soldier who had fallen from his horse was propped up against the litter, conversing quietly with the other household knight, hand pressed up hard against his bloodied shoulder.

Matilda drew herself up to her full height, which annoyingly, seemed only a shade above this disquieting man's shoulder. 'Please don't let me, let us, keep you from anything,' she intoned formally. Even to her own ears, her voice sounded jerky, too precise. 'I'm sure there is somewhere that you would rather be.'

'There is.' He inclined his head to one side, a gesture of agreement. 'But the laws of chivalry prevent me from leaving a damsel and her sister in distress.'

His hair was quite an incredible colour, thought Matilda. Pale gold, like washed sand on a deserted shoreline. The strands glowed in the sun with a bright star's incandescence. A heated flutter stirred her stomach, coiling slowly; she ducked her eyes, toeing the ground with the damp, squishy leather of her slipper.

'Oh, I don't believe in all that chivalry nonsense.' She waved one white hand at him airily, attempting to keep her tone light, practical. 'Katherine doesn't, either. Look, our servants are fine, and I think our knights will live. So we really don't need you any more. Thank you for what you've done, and…and everything.' Her sentence trailed off at the end, lamely.

He was being dismissed. Gilan watched her hand flick through the air at him, as if she were shooing away a fly. A small, insignificant fly.

His eyes gleamed. 'I'll help you find her, at least.'

Matilda's shoulders slumped forwards, a visible sign of defeat. Why did she object to his presence so much? Most women would be clinging on to him by now, weeping on his shoulder about the outrages of their attack, begging him to help, but this maid? Once she had realised he was no threat to her, her whole demeanour moved to the defensive, indicating in no uncertain terms that she wished him to disappear.

'Don't feel you have to,' she tried once more. Her voice was limp.

'I *want* to,' he lied, knowing this would annoy her even more. Her abrasive manner intrigued him; he couldn't remember a woman being quite so stubborn, so *ungrateful*, as this pert-nosed chit. His lips twitched at the disgruntled set of her shoulders as she turned away from him, intending to head into the woodland behind the tower. His fingers reached out, snaring the soft flesh of her upper arm, stalling her. 'I suggest you remove your cloak. The wet fabric will slow you down,' he said.

Matilda whisked around, glowering at him, then wordlessly raised both hands to the pearl-studded clasp at her shoulder. Her frozen fingers struggled with the intricate fixings.

'Here, let me,' he offered, exasperated, tough fingers dealing quickly, efficiently with the stiff fastening. One rough knuckle brushed the sensitive skin of her neck, below her ear, and she gasped out loud. A sweet, looping sensation plummeted straight to her belly. Astounded by her response, she staggered back, her mind draining of conscious thought. Her breath disappeared. The cloak slithered down her back, over her slim hips, pooling into loose folds around her ankles.

'There,' he announced. 'Now we can get on with the business of finding your sister.'

Hating the man at her side, this stranger who dogged her steps, who refused to go away, Matilda strode into the woodland, her skirts swishing angrily through the drifts of spent cow parsley, across collapsed bluebell stalks, sweeping her gaze across the shadowed green beneath the spreading beech, searching for the blotch of colour that would be Katherine.

'She's wearing a red gown,' she chewed out grudgingly. The sooner they found Katherine, the sooner this horrible man would be on his way. Her hand crept up to the spot below her ear, still throbbing from his touch, amazed at her reaction to him. Her fall into the river had obviously shaken her up more than she realised. Men did not often have the power to affect her in such an adverse manner.

'Easy to spot, then,' Gilan replied mildly. For some reason he could not explain, he was quite enjoying himself at the maid's expense. Something about the chit drew him, her truculent manner maybe, the fact that she didn't want him around. It intrigued him, made him determined to linger, despite knowing that Henry would be wondering where he was.

'There!' Matilda pointed.

Braced by a large trunk, Katherine's ebony head lolled against the ridged bark. Her eyes were closed, her mouth partially open. A faint snore emerged from between her lips.

'She's asleep!' Matilda blurted out in surprise, working her way steadily through the undergrowth towards her, arching brambles snaring the fine silk of her gown. How could her sister have possibly fallen asleep, with all that had been going on? 'I think you should stay here.' Matilda held up her arm to prevent Gilan moving any farther forwards.

A tightly buttoned sleeve, unbelievably tiny small pearl buttons, encased her narrow wrist, the material reaching to her knuckles. Her ringless fingers wagged bossily in front of his face and he wondered again at the temerity of the maid. What or who gave her the right to order him about like this? She was obviously unmarried, so had no protection or guidance from a husband. But maybe her father or a brother had been so lax or indulgent in her upbringing that it had given her a misguided sense of her own authority.

He shrugged his shoulders. It, or rather she, was none of his concern. Should the need arise, he was perfectly capable of putting the maid in her place. But at the moment, he relished her display of wilful bossiness, her grumpiness at his continued presence, enjoying the easy diversion to the afternoon and his normal rigid, constrained existence. His gaze slid to the woman at the base of the tree, endeavouring to keep his expression neutral. The girl had not been lying about her sister's pregnancy. From the size of her stomach, she looked like she was about to go into labour there and then. He raised his eyes heavenwards, sent up a silent prayer.

'Katherine! Wake up.' Matilda bent over her sister, jogged her elbow carefully.

Katherine opened her eyes, a small smile crossing her face. 'What?' she murmured hazily. 'I was having the most wonderful dream, about the baby...' she smoothed one hand across her stomach '...and what he would be like when he was born and...' her eyes drifted over to Gilan's tall figure, standing in the shadows '...and...who is that?'

'Don't let him alarm you,' Matilda said, as she helped Katherine to her feet. 'He came to help, when we were attacked.' She tried to keep her tone even, on the level. Any kind of shock at this stage could jeopardise her sister's labour. Her mind scampered for a discreet way of alerting her sister to the fact that the man was riding with their enemy.

Katherine smiled at Gilan, lurching forwards with her arm outstretched, a pretty blush washing her face. Distorted by her vast belly, the pleated front of her gown rose up at the front, revealing her pink satin slippers. 'My pleasure,' she said, 'Lord...?'

Gilan smiled, skin creasing either side of his mouth, teeth white in his tanned face. 'No, not a lord, mistress. My name is Gilan, Comte de Cormeilles.' He bowed low, deep from the waist.' At your service.'

Katherine extended her hand towards him and he took her fingers, glittering with heavy gemstones and kissed the top of her hand, as was the custom.

'Then you are from France?' Katherine peeked coyly at him from beneath her long eyelashes. Matilda stared at the two of them in horror. Was it her imagination or was Katherine flirting? His display of courtly manners seemed so at odds with her own first encounter with this man, this *Gilan*, whatever his name was, only moments ago! Half drowned by him, then thrown down on the grass, shaken roughly back to consciousness, assaulted by those piercing, silver eyes. And now, her sister was patting him on the shoulder, thanking him profusely for all he had done! If only she knew!

'I am English, but my mother is from France—my title comes from her family. I manage her manor and estates over there. In Cormeilles.' Gilan crooked his arm and Katherine tucked her hand through it companionably, throwing a running stream of questions up to him. Matilda's heart sank as she trailed after them, snatching up her sodden cloak on the way. She had hoped to walk with Katherine so she could have a quiet word, warn her about this man, about who he was. It was not to be.

* * *

As the three of them approached the spot where the sisters had been attacked, Katherine picking her way carefully down the cobbled slope of the bridge with Gilan's help, Matilda saw that the numbers in their original entourage had swelled. Beneath the low, swaying branches of the beech trees, arching over the track, stood a stocky, russet-haired man, face ruddy with sunburn. He called out to Gilan, raised his arm in greeting. He wore a surcoat over chainmail, a dark blue surcoat emblazoned with a distinctive coat of arms: three gold lions on a red background, quartered with three gold fleur-de-lis on a blue background.

Henry of Lancaster.

He had brought knights with him, knights wearing the same livery: a dozen or so men on horseback. They stretched along the track, horses nose-to-tail in single file, men's features impassive beneath steel helmets, lances pointed rigidly into the air, steel tips flashing in the sporadic rays of sunlight that slanted through the whispering trees.

'Now I see what's been keeping you!' Strutting forwards to greet them, Henry clapped Gilan on the shoulder. 'You had me worried back there!'

'You, worried?' Gilan raised his eyebrows in mock surprise. He escorted Katherine to the side of the litter and she clutched on to one of the up-right struts gratefully, clamping one hand to the small of her back as she leaned over.

Henry laughed. 'You're right, I wasn't worried, merely impatient at your tardiness. But now—' he swept his gaze over the two women '—it all becomes clear. Ladies,' he addressed them both with a short, sharp bow, 'may I have the honour of knowing your names?' Removing his mail gaunt-let, the individual iron links glittering like fish scales, he handed it to his manservant, who hov-ered nervously at his side.

'I am Katherine of Neen.' Katherine performed a small, wobbling curtsy, extending her hand. 'And this is my sister, Matilda of Lilleshall.' Henry kissed the top of both their hands in turn. If he no-ticed Katherine's advanced pregnancy at all, then he made no indication, no comment.

'Delighted,' he pronounced, clapping his hands together. 'Your knights have explained what has happened to you. I understand that you were on your way back home from a shrine?'

Katherine nodded.

'Then allow me…us—' he waved his stubby fin-gers in the direction of his knights '—to escort you home…'

'There's really no need…' Matilda protested.

Henry laughed. 'Forgive me, madam, but it's no trouble. Besides, I have an ulterior motive. My men and I seek board and lodging for the night.'

'Oh, yes! Yes!' gushed Katherine. She wasn't too sure exactly who Henry of Lancaster was, but she did know his grandfather was King Edward III and that was good enough for her. More than good enough—why, he was royalty! What a feather in her cap, to entertain such a person! 'John will want to see you rewarded for what you have done for us today.' She flicked her eyes appreciatively in Gilan's direction.

Oh, Lord, thought Matilda, hitching her shoulders forwards in her damp gown. Things seemed to going from bad to worse. Katherine obviously had no idea of Henry of Lancaster's true intentions in this country. In fact, Matilda doubted that her sister really knew who he was.

Once Katherine was comfortably installed in her litter, her entourage—swelled in ranks with Henry's knights— began its slow progress eastwards once more. The servants who carried the wooden struts on their shoulders had emerged from the attack relatively unscathed; the youngest manservant dabbed sporadically at a split lip, but apart from a few bumps and bruises, no great injuries had been sustained. The household knight with the injury to his shoulder had to be helped up into his saddle but seemed to be holding his seat tolerably well, following Henry's knights, who rode up front, the rumps of their muscled warhorses glossy, shiny.

The track was dry and flat; they would make good progress now. John and Katherine's home lay only a mile or so farther up the expansive, fertile valley. In the strip of rough, uncultivated land between the river and the path, white hogweed grew, proliferated: great lacy umbels like dinner plates reaching up beyond the mess of inferior weeds, frilled flower heads against the deep blue of the sky. A brilliant green-backed beetle ambled across one of the flowers, black whiskered legs crawling slowly.

As they emerged from the dimness of the woodland, and into the scorching radiance of the open fields running either side of the river, Katherine sank back on her cushions, a smug, self-satisfied look on her face. 'John will be so pleased with me,' she announced, stretching her hand out limply to Matilda, who walked alongside the litter. 'Such important guests that I am bringing home to him! How fortunate we are that they turned up.'

Ignoring her sister's hand, Matilda scuffed her leather boots along the track, deliberately kicking up dust. Hanging across the path, a teasel head, brown and withered from the year before, scraped along the fine blue wool of her sleeve. A pair of brilliant pewter eyes danced across her vision. She pursed her lips, determined to scrape the memory from her brain. He was nothing, not important.

'And such a lot to prepare, if they are to stay tonight!' Katherine's eyes widened. 'What do you think, Matilda, should we put Henry in the south tower—you know, the one with the gold brocade hangings around the bed? Will he think it too shabby?'

Keeping pace with the litter's progress, Matilda folded her arms across her bosom. 'Katherine, do you have any idea who these men are?' She nodded up ahead, indicating the broad, stocky back of Henry, Gilan's tall, muscular frame riding alongside him. His dark blue cloak spread out over the rump of his horse, the gold fleur-de-lis embroidered along the length of cloth twinkling like tiny stars.

A deep shuddering breath burst from her lungs at the sight of them; individually, these men were formidable enough, but together as a group, with plate armour burnished and shining and helmets obscuring their features, their horses with hooves the size of a man's head, they presented an intimi-

dating force. Her heart flailed, searching for purchase, for direction, the memory of that stranger's
tanned handsome face, *Gilan's* face, so close to her
own she could still smell the musky woodsmoke
on his skin. In the face of such powerful masculin-
ity, such strength and vigour, she was at a momen-
tary loss as to what to do next. Fear had emptied
her mind.

She turned away, back to her sister, a wave of
panic pulsing through Matilda's veins. The thought
of these men in her sister's home, that they would
discover where John and Katherine's true loyalties lay, not with them, but with the king, made
her legs shake.

'Do you have any idea?' she repeated, her voice
low, insistent.

'What's the matter with you?' Katherine replied,
her voice rising shrilly. 'Of course I know who they
are. Henry is the grandson of King Edward III...'

'...and he's been exiled, Katherine. King Richard exiled him to Paris. He's not even supposed to
be in this country.'

Katherine frowned, her mind trying to make
sense of the information. 'But...but I didn't know
that!' she protested. 'Why would I have known
that?'

Matilda shook her head. Why, indeed. Her sister showed little or no interest in the politics of the country. Henry had been exiled on the death of his father, John of Gaunt, simply because, as sole inheritor, he would have become more powerful than King Richard himself. And Richard resented that, viewed his cousin as a threat, confiscating Henry's lands for no good reason.

'What can we do?' cried Katherine.

'We must keep quiet,' advised Matilda, trying to remain calm for her sister's sake. 'And hope that John keeps his wits about him when he sees their colours riding towards the castle. If we are careful, then they won't find out that John is a staunch supporter of the king. And serve them horrible food—that will send them on their way a bit quicker.'

'Mother of Mary! What's John going to say?'

'Hopefully, he will say nothing, at least while they are in the castle.'

The Castle of Neen rose up in the middle of the valley, at the point where two gentle slopes intersected at the river: a silver ribbon cutting through fields thick with a ripening wheat crop. Cattle and sheep grazed on the upper slopes, the poorer ground, before the land rose into a steep escarpment, blotched with yellow gorse. The castle was unusual, built in the French style, a rectangular building with round towers on the four corners, each topped with a conical roof in slate. Great carved corbel stones supported projecting parapets, protecting any knight who stepped out onto the narrow ledge surrounding the roof above. In the dropping sunlight, the polished limestone walls, studded with shells from prehistoric times, glowed pale and luminous.

'Enchanting,' breathed Henry, raising gingery eyebrows in appreciation at the pretty building, as they slowed their horses to clatter through the gatehouse and into the bailey. The river they had been following flowed beneath the outer walls and into the deep moat surrounding the castle before disappearing out the other side, providing a constant supply of fresh water.

Henry turned in the saddle, leather creaking beneath his burly thighs. 'We should allow the ladies to go in first, announce our presence.' With one touch of his knee he shifted his horse out of the way, Gilan performing the same manoeuvre. The litter was carried past them, Matilda striding alongside, head held high, eyes fixed straight ahead. Her wet gown had picked up all the dry dust of the road, and the blue material was now coated in a clay-coloured paste almost up to her knees. The silken ebony of her hair drooped forlornly in its inadequate pins, her circlet and veil set askance on her head.

'What has happened to that maid?' Henry said pointedly, beneath his breath. 'She looks like she's been dragged through the mire.'

She looks beautiful. The words strove, unbidden, into Gilan's brain. He snatched up the reins in surprise, angry at his own musings. Why was he even thinking such a thing? The girl was a mess, plain for all to see.

'She's had a busy day,' Gilan replied drily, bunching his reins into one fist as his horse sidled beneath him. 'She almost took my head off with an arrow, then fell into the river when I went to stop her.' He grimaced, guilt flooding through him at the memory: outraged blue eyes, firing hostility; the sweet curve of her bosom as she lay, unconscious, in the warm grass.

'Impressive,' murmured Henry, his eyes narrowing on the diminutive figure as she helped her sister alight from the litter.

'More like misguided,' replied Gilan, watching as Katherine sagged dramatically against Matilda, making her stagger. 'The stupid chit made the situation far worse for herself than if she had just stayed put.'

'One can't help but admire such bravery in a woman,' Henry said.

'Perhaps.' Gilan shrugged his shoulders. 'But sometimes it can lead them into greater danger.'

Chapter Four

Matilda curved her arm beneath Katherine's, and hauled her up and out of the litter. The main entrance to the castle was only a few steps away, across the uneven cobbles of the inner bailey. As Katherine reared upwards, her movements ungainly, awkward, she clung to Matilda for support.

'Ugh! You're all wet!' Katherine exclaimed. Her gaze drifted down, noticing the grey dust adhering to the fabric. 'Oh, Matilda, what have you done to my gown? I doubt it will ever be the same again!'

Matilda began to steer Katherine towards the studded-oak doorway, the muscles in her back pulled into a rigid line. Even though she couldn't see them, she knew all eyes were on them. Henry and his men were watching, respectfully waiting to dismount. And he was watching her. Gilan. She could feel those silvery eyes following every detail of her movement, making her feel flustered, unsettled. In the damp dress, an involuntary shiver chased up her spine.

'It will wash out, Katherine, don't worry.'

Up the stone steps they went, one at a time, a slow progress. Matilda breathed out slowly, a long quiet sigh of frustration. She would be relieved when this baby finally made an appearance in the world, for it would make everyone's lives a whole lot easier. At this time of the year, the work at her own home of Lilleshall was mounting up: the continual planting and maintenance of crops, care of the animals and the beginning of the harvest. Someone needed to supervise the work, and now that her mother had decided to withdraw from public life, and she had heard nothing from her brother in the past year, the role had fallen to her.

'I hope so,' grumbled Katherine, breathing heavily as she reached the top step, placing one hand on the carved stone surround of the door. 'Hold for a moment, sister, I need to catch my breath.'

'We're nearly there,' Matilda reassured her. Without thinking, she glanced back down in to the inner bailey, her eyes immediately drawn to a shock of blond hair, feathered across the tall man's tanned brow. Threads of unravelling excitement shot through her veins. What was the matter with her? It wasn't in her nature to be so disturbed by a masculine presence, even one as intimidating as Count Gilan of Cormeilles. Having grown up with a loving brother and father, she was not in awe of men, quite the reverse, in fact. Most of the time she ignored them. She simply couldn't explain these odd feelings that roiled around her body, the way his company set her nerves on a jittery edge.

As the sisters moved into the hallway, Matilda blinked once or twice, adjusting her eyes to the dim interior, inhaling the damp, gritty scent of the thick stone walls. Above their heads, ribs of stone fanned out from a central boss: a carved-stone trefoil beset with finely chiselled leaves and flowers.

'Good! Good! You're back at last!' John burst out from the curtain strung across the entrance to the main stairwell, pushing aside the weighty material with impatience. He was a stout man, small brown eyes set deep in a flabby face, the belt around his high-necked, pleated tunic straining across his portly waist. 'You've been ages!' Grabbing his wife's hands, he squeezed them strongly. 'You need to change, quickly, my dear. My guards tell me you have brought guests. Important guests.'

'Yes, but…' Matilda began to explain, to warn him. Had no one thought to tell John of the colours that these 'important guests' wore? But John had already walked past them, out through the arched doorway, out into the open air. Matilda sighed. He would know soon enough. 'Come on,' she said to Katherine, placing a protective arm around her sister's shoulders. 'Let's go upstairs to your chamber.'

Shielded by a heavily embroidered screen, Matilda sank deeper into the hot water, a small sigh of pleasure escaping her lips. She listened to the sounds of her sister's maidservants, two of them, fussing around Katherine. They sounded like hens, clucking with their tongues, sympathising, commiserating, whilst they bustled and rustled around the chamber, placating her sister with their soothing words.

Matilda leaned back in the wooden tub, the water swilling across her exhausted limbs, easing her muscles. Katherine had insisted that she take a bath, practically ripping the destroyed dress from her shoulders, and for once, Matilda had agreed with her. The hot water, dried rose petals scattered across the surface, was gradually soothing her frazzled nerves, calming her. In the corner, coals glowed in a charcoal brazier, sending out more heat, and she welcomed it, rolling her tired shoulders forwards. Through the glazed window, swallows, wings like black knife blades, sliced across the deepening blue. A bright fingernail of a new moon appeared in the sky through the leaded grid of the window, the herald of evening.

There was enough daylight for her to return to Lilleshall, Matilda thought. That way she could meet with her bailiff this evening and make—

The door to Katherine's chamber crashed back on its hinges, swinging back against the wood-panelled wall.

It was John.

'Do you know who you've brought here, you stupid cow?' he roared at his wife.

'John! John? Whatever's the matter with you?' Katherine twisted up on to her side, half rising from her recumbent position on the feather mattress.

Her husband plonked his portly girth on to the side of the bed, stuck his hands in his grizzled hair, distraught. 'You've only gone and brought Henry of Lancaster into our home! Henry, Duke of Lancaster! Have you any idea who he is?'

'I...er...'

'No, you don't, do you? Because you have no idea about anything!' Clenching one fist, he knocked the side of Katherine's head, not gently. 'Because you have nothing up there, do you, my sweet one? Nothing at all, just sawdust.'

Adrenaline thumping through her veins, blood

rushing, Matilda rose quickly out of the water, grabbed at a voluminous chemise and pulled it swiftly over her head, down over her wet, bare body. She had no intention of John seeing her naked in her sister's bathtub. The scum of soap adhered to her knees as she stepped out on to the curly sheep's fleece that covered the bare floorboards and soaked up the wet trickles from her toes. Her breath snared; she knew what John was capable of, knew how he treated her sister when he was displeased. Catching up the thick, linen towel, she threw it over her shoulders, anxious that not an inch of flesh was on show for John to ogle at. She moved out from behind the screen, her unbound hair swinging in long, curling ropes down her back.

John turned, squinted nastily at her. His top lip curled down into a sneer. 'Ah, you! I want to talk to you, too! What were you thinking?'

'We were attacked, John,' Matilda explained, keeping her voice low and calm. She would not allow John to rile her. 'Those men saved us. If they hadn't come along, then the outcome might have been a lot worse. We had to thank them somehow.'

He shook his head. 'If it had been anyone else...'

'I know, John,' Matilda said, deflecting his attention away from her frightened sister, cowering back on the pillows with her eyes large, round, luminous with fear. 'I know who they are. But they have no idea of your allegiances, where your loyalties lie. Keep quiet. Give them board and lodging for tonight, and by tomorrow morning, I'm certain they will be on their way.'

'Spoken like a true diplomat,' replied John. 'Well, I praise the Lord that at least one sister has a head on her shoulders.' He placed his tubby fingers flat on his bulging thighs, pressing down so that he rose from the bed, throwing a mocking glance down at his wife. Katherine hadn't moved, pressed up in terror against the pillows, her mouth partially open, breathing shallowly. She looks like a wild animal, thought Matilda, an animal who is trapped and vulnerable, unable to move, or to think, for itself.

'Get dressed, both of you. I want you downstairs to help me entertain our guests.'

'Oh, but I need to...' Matilda stepped forwards.

John pushed his face up close to his sister-in-law. He was about the same height as her; she could smell his fetid breath, see rotten teeth crowd the interior of his mouth. 'No, Matilda, not this time. You cannot run away to your precious estate, to your mother. You brought these men here, you entertain them. And if they find out who we support, then God help you both.'

* * *

The great hall at Neen was situated unusually on the second floor, with the kitchens and servants' quarters on the floors beneath. The dressed-stone walls, pale limestone, glowed in the evening light that spilled down from the huge windows, striking the swirling dust motes rising from the wooden floorboards.

'Not bad,' said Henry, reaching for another chicken leg, chewing hungrily. 'Not bad at all.' He looked around him appreciatively, at the fine tapestries hanging down from the walls, the expensive carved furniture, the plentiful food. His eye caught on two banners, hanging down from the wooden gallery at the opposite end of the hall, sweeps of blue-and-red cloth impaled with the golden arms of royalty. 'Although a bit too much evidence of King Richard, I think.' He smirked at Gilan, sitting next to him. 'Do you think they'll murder us in our beds tonight? Or clap us in arms?'

Gilan crossed his huge arms across his chest, leaning back into the oak chair. Then leaned forwards again as the ornately carved wood poked uncomfortably into his spine. 'No, they wouldn't dare. I'm sure John of Neen realises how weak King Richard's rule has become. It wouldn't be in his best interest to thwart us.'

'No, I suspect he's the type to change sides at the drop of a cloth,' Henry mused. He leaned past Gilan, lifted a floury bread roll from an oval pewter platter. 'I don't think we have anything to fear from this household. And good food, too. Not quite like the fare we're used to, eh?'

No, indeed, Gilan thought, staring out across the busy hall. Henry's soldiers clustered along the ranks of trestle tables, talking, laughing, joking with each other, piling the food into their mouths. They deserved it, these loyal men. They deserved a taste of this good life. Having ridden on many of Henry's crusades, they had endured all manner of harsh conditions, days on meagre food rations, days when the air was so raw it froze the tears in their eyes and turned their fingers black. He looked along the happy laughing faces, dishevelled hair released from helmets now resting by their feet, their faces ruddy and flushed from the strong sun. A sense of utter loss pierced his heart. There should have been another face amongst them. A face that looked like his, hair the same startling blond, the frame a little leaner and shorter. His older brother. Pierre.

Grief, bitter, unrelenting, scythed through him, and he wrenched his gaze from the men, glowering down at the table, his plate, the piles of food spread out along the pristine white cloth, anywhere that wouldn't remind him of that horrible time. His heart tore at the rift so deep, he wondered whether it would ever heal. Guilt cascaded through him, a numbing black bile, clagging his chest. He gripped the stem of his pewter goblet. If only he hadn't insisted, if only he hadn't goaded his brother, pushed him on, teased him. Then the accident would never have happened.

'Come on, Gilan, eat up!' Henry jostled his elbow. 'Once the lady of the manor arrives, we'll be forced to talk, not eat. Get something down your throat at once! That's an order!' Henry began to pile food in front of his friend: a couple of slices of ham, some cooked vegetables, a hunk of bread. He raised his eyebrows towards the door, a flicker of movement catching his eye. 'Too late.'

Gilan looked up.

Framed by the stone archway with Katherine at her side, Matilda hesitated, as if stunned by the crowds of men in the great hall. Her appearance arrested conversation, reduced the bursts of laughter to soft murmurs of appreciation. She ducked her head, a stain of colour creeping across her pale cheeks, not wanting the male eyes upon her, embarrassed. Her hair was dry now, coiled in intricate plaits on either side of her neat head, the wisps contained by a silver net, delicately wrought. Her circlet, etched silver, gleamed as she moved forwards tentatively, her sister hanging on her arm.

She wore a simple overdress cut from a rose-coloured fabric, shot through with threads of silver; the material shimmered against her slender frame as she walked. The wide, angular-cut neck exposed her collarbone, the shadowed hollow of her throat. As was the fashion, her sleeves were fitted on her upper arms, before hanging down loose from her elbows, revealing the tightly buttoned sleeves of her underdress, a rich scarlet.

'My God!' murmured Henry as the two women approached, John bustling up behind them, chivvying them up to the dais as if they were cattle. 'What a beauty.'

'My lords, both of you, so sorry to have kept you waiting…' John practically shoved his lumbering wife up the wooden steps. Katherine clutched at the wooden bannister for support, dragging herself up. Matilda led her sister to the empty chair between Henry and Gilan, intending to help her into the seat.

'No, no, what are you thinking?' John protested, grabbing Katherine's arm and forcing her down between Henry and his own place. A pained expression crossed his wife's face; she paled suddenly, biting down hard on her bottom lip.

'My lady?' Gilan quirked one blond eyebrow up at Matilda, who hovered behind the backs of the chairs. 'I believe this is your seat?' He indicated the empty chair between himself and Henry.

Her toes curled reluctantly in her pink satin slippers, stalling any forward movement. Every muscle in her body, every nerve tightened reflexively at the sight of him, bracing, readying themselves for some further onslaught. She needed to arm herself against him, to shield herself from the devastating silver of his eyes, the implacable force of his body.

He read the reluctance in her face, and smiled. 'Have no fear my lady, I'm not about to shove you into the nearest pond.'

'No...I...' Her voice trailed off, mind incapable of finding any explanation for her hesitation. He thought she was frightened of him, but that wasn't it. She couldn't identify the strange feelings that pulsed through her body. Odd feelings that flooded through her veins, making her heart race. Not fear. Excitement.

'Oh, for God's sake, Matilda, sit down!' John bawled at her from the other side of Henry, lines of strain stretching the fleshy skin on his face.

She slipped between the two chairs, carefully,

avoiding any contact with the man on her right, sliding down on to the hard, polished seat, thinking she would rather be anywhere but here. Gilan lifted the heavy jug, pouring wine into her goblet.

'Thank you,' she murmured, staring straight ahead.

'Tell me, my lady, have you recovered from your ordeal this afternoon?' Henry said conversationally on her left. 'It sounds like you were extremely brave.'

'Or extremely stupid,' Gilan muttered under his breath, so that only Matilda could hear.

Eyes blazing with blue fire, she shot him an angry look, grazing the sculptured lines of his face, the corded muscles of his neck. He had dispensed with his breastplate and all other visible signs of armour, but the pleated tunic that he wore served only to emphasise the huge power of his shoulders, his chest.

She swallowed hastily, her mouth dry, arid, then turned back to Henry.

'I didn't have time to think about it,' she replied, honestly, smoothing her hand across the white tablecloth. To her surprise her hand shook, fingers quivering against the soft fabric. The skin on the right side of her neck burned—was he staring at her? She clamped her lips together, annoyed with herself, with her unwanted reaction to him. Men meant little to her; scornful of their appreciative glances, mocking even, she was not in the habit of paying them any attention and had no wish to marry, especially after witnessing John's treatment of her sister.

'Where did you learn to shoot like that?' Henry took up his eating knife and began cutting thin slices of roast pork that he popped into his mouth at intervals. Grease slicked the sides of his mouth and he rubbed at his mouth with a linen napkin, throwing the crumpled fabric back into his lap.

'My brother taught me.' Matilda rubbed at an errant spot of spilled wine on the cloth, frowning.

'Your brother?' Henry raised his eyebrows. 'And where is he?'

Where was he, indeed? Matilda fixed her eyes on the colourful banners at the end of the hall. As far as she knew, Thomas was with King Richard, fighting his cause in Ireland. Her brother had no idea that their mother had given up all intention of running the estate at Lilleshall, that the responsibility had fallen to his younger sister. He had been away for over a year now; she had heard nothing from him.

Bringing her hands into her lap, she twisted her fingers together. What could she say to Henry?

She couldn't tell him the truth, because that would underline John's allegiance, *their allegiance*, to Richard. 'My brother…er…he's…at home.' Her answer stumbled out. 'Dealing with things,' she added vaguely.

Beside her, Gilan shifted in his seat. His forearm lay along the wooden arm of the chair, his hand rounding the carved end, strong fingers splayed. She could see the raised sinew on the top of his hand, the lines of blue veins tracing beneath the skin, knuckles roughened, scratched. The hands of a working soldier, a knight.

'My lady?' Henry was speaking to her.

'I'm sorry? What did you say?' She blushed furiously, a wild scarlet chasing across her cheeks.

'I asked you where your home is, my lady?'

'Not far from here,' she answered lamely.

The little chit's lying through her teeth, thought Gilan, lifting his pewter goblet to his lips and taking a large gulp of wine. The heady liquid slid down his throat. Not that it was any of his business, but it was intriguing, all the same. Her shoulder was turned rigidly away from him, her manner overly attentive to Henry; it made him want to laugh. He wanted to tell her it didn't matter, whatever she did would have no effect on him. She could be as rude or as coquettish towards him as she liked. She could fall all over him or slap him in the face. He was immune to the many wiles of women, to their tempers and their masquerades, his body remaining in a constant state of numbness, of bound-up guilt and grief, unable to love, unable to give. His brother's death had removed the very spirit of him, driven out his soul so that only the shell of him remained. A husk of a man.

Chapter Five

As the sun dipped low in the sky, inching away from the long, rectangular windows, servants moved around silently with flaming tapers, lighting the thick wax candles in their iron holders, thrusting lit torches into the iron brackets secured around the walls. The cavernous chamber filled with a flickering luminescence, dreamlike, which cast odd shadows, illuminated chattering faces with rosy glows.

'And our last crusade was up around the Baltic...' Henry droned on, his nose reddened, cheeks flushed from too much wine. 'And, oh Lord, I can't even begin to tell you how cold it was...'

Crumbling a soft bread roll between her fingers, paddling the cooked dough into a smaller and smaller piece, Matilda forced herself to concentrate on the story Henry was telling her. She had smiled and nodded all through this interminable evening, aware that for the whole time Gilan sat to her right, silent, and that she was ignoring him. The muscles in her cheeks ached with the constant effort of maintaining an impressed, amenable expression towards Henry.

'But how did you keep yourselves warm, if there was so much snow?' To be fair, Katherine was doing a very decent job of listening to Henry, prodding him with a question now and again to show interest and keep his stories flowing.

Henry grimaced, lowering his eyebrows in an exaggerated frown. Coarse russet hairs straggled out from his brows, haphazard, messy, giving him the look of a farmhand, as opposed to a cousin of the king. A roar of ribald laughter broke out from the soldiers below and he paused, allowing the noise to die away before he answered, 'Well, my lady Katherine, I have to tell you, it wasn't easy, was it, Gilan?'

Matilda sensed, rather than saw, Gilan's slight shake of his head. Then saw her sister's face, her profile clenched, delicate jaw rigid with pain.

'Katherine...?'

Henry's story faltered to silence as he turned to observe his hostess. Katherine's face was set in an expression of sheer horror, her mouth screwed up, as if braced against an unknown onslaught, her eyes squeezed tight. The blood had drained from her lips.

'Katherine…!' Matilda shot up from her seat, turning abruptly to push past Gilan in a desperate attempt to reach her sister. Her hip brushed against him, the soft curve of flesh beneath her gown yielding against his upper arm. He drew a sharp unsteady breath.

'For God's sake, woman! What's the matter with you?' John shouted at his wife, at her rounded eyes that stared unseeing straight ahead, at her skin: red and sweating. He threw down his napkin into the middle of the table, a flare of annoyance crossing his portly face. 'I'm so sorry about this, my lord…' he inclined his head towards Henry '…she's not normally like this. It must be the shock of today.'

Rushing to Katherine's side, Matilda saw the growing puddle of water beneath her sister's seat, the sopping hem of her gown, watched her hands grip the armrests of the chair. 'She's in labour, John,' Matilda bent down to murmur in John's ear, laying one hand on her brother-in-law's forearm.

'What? What are you talking about? It's too soon, isn't it?' John babbled, his fetid breath wafting over her, his face contorting into a look of sheer horror. His lips curled at the water spreading across floorboards, staining the wood. 'What on earth is that horrible mess?'

'Her waters have broken, John. We need to carry her upstairs!' Matilda's voice was more urgent now. She bit down hard on her bottom lip, forcing herself to think logically, clearly, against the brimming tide of fear pushed around the edges of her consciousness, a push of bulging breath expanding her lungs. She couldn't, wouldn't panic!

'Take her away, then!' John hissed at her. 'This is so mortifying! Get her out of here!' He fluttered his hand at Matilda, in the manner of dismissing a servant. A dull red flooded his pouched cheeks.

Aghast at his lack of assistance, Matilda gawped at him, her arm slung across Katherine's back. Her sister was panting now, fingers fixed around the edge of the table, trying to subdue the cramping waves of pain.

'John, you need to carry her!' Matilda squeaked at the bullish back of his neck, hating him, horrified by his ignorance, his sheer stupidity. Did he truly mean for Katherine to deliver her baby here, in the great hall, in front of all these men? 'There's no way she can walk!'

'With the state my leg's in at the moment? You know I'm injured! Ask one of the servants to do it!' John raised his eyebrows at Henry in mute apology, who was observing the whole proceedings with a bemused, drunken demeanour. 'Women, eh?' John burped loudly, shaking his head with a nonchalant, unconcerned air. 'What can you do with them? Always some little problem to deal with!'

'Let me help you.' A low, velvety voice cut across Katherine's stifled gasp. Gilan appeared at Matilda's side, bending down over her sister, bright hair falling across his forehead, wayward. Katherine made no demur as he shifted her rounded body up into his arms, levering her easily out of her chair.

'I...er...no, we have no need of your help,' Matilda protested, agitated, her hands flapping towards him as if to ward him off. How had he managed to lift her pregnant sister so swiftly? Gilan shifted Katherine's body so she rested easily against his chest, her head rolling back against his shoulder.

'Why, were you intending to carry her yourself?' His sparkling eyes swept over Matilda's diminutive stature, the close-fitting sweep of her dress, immediately mocking. 'Which way?'

'Follow me, then,' she replied, stalking off in front of him, her head held high. Her long hem trailed treacherously across his leather boots as she swept past him and she flicked the material away, huffily, annoyed that she had no choice in this matter. Despite her reluctance, she would have to accept his help, as Katherine's husband was demonstrating, once again, the whole wretched expanse of his uselessness. John's behaviour had forced her to accept a stranger's help. At the door, she turned, fixing her sister's husband with a cold, hard look. 'Send someone to fetch a midwife, John, and do it now!'

'Good luck, my lady Katherine!' Henry called out, lifting his pewter goblet in a toast, his speech slurred and warbling.

Gilan followed Matilda's neat figure through an arched doorway in the corner of the dais which lead directly on to the circular stair. Her hips swayed seductively beneath the twinkling gown, the whispering train of the overdress slipping across the floorboards. At once they were plunged into a dank shadowy space, lit only by one flaming torch slung into its iron holster on the cramped landing. Steps curved away from them, down as well as up.

Seizing the torch from its holder, Matilda thrust the spitting flame aloft, bunching her skirts in the other hand. 'This way,' she murmured tersely, climbing up the narrow, curved steps. Behind her, Gilan carried her sister's pregnant form effortlessly, and surprisingly gently, as if it were a manoeuvre he performed every day. They climbed steadily, with only Katherine's moaning gasps breaking the silence; suddenly, she arched over, letting out a long, low howl of pain. Caught unawares, Gilan staggered forwards at the jerking violence of the movement. Instinctively, Matilda reached down and grabbed his upper arm, attempting to steady him.

But he had no need of her bracing hand; his feet were already planted firmly again, one step below her. Beneath the dancing flame of the torch, his carved features were inches from her own, his eyes mineral dark.

'I have her.' He glanced at Matilda's hand clamped around his upper arm, not steadying now, but clinging to him, as if for support. Beneath his tunic sleeve, the roped muscle was hard, like an iron bar. She snatched her hand away, face flaming, speech stalled. Why couldn't John have carried his own wife upstairs? She had no wish for this man, this stranger, to be involved with her family affairs. He seemed too close to her, too intimate in this confined, shadowed space, scattering her senses, befuddling her.

'Hurry, this way!' Matilda whisked away from him, climbing the circular steps two at a time, pushing through the planked door of Katherine's chamber. In a moment, Katherine's ladies-in-waiting were all around them, like colourful butterflies, clustering around Gilan as he carried Katherine to her bed.

He laid her down with infinite gentleness.

Stuck in the doorway, Matilda watched the scene with growing incredulity, still holding the sparking, spitting torch. The light arched over her, casting flickering shadows down across her cheeks. Who was this man, his body built for a life of fighting, of soldiering, to perform such an act of kindness? His tough, muscular frame looked out of place, all angles and hard lines in this lady's bedchamber. He towered over Katherine's ladies-in-waiting. He had helped, where John had not. She frowned, unable to untangle her reasoning.

'Matilda!' Katherine screeched, hunching over in a foetal position on the bed furs, clutching dramatically at her belly. 'Matilda, come here! I need you!'

Starting at the sound of her sister's voice, Matilda shook her head: a quick movement, wanting to rid herself of these troubling thoughts. She moved towards Gilan as he straightened up from the side of Katherine's bed. Against the blood-red of the velvet bedcurtains, his hair shone out like spun gold, glimmering fire.

'Fetch linens, towels, hot water…now!' she ordered the women fussing about the bed. They sprang away from their mistress at the sound of Matilda's voice, following her commands without question. 'And you,' she said, tipping her chin towards Gilan, 'you can go now.' She thrust the flaming brand towards him, as if to emphasise her point. Her tone was brusque, dismissive.

'Careful with that,' he murmured, jerking his head back. 'You'll set my hair on fire.'

'Have it,' she said briskly. 'You'll need it to find your way back downstairs.'

He took the torch from her hand, strong fingers grazing against her own, reading the fear behind the veneer of bravado in her manner. 'I can stay, if you need me.' His voice was a low rumble of reassurance; for one tiny, inconceivable moment, she considered the possibility of him staying, of helping, wanting that implacable strength beside her as she assisted her sister through this ordeal.

She glared at him, astounded by her own thoughts, annoyed with such weakness, the weakness that would drive her to ask this man for support. When had she ever asked a man to help her? Her fingers moved swiftly along the row of pearl buttons that secured the fitted sleeve of her underdress, undoing them. 'Are you mad? This is women's business!' She dropped her voice to a hush, so that Katherine wouldn't hear. 'Do you really want to stay—to witness all that blood and gore and screaming?'

No, he didn't. But he didn't want to give the bossy little chit the satisfaction of knowing that.

He shrugged his shoulders. 'It's nothing that I haven't seen before.' Not childbirth, admittedly, but blood, and gore and screaming? He'd seen enough of that to last him a lifetime.

She arched one dark eyebrow at him in disbelief, a perfect curve above her shimmering eyes, the soft blue of forget-me-nots. 'Really? You do surprise me.'

Her caustic tone made no apparent impact. 'Call me, if you need any help.' Gilan strode towards the door, leather boots covering the distance in three big strides.

'We won't,' she replied rudely, pivoting away from him with what sounded like a snort.

And she would make sure of that, he thought. The maid had done an excellent job of making him feel like he would be the very last man on earth to whom she would turn for help. As if she knew who he was; as if she had peeled back the vast wall of chest muscle and seen the dull, numb beat of his cold, black heart. As Gilan moved through into the stairwell, he glanced back through the open door. For all the chit's bravado, for all her spurning, he knew she was scared. Her small hands trembled as she smoothed them down the front of her gown, delicate blue veins in her dainty wrists revealed by her loose flapping sleeves.

Perched up beside her sister on the big bed, Matilda raised one arm, wiped the gathering perspiration from her forehead, holding on to Katherine as she let out a long, wavering moan, a cry of despair. At her sister's feet, crouched on a wooden stool, an old lady sat, her face wizened, crumpled with age: the midwife.

'Open that window, there!' Matilda pointed over to a small single-paned window set into the west wall. 'We need more air!' Mary, one of Katherine's ladies-in-waiting moved swiftly across the room, twisting the wrought-iron handle set into the glazing bars. Now all the windows were open, set out as far as they could go on their hinges, yet the chamber was still muggy, hot, full of the heavy scent of sweat, of blood. Exhausted by her fruitless labouring, Katherine lay on a linen sheet, the fabric creased and crumpled beneath her. Between her screams that accompanied each tightening contraction of her womb, her ladies had managed to remove her dress, easing her into a loose night-gown, which had provided her with some temporary relief. But the baby refused to come. Her belly was rigid, the skin pulled tight as a drum, distended.

With every one of Katherine's screams, the old midwife had nodded importantly, running her leathery hands across Katherine's stomach, before plonking herself back down again.

'What is happening?' Matilda said. 'Why does the baby not come?'

From the shadows at the base of the bed, the midwife smiled her toothless smile. 'It's all happening the way it should, mistress, do not fret. Some babies like to take their time.'

'But she's been labouring for hours. She's exhausted.'

'Sometimes, babies take days to arrive,' the midwife supplied unhelpfully.

One hip hitched up on the bedclothes, Matilda leaned over her sister. Something was not right. She spread her palm across Katherine's belly, feeling the various lumps and bumps of the baby beneath the distended skin. At the top of the high curve, pushing up into Katherine's ribs, Matilda could feel a rounded shape. Was it the curve of the baby's bottom, or, far worse, was it the baby's head? Fear flowed through her instantly, like water. Leaping from the bed, she strode over to the midwife, eyebrows drawn into a worried frown.

'Tell me, do you think the baby might be the wrong way around?' Not wishing to alarm her sister, Matilda forced herself to keep her voice low, equable. 'You might need to turn the child.'

The midwife cackled up at her, waving her hands in the air. 'Nay, mistress, I think he's pointing the right way. Don't fret, he'll arrive when he's good and ready, mark my words.'

'Matilda, where are you?' Katherine yelled out, her mouth gaping, contorted with fear as another contraction gripped her body, her head thrashing from side to side on the flock-filled pillow. Two thick candles set either side of the canopied bed sheened the sweat on her skin. Her hair straggled across the gauzy embroidered fabric of her night-dress, rippling strings of seaweed across a sea of white. 'Why does he not arrive?'

'I'm not certain, Katherine,' Matilda said, moving back to her sister's side. 'The midwife says all is well, everything is happening as it should be.'

'Something's wrong, I can see it in your eyes!' Katherine screeched at her. Her hand flung out in desperation, clutching at one of the bed curtains, half hauling her body into a sitting position. 'Get rid of her!' she pointed with one shaking finger at the midwife, 'and fetch our mother. She'll know what to do!'

'But Katherine, our mother...'

'I don't care. She'll come for me, she'll come out for my baby. She knows how important this child is to me, for John.' The words stuttered out of her, barely coherent. She gave Matilda a little shove. 'Go, go now! Mary will stay with me.'

Racing down the circular stairs, one hand sliding down the cool, curving banister, Matilda burst through the door into the great hall. Dismay flooded through her as she skidded to a sharp stop at the edge of the dais. There were men everywhere: drunken men, soldiers, knights, their snoring bodies heaped over tables, or lying prone beneath them. The thick, heady smell of wine, of mead, filled the air with a soporific stupor. She needed to find just one, one lowly knight who she could trust not to say anything of their destination, but would be willing to escort her to Wolverhill, the priory where her mother now lived. Her eyes scanned the hall, seeking, searching the snoring bodies.

But there appeared to be no one. Not one man

visible who hadn't drunk a vat full of John's expensive French wine.

She sighed. On reflection, it might be safer if she went alone. She couldn't risk John finding out that her mother had renounced her widow's right to own and manage their family estate at Lilleshall, couldn't risk one of his knights leaking the information back to him. John believed her mother still lived there, still believed that the strong bossy widow was in control.

Matilda sought out John's portly frame, slumped over the top table next to a snoring Henry, a thin, sparkling line of drool dropping from his gaping mouth on to the tablecloth. If he discovered that Matilda, in her mother and brother's absence, had picked up the reins of running one of the largest and most profitable estates in the country, he would seize it, claim it as his own. In the eyes of the law, unmarried women were not allowed to hold property in their own right. They were not allowed to do anything without the consent of a male guardian, be that father, brother or husband.

Pivoting sharply on her heel, she whisked away from the great hall in disgust. She would go alone. Wolverhill was not above four miles from here; she could walk it easily and still be back before the midnight bell rang out on the chapel in the village. But a horse would be faster.

No guard at the main door to the castle stopped her. The entrance hall was empty. It seemed everyone had decided to take advantage of the celebrations, to take part in the welcome of John's important guests. As she heaved open the door, thick oak planks fitted with iron rivets driven into the grey wood at intervals, no one asked her where she was going.

The night air was cool, stirred by a faint breeze, a balm on her flushed face. The pale illumination from the moon, half risen in the dark blue nap of the sky, pooled down on the cobbles of the inner bailey. In the limpid sheen of the moon, she picked out the gable end of the stable block and sprang across the uneven yard towards it. No voice hailed her, no one shouted at her to stop, to halt; the whole place was deserted, cloaked in a deafening silence. Lord help John if someone decided to attack at this precise moment; the castle was completely defenceless. Her small feet covered the short distance quickly, and as she rounded the corner of the stable block, she glanced behind her, checking to see that no one was following.

And collided with something. *Someone.*

'Oooh!' she squeaked out in shock, pressing her

palms against the tall, solid bulk, pushing herself backwards, away, away from whoever it was. But she knew who it was. Her heart thumped dangerously, excitement slicing through her, rivulets of fire.

In the moonlight, Gilan's hair shone like silver thread. He stood before her, folding his arms across his massive chest, his head tilted to one side, assessing her quietly. His eyes gleamed out from the darkness, piercing, unreadable.

'You!' she breathed, clapping one hand over her mouth, trying to gather her scattered senses. 'Why are you here?' Her accusing tone echoed around the silent bailey; she frowned back at the lit windows of the castle, as if the power of her thought could place him back where he should be. Why wasn't he in the great hall, snoring over the trestles with the rest of his companions?

'You mean, why am I not drunk out of my skull?' he replied drily.

'Well…yes, I suppose. All the rest of your companions are,' she said scathingly. His implacable regard bore into her, unnerved her. She toed the ground awkwardly with her soft leather slipper. 'I mean…you can do what you like. I was surprised to see you here, that's all.' The brittleness of her own voice startled her, shamed her, but, in the face

of his intimidating presence, her behaviour immediately became wary, aloof—her only defence.

'I came to check on our horses,' Gilan supplied
by way of explanation. She had forgotten to but-
ton her sleeves again, he realised; the skin of her
forearms was milk-white, like pouring cream. If he
rubbed his thumb upwards, from her wrist to her
elbow, would it feel like silk? Desire kicked him,
sudden and unbidden, deep in his solar plexus.

'Um, look, I'm sorry, would you excuse me?'
Matilda hopped anxiously from one foot to the
other, tucking her fingers into her belt in a vague
attempt to do something with her hands. The
breadth of his body filled the entrance to the stables—would she have to push past him, or would
he give way? 'I have to fetch a horse...my sister...'

'How is she?'

'Not good...' Tears gathered suddenly at the corners of her eyes. She jerked her head upwards, biting fretfully at her bottom lip, fighting the tremble
of her mouth. 'Not good at all...' her voice wavered, emerging in a breathless rush '...and I have
to fetch someone, someone who can help her.'

'A midwife?'

'No, she has one of those, a woman who is prov-
ing to be useless!' Matilda began to edge around
him, squeezing herself flat against the inner wall

of the stable entrance, grazing her spine against the cool stone so that no part of her body came into contact with him. He turned, watching her. Once free of his disquieting stance, she moved along the stalls, her step quick and fleeting, gown skimming across the loose straw on the packed-earth floor. Where was the grey mare, the docile animal that she always rode when she stayed with her sister? Ah, there she was.

Aware of Gilan's diamond gaze surveying her from the entrance, she lifted the bridle from the rusty hook and raised the iron latch on the wooden half door, pushing it open. Standing on tiptoe, she managed to slide the bridle over the horse's head, settling the metal bit between the animal's teeth. The mare whinnied softly, moving big teeth across Matilda's hands, searching for the carrots, or apples that Matilda normally brought for her.

'Sorry, I have nothing for you.' Matilda patted the horse's nose. With a gentle tug on the reins, she led the animal from the stall and out towards the entrance. There was no time to fit a saddle to the animal and she certainly wasn't going to ask *him* to help

Gilan's broad frame stood silhouetted in the arched entrance, long muscled legs planted firmly astride, blocking her path. His mouth was set in a firm, hard line.

'Would you let me pass, please? I have to be quick!' Urgency plucked at her voice.

'Who is going with you?'

She gave a quick shake of her head, dismissing his question. She would pretend she hadn't heard him; the less this man knew about her domestic circumstances, the better. Hitching up her dark pink skirts, she climbed the flight of steps that served as a mounting block inside the stables and slid herself over, astride, on to the horse's back. Her feet poked out from the bottom of her dress, and to her dismay, one of her leather slippers peeled off the back of her heel and plopped to the ground.

Moving into the shadows of the stable, Gilan bent down and picked it up, holding the pink leather between his fingers. Matilda eyed him warily.

'I said, "who is going with you?"' His voice held an edge of steel.

'Can I have my slipper back, please?' she asked, her voice petulant. The thin leather of her slipper looked incongruous against the muscled strength of his fingers, pinpoints of fire streaking out from the diamond cluster decorating the toe. She held out her hand, but realised, in shock, that he had grasped her ankle, clad in a silk stocking. He slipped the shoe back over her foot, the heat from his hand travelling up her leg, driving every muscle in her body to rigid alertness. The breath drove from her lungs, she couldn't speak, or protest…

Fury rose at his outrageous manhandling. Alarmed by her own response to his touch, she kicked out, toes colliding with his chest. His fingers twisted swiftly, almost as if he anticipated her movement, crushing both foot and slipper against a solid wall of muscle, one big thumb pressed up into the tender skin of her sole, sending sparks of… of what? Of sheer pleasure, scything up her leg? She glared at him, astounded, and tugged her foot once more, to no avail.

'Let go of me!' she hissed down at him. 'Your behaviour is unspeakable!'

'Not until you tell me who is going with you.'

His head was on a level with her chest, his glinting hair inches from the spot where her hands grasped the reins. The urge to sift her fingers through those glimmering strands surged up within her; she smashed down the scandalous thoughts, wondering at her own sanity.

'They're all drunk to the world up there! Completely wasted.'

'You cannot go out alone. A young maid, riding through the woods at night, dressed in all your finery? You'd be attacked, or worse.' His eyes raked her slim frame, her low-cut bodice, his meaning obvious. 'There are a lot of lonely men out there, looking for companionship.'

She hunched her shoulders forwards, embarrassed by his scrutiny, his allusions. 'I am fully aware of the dangers out there,' she replied, her voice quiet, 'but my sister is in trouble. I have no choice. There is no one to go with me.'

He shrugged his shoulders. 'I can. I can go with you.'

Chapter Six

'You?' she blurted out, astonished. 'How can you possibly go with me?'

'Easy. I fetch my horse—' Gilan pointed back into the gloom of the stables '—and I climb on his back and ride with you.' He released her foot and she tucked it hurriedly against the horse's flank, conscious of the lingering imprint of his fingers.

'But…but…' she spluttered, frowning as he moved along the stalls, his stride purposeful, 'you can't come with me. You're a stranger. I hardly know you!'

Gilan led out a huge stallion, coat glossy and smooth, muscles rippling beneath gigantic haunches. Hefting up a saddle, he then looped a bridle over the animal's head. 'I think I might be your only option.' He glanced meaningfully in the direction of the great hall, sticking a booted foot into the metal stirrup to mount up. The movement was graceful, practised; of course, he would have done it hundreds of times before. The silver light casting through the gaps in the cob wall patterned his body with stripes of dark and light; the gemstones on his sword hilt gleamed, red and violet streaks of fire.

'You don't have to do this,' she said, stumbling over her words in an effort to dissuade him. The thought of spending any length of time in this man's company sent her heart skittering off in panic. She seemed incapable of even looking at him without a surge of unwarranted emotion, of tickling excitement. 'I grew up round here. It's very safe. I can look after myself.' She chucked the words out to him without logical thought, like weapons, hoping to deflect him. Her mare sidled gently beneath her slim stature, the air from its lungs blowing out through rounded nostrils: a stifled, impatient sound. Matilda leaned forwards, patted at the flowing mane.

He brought his horse alongside her, hooves clattering against the cobbles. 'Like this afternoon, you mean?'

She flushed beneath his silvery perusal. 'That was different. Those ruffians saw the expensive hangings on the litter and thought there might be coin to be had.' Through the side split of his tunic, she could see his bulky thigh muscles pressing against the fawn wool of his chausses.

'And what do you think those same men would do if they saw a well-dressed lady, riding alone in the middle of the night?'

'Why…they…they wouldn't dare!' Heat flooded her body at her feeble response. She was losing the argument and she hated him for it.

He cocked his head to one side, his mouth curling upwards, faintly mocking. The shadows beneath his high cheekbones made them look like they had been carved from stone. 'I think you're living in a dream world, my lady. Do you think you're invincible? That you can ride unmolested through the dark and remain secure from the harsh realities of life? Of what hot-blooded men in the need of solace might do?'

She flinched at his harsh words, fingers tightening around the leather reins. *Yes!* she wanted to shout at him. *Yes, I am invincible!* Oh, how she wished it were so, how she wished she didn't have to rely on male protection. Instead she glared at him, her expression mutinous.

'Forgive me, my lord, but for all I know, you might be one of those ruffians,' she answered boldly. 'How do I know that I can trust you?' She stuck her chin in the air, openly defiant. 'You might be tricking me. You might be the one who ends up attacking me!'

His eyes darkened. 'Is that what you think? That I would pin you to the ground and throw your skirts above your head? What a low opinion you have managed to form of me in such a short time.'

'No! No!' she gasped out, head rearing back in shock at his deliberately coarse speech, eyes flicking upwards in alarm at the detailed image he portrayed. Her knees and legs trembled; if she hadn't been sitting on the horse, she would have fallen. 'You go too far with your words, my lord,' she whispered out on a scant amount of breath. She shook her head vigorously, blotches of violet exhaustion appearing beneath her beautiful eyes. 'Stop saying such horrible things to me!'

Gilan watched the colour drain from her face; her whole stature seemed to shrink before his eyes, reducing her appearance to that of a pale ghost, wan and shaking. He hadn't meant to frighten her, only to warn her, to make her aware. But she was correct; he had gone too far. A wave of unexpected guilt surged through him. 'My words will not hurt you, my lady Matilda,' he said, more gently. 'But men can, and will, if they have a chance. Don't give them that chance.' He shrugged his shoulders. 'You have nothing to fear from me. Remember, I have already saved your skin today. With many opportunities to take advantage of you, I might add. Opportunities which I have not taken.'

'When?' she blurted out, unthinking, drawing her eyebrows together in a deep frown.

His mind tacked back to the hot afternoon, a vivid picture forming in his mind. 'When you lay unconscious on the grass beside me, scarcely breathing, when we walked side by side into the forest by the tower, when…'

'Enough!' She held up her hand to silence him. A rapid blush flooded her cheeks; she hoped he wouldn't notice. To her dismay her fingers shook from his earlier words; she tucked them away. She had no wish to be reminded of her own vulnerability, no wish to recall her humiliating fall from the tower, her defeat at his hands.

'You can trust me, Matilda.' He tapped his heels against his horse's rump, the fractional movement enough to set his horse in motion, to move out into the bailey. She was more than safe from him. How could he tell her he was immune to the ways of women, incapable of feeling, his spirit deadened from the moment his brother's body fell from the scaling ladder through the thin, frosty air and hit the hard, icy ground.

Matilda peered after him, hating his arrogant assumption that she would follow without further argument or question, that she would allow him to accompany her as if she were a grateful lapdog or some pathetic piece of doe-eyed femininity. Let him think that, if he wished, but she was none of those things, and above all, not in the least bit grateful to him. She didn't want him there at all.

'Can you ride like that?' Gilan asked, eyeing her slipping seat doubtfully. His horse shifted beneath him, front hoof scraping against the cobbles of the bailey, ears pricking up with excitement.

'Of course,' Matilda scoffed at him, squeezing her knees into the mare's rounded sides. 'I've been riding like this since I was a child.' She leaned down, wrenching the hem of her gown over her ankles, as her horse trotted through the yard.

'Astride?' His voice was a low, seductive rumble.

'Yes,' she admitted. 'But most times when I knew no one was looking.' She threw an anxious glance up at her sister's window, before fixing Gilan with a more disparaging glance. 'We'd better go then.' She couldn't have sounded more reluctant if she had tried.

He followed her out of the inner bailey, through the gatehouse and across the shining moat until they rode out into the gently undulating countryside. The night held the heat of the day, a thick muggy air that stuck fabric to skin. Perspiration gathered at Matilda's brow; her circlet pressed against her forehead, hot against her temples. Her gown bunched up beneath her, two gowns, in fact, two layers of material to make her even hotter. The material gathered around her thighs, annoying and cumbersome. She eyed Gilan's pleated tunic and fitted trousers with annoyance. How easy it was for men, with the simple cut of their clothes and the absence of endless layers. He appeared cool, self-assured in the saddle, while she must look like an overheated fishwife. No matter. She wasn't out to impress him.

They rode across a landscape soaked in moonlight, a pearly shine from a navy sky. Freed from the towering confines of the castle walls, they broke out into rolling, open grassland, fields stretching away from the dusty chalk track in a series of haphazard gridlines. Scrubby hawthorn hedges delineated the rough squares of pasture; sinuous lines of willow denoted a watercourse, or spring line. Towards the west, towards the estuary, the sky lightened, imperceptibly, the fading mark of a dying sun.

Acutely aware of the man following her, Matilda fought hard to maintain an upright seat on the mare; riding bareback was far harder than she remembered, despite her brave assurances towards Gilan. Along the narrow rope of her spine her muscles protested with clenched exhaustion, but she would not give in, would not slump in front of this man. He had seen her weakness once, after she had fallen from the tower; she would not give him the satisfaction of seeing it again.

She curved her body around in the saddle, searching him out in the shadows. The embroidery on his tunic glimmered; she caught the flash of gems from his sword hilt. 'We can gallop along this next bit,' she explained, chewing at her lip. 'The track runs straight for a good mile now.' The breeze from the coast tussled at his hair, sending a few glinting strands wayward. Her heart constricted and she turned smartly back in her seat, eyes fixed on the horizon line, brows drawn together sharply, puckering the skin on her forehead. What was it about this man that made her heart pound so?

Laughter bubbled in his chest, eased the constricting band that seemed permanently strapped across his torso. The chit made it sound as if she were apologising for the fact that he had to gallop, as if he were unable to perform such a manoeuvre, that she doubted his dexterity on a horse! Her way with words was delightfully obtuse, unconventional. Another man might have taken offence at her speech, but with him? Nay, it made him smile.

Matilda kicked the flanks of her mare, picked up the pace. Her horse's tail fanned out, picking up the shift of air. She hunkered down against the animal's back, gripping the bridle, gripping the mane, anything that would help her to maintain her seat.

After what seemed like an interminable length of time, but was perhaps in fact not longer than a mile, she spotted the substantial outlines of Wolverhill against the dusky sky: the dark heft of the grain barn, the rising stone walls of the priory. A flame burned in the small church tower which also acted as a lighthouse, a marker for any ships out in the estuary.

Sighing with relief, Matilda hauled on the reins, slowed the mare to a walk in front of the small gatehouse. Her leg muscles burned from the amount of effort she had exerted in trying to stay on the horse at speed and she rubbed the tops of her thighs surreptitiously. There was no guard, no soldier to challenge them or prevent them entering. The whole place was quiet, save for the whisper of breeze through the willows along the drainage ditches, an owl hooting in the distance. The nuns were safely tucked into their hard, narrow beds at this hour, bolted into their grey stone cells. Gilan drew along-side her, his knee jogging into her hip as he skit-tered his horse to a stop.

'What is this place? Whom do you seek?' Gilan asked.

'It's a nunnery,' she explained. Her veil, a diaph-anous shift of white silk, blew forwards, around her face, and stuck against her cheek. She pulled it away. 'There is a woman here who is skilled in the art of childbirth,' she explained, edging her horse carefully away from him. He didn't need to know that the woman was her mother. 'She has the abil-ity to turn babies who are the wrong way around, breech babies.'

He nodded. 'You'd better go in alone. I don't want to scare the living daylights out of a bunch of nuns.' Leaning over, he grabbed her reins. 'I'll stay here, hold the horses.'

She slithered awkwardly down to the cobbles, staggered back a little under his astute gaze. Brush-ing down her skirts, she stalked towards the open archway and disappeared.

'No, I can't do it, Matilda! You can't ask that of me!' Her mother stared at her, shocked and terri-fied.

'Mother, listen to me! This is Katherine's baby

we're talking about. Your own daughter! I'd understand if I were asking you to attend some stranger,
but this…this is Katherine! You know how much
it means to her for this baby to survive! You know
the problems she has endured.'

Her mother sat on the side of the truckle bed,
hunched over. Her long dark hair was bundled
into a thick plait that fell over one shoulder. Her
nightdress flowed out from her neck, voluminous,
a wealth of undyed linen, plain—no embroidery,
no adornment. Through the slit window, Matilda
could see a strip of midnight-blue sky, sparkling
with stars. She sighed; she had been here for too
long already, pleading with her mother, cajoling
her…begging her.

'You know my situation, daughter—' her mother
raised tear-soaked eyes towards her '—since your
father died, I…I sought seclusion, I sought a way
forwards without the man I loved.' She scrunched
a white linen handkerchief between her fingers,
the fabric sodden with tears already shed. 'And I
found it here, with these good nuns. I haven't been
out in the world for nearly two years. Katherine
will understand.'

Matilda shook her head. A stump of flickering
candle cast her mother's jittery shadow on the wall.
Damp gleamed from the thick white stone like a

skin of sparkling sweat. 'I'm not certain she will, Mother. Not this time. John is putting great pressure on her. I suspect it might be her last chance to provide a viable heir.'

Her mother placed her face into the palms of her hands, weeping openly. 'Please don't do this to me, Matilda, please don't make me do this! It would kill me to go out there, you know it would. Since your father...' Drops ran from her chin, plopping down into the coarse-weave nightgown covering her lap.

Matilda closed her eyes with despair, squeezed them so tightly, she could see flickers of light cross on the red insides of her eyelids. Her mother was not going to come. Katherine's baby would die. Her shoulders slumped with misery, with disappointment. She had failed.

'Matilda!' Outside in the corridor she could hear a rough male voice calling her. 'Matilda!' And alongside the deep, masculine tones, an outraged tirade, overlaying his constant shouting. *Oh, good Lord,* she thought, *what is he doing here?*

Her mother lifted her head, startled by the unfamiliar noise, then shrunk back into the corner of her bed, huddling, drawing her knees up to her chest. Springing from the bed, Matilda wrenched open the door, stuck her head out into the musty corridor. Gilan was marching down the stone passage, banging his great fist on every cell door, calling her name with every thump. And at his side, her lined face screwed up, little mouth puckered with anger, the prioress, no doubt pulled from some deep slumber by his bellowing, her sparrow-like frame skipping frantically to keep up with his long-legged strides.

'My lord, this is totally improper!' she was berating him. 'Men are not allowed in the priory. You need to leave—now!'

'Not until I find who I'm looking for,' he roared at her, hammering on the next door with a raised fist. The noise ricocheted up and down the dim corridor, squeaks of feminine alarm erupting from behind the closed doors.

Matilda moved out into the corridor. 'Gilan, stop,' she called out to him. Was that the first time she had used his Christian name? The word felt strangely intimate coming from her mouth. 'I am here. You have found me.'

He strode towards her, covering the stone flags swiftly. 'You were gone too long,' he pronounced by way of explanation. His eyes swept over her, glinting, diamond-cut.

'What on earth could happen to me, in a house full of nuns?' Matilda hissed at him. 'Now, you truly have scared them half to death!' Beyond his shoulder, she watched the prioress move along the chamber doors, murmuring reassurances to the awakened nuns, coaxing them back to their beds.

He shrugged his shoulders. 'Who knows what might have happened? I thought you had spent too much time in here.'

Matilda shook her head, her lips tight, disapproving. 'You can't go around terrorising innocent people! Especially good people such as these. This isn't the Baltic, you know. You're not on crusade anymore.'

His face clouded, like a veil dropping. She peered up at him in horror, watched as the spark in his eyes snuffed out, deadened. Had her angry words forced him across some invisible boundary, pushed him into forbidden territory? The shadowed air between them pulled tight, time vanishing. She resisted the urge to move away from him, to retreat from the sudden bleakness of his expression, the hardening of his jaw; instead, she wound her arms tightly across her bosom, barricading her soft curves against whatever onslaught was to come.

He scowled down at her, eyes fathomless pools of black liquid. 'Do not speak of what you do not know,' he growled out. 'Just fetch the woman and let's get out of here.'

'She refuses to come.' Matilda sighed, shaking her head, relieved at his reaction to her harsh words. 'I have spent ages trying to persuade her, but she will not budge.'

'I'll budge her,' Gilan said gruffly. 'Surely this is her livelihood? Why does she refuse?'

Because she has given up, thought Matilda, despondently. *My own mother, who I used to think so strong, so capable, has been reduced to a shivering wreck by the death of my father. A woman incapable of facing the outside world, who has hidden herself away in this house of prayer.*

Gilan watched the fleeting sadness cross Matilda's face. 'Let me fetch her out for you,' he suggested, more kindly. 'I'm sure she can be persuaded to come.' He took a step forwards, indicating that Matilda should move out of the way. But she huddled into the archway, pressing her hands up against the stone to stop his forward progress; the huge blocks of cut limestone framed her slender build, emphasised the fragility of her bones, the delicacy of her collarbone.

He took another step forwards. 'Out of the way, Matilda.' His knees brushed against hers through the fabric of her gown.

'No,' she managed to force out, one hand flying up instinctively to push against him. He was too close, crowding into the archway with her!

The wooden door pressed into her back, the iron latch jabbing at her shoulder blade as she hitched away from him. She would not allow him to enter the chamber, to terrorise her mother. Her fingers splayed across the pleated tunic, unconsciously rubbing at the ridges of tough muscle beneath the layer of material.

He was so close that the rush of his breath stirred the wisps of hair on her forehead. Angling his gaze, he pinpointed her fingers fanning out on his chest, her touch sending darts of desire through his hard frame. In the shadows he picked out the spikes of dark feathered lashes, the limpid profile of her flushed cheek, the etched curve of her top lip. A lick of pleasure, of anticipation, rushed through him, treacherous, wild, unstable. One step, one step closer and he could have her pinned against the solid wood of the door, her delectable body crammed against his, his mouth against hers. On those soft, rose-petal lips. If she tilted her head up slightly, then…

'I must ask you both to leave.' A censorious voice broke into the sensual luxury of his thoughts. The prioress. She stood beside them, addressing Gilan, poking a bony finger into his upper arm. 'Your behaviour has been most improper. Who is your lord? I will make a formal complaint…and make sure the bishop gets to hear of this!' Her brown beady eyes alighted on Matilda, huddled in the doorway. 'And you, young lady! I had expected better behaviour from you with all your mother has been through!'

Mother? Gilan frowned. What was the prioress talking about?

'We're leaving...now,' Matilda said, hurriedly. Breath whooshed from her lungs. Her hand dropped from Gilan's chest and she twisted her fingers together guiltily, cheeks flaming. 'I'm so sorry for all the trouble we've caused.' The stone wall scraped against her spine as she edged awkwardly past Gilan, head hanging. What was it that made her body leap in response to the merest brush of his arm, or hand? She marched off down the corridor, neat shoulders set in a rigid line, without turning back to see if Gilan was following.

He wasn't.

'Mother?' Gilan repeated his thoughts out loud, indicating with an incline of his head towards the prioress that he expected an answer.

'Yes, that's her mother in there, didn't you know? And I'm probably going to have to spend the rest of the night trying to settle her back to sleep, more's the pity!' The prioress pushed irritably at the door of the chamber, squeezing her wiry body through the narrow gap and slamming the door in his face.

* * *

Once clear of the Priory gatehouse, Matilda kicked her horse into a gallop, angry, frustrated at her mother's weakness, her pathetic demeanour. Disappointment flooded through her, weakening her knees, her wrists; what an utter waste of time the whole trip had been! She wanted to cry, to weep, but *he* was there, the hooves of his destrier thumping up the track behind her, sending up clods of chalky mud, dogging her steps.

As the path narrowed, she was forced to slow her horse to a walk. Gilan nudged his horse in beside her, tugging on the reins to match his animal's pace to her own. 'That was your mother in there?' he questioned mildly. 'What's she doing with the nuns?'

The wind had picked up, blowing in fresh and strong from the estuary, bending the tough tussocks of bleached grass. Matilda shivered, hunching over in the saddle. 'She prefers it there,' she mumbled in reply, keeping her eyes set on the track ahead.

'Why would she not come? Why would she not help her own daughter?'

'Because she's frightened, Gilan. Not strong enough for the outside world.'

'Not even to help her own daughter?'

Matilda pushed her flapping veil back around her shoulders. 'Not even for that.' A vast shudder clenched at her heart; Katherine would lose her baby now and it would all be her fault.

'Is that why you live with your sister?' he asked.

'What...?' Snared by the worry about Katherine, Gilan's next question was unexpected. She sucked in her breath. How much to tell him? The man would be gone by tomorrow morning, riding away from her sister's castle with Henry and his men. Did it really matter if she told him the truth? She doubted he would be that interested in her domestic arrangements anyway.

'No, I don't live with my sister.' Matilda forced her tone to remain neutral, hoping he wouldn't ask any further questions. 'I come over to see Katherine almost every day at the moment.' She lifted blue eyes towards him, haunted but determined. 'She needs me. And right now, she needs me more than ever.' A wave of panic crested over her, clamping her lips together, Matilda tried to prevent the bubble of tears welling up, sadness snagging at her chest. Jaw set, she focused on the bobbing mane of her horse, willing herself not to cry, not to burst into tears in front of this man. 'How can I tell her that there's no one to help her, that I've failed?' Her voice wobbled with tiredness, with misery.

Sympathy crashed through him, potent, visceral, hitting him in the solar plexus with the force of an axe. Surprisingly, he understood. She would do anything for her sister, such was their bond of sibling love. Just as he would do anything for his brother. For Pierre.

Would have done.

Pain hit him, scythed through his gut. He had run through the hail of arrows, the great gobs of hot tar splattering down from the turrets to reach his brother. Cradled his fallen body in his arms. Idly, he rubbed at the top of his thigh, ground his fingers down into the hard muscle. A flick of hot tar had burned through his woollen leggings, burned into skin unprotected by leg armour as he had run, and now the scar itched. A legacy. A reminder of that terrible day.

Rags of cloud swept across the dark sky, shifting the limpid shine of the moon. Matilda caught the flash of pain in his eyes, a shocking bleakness. Ducking her head, she lifted her fingers to her circlet and patted the coils of hair over her ears—self-conscious gestures. 'I'm sorry,' she croaked. 'It's no concern of yours.'

But it was, he thought suddenly, surprisingly. He wanted to help, to find out more about this unusual woman who had sprung so unexpectedly into his life. 'You want to help your sister,' he replied. 'It's understandable.'

'I've failed her.'

'No,' he said, his voice low and calm, so strong. 'From where I'm sitting, you're doing everything in your power to help that baby survive.'

Astonishment coursed through her. Was he complimenting her?

'Is there no one else who can help? No other midwife?'

She scrubbed at her eyes with small fists, beating back the tiredness. 'The only woman for miles around is sitting at my sister's feet. There's no one else.'

'There's you.'

'Are you mad? I have no knowledge of how to do such things! I can't do it, don't you realise? That's the whole reason I went to fetch my mother!' But even as the words were out, she knew she lied. She had attended many births with her mother and watched the various techniques performed, even helped on some occasions. But never on her own. 'I've seen it done.'

'Well, then.'

Listening to the steady tread of the horses' hooves, she bit her lip. Why hadn't she tried to help her sister before she had made this fruitless journey? Because she had felt she wasn't capable? Yes, that was it, the fear of failure. If someone else turned the baby and it didn't work, at least then she wouldn't be culpable.

But surely...surely her help was better than none at all. 'I could try...' she said doubtfully.

'What's the matter?' he said. 'I think you can do it.'

'Who are you to tell me what I can and can't do?' she flared back at him, truculent. 'You scarce know me!'

'I know that you didn't balk when those ruffians attacked you this afternoon,' Gilan replied. The brass on his bridle jangled as he shifted position in the saddle. 'I know that your hand was steady enough to nearly shoot my ear off.' She caught the wry, upward curl of his mouth. 'I think you are capable.'

In astonishment, she tipped up her chin up to him, met his gaze with puzzlement. No man had ever spoken to her like this before. Her father—God rest his soul—John, and even her beloved brother, Thomas, all of them had chastised her for her hoydenish ways, implored her to be more lady-like, more restrained. But this man? He sounded like he was paying her a compliment!

'Should we gallop?' he asked, nodding at the

widening track before them, the spread of extensive countryside.

Matilda nodded, a new confidence growing within her, fortifying her limp frame. She had made up her mind. And he, Gilan, this daunting knight who had appeared in her life from nowhere, had helped her. 'Yes, let's go,' she said, squeezing her knees against the sides of her mare.

Chapter Seven

'It's a girl!' Matilda declared, handing the squalling, red-faced bundle up to one of Katherine's ladies-in-waiting. A wave of relief crested through her; she sat back on her heels, exhausted. Tired, but happy. It had taken the remainder of the night, and a good part of the next morning, but finally, finally, after long hours of pushing and cajoling, of tears and screaming, John and Katherine's daughter had been delivered safely. She thought of Gilan's encouraging words last night and realised she wouldn't be able to thank him; he and Henry would be long gone by now. The ten o'clock bell had already rung out on the chapel in the outer bailey, and sunlight crept across the woven rugs scattered across the floor of the bedchamber, picking out the madder-dyed red of the pattern.

The baby continued to bawl, the noise becoming louder as one of Katherine's ladies dabbed the new pink skin with a soft cloth dipped in warm water, its limbs jerking out at all angles in protest. Still kneeling at the foot of the bed, pins and needles beginning to run up her feet and calves, Matilda watched the new baby's antics with a smile on her face. A feeling of exhausted contentment washed over her; she was happy for her sister. The baby girl was alive and healthy, and that was all that mattered. After Katherine's string of disappointments, her miscarriages, this moment was one to celebrate.

Emotion crimped her heart. Her gaze lingered on the water sparkling down from the violent, kicking limbs and she bit down hard on her bottom lip. She would never have this, never hold a child of her own in her arms. She had realised long ago that wedlock was not for her; she was too wayward, too bossy for most men, and she had no intention of curtailing her ways, of becoming someone she was not. If that meant not having children, or marriage, then so be it. Her mind zigzagged back to the evening before, to Gilan standing over her at her mother's chamber door. His big frame folding around her, the musky smell of his skin, the husky rasp of his voice. Delight skipped through her veins at the memory. It was the closest she had ever been to a man. Ever.

She tightened her mouth, fighting a flicker of disappointment. Nay, it was better that he had gone. Lord knew what his constant presence would have made her do next. He had made her behave out of context, sent her mind into disarray, looping illogically out of control. She was in no doubt that any further contact with him would be disastrous; at least now, her body and mind were her own, firmly embedded within her control.

With a soft moan, Katherine turned her face away from the window, away from her new daughter. Her sable locks strung out across the stark white of the pillow, like straggling seaweed on the beach; the hair was matted, unkempt after her night of exertion.

'Katherine?' Jerking out of her reverie, Matilda eased herself up from the floor, bundling the stained linens together in a pile for burning. Her limbs ached from being in a confined position for so long and she stretched her legs and toes out, raising her arms above her head to stretch out the kink in her spine as she moved slowly, awkwardly, towards the head of the bed.

'He will kill me,' Katherine whispered. Her wrecked, tear-stained face was pinched with sorrow as she turned towards Matilda.

'No, Katherine. You don't understand. Your baby

daughter is alive and well. Look. Look over there!'
Matilda gestured towards the window, where one
of Katherine's ladies was now using a soft towel to
dry the yelling, indignant newborn. A sable fuzz
of hair peeked out above the crook of the lady's
arm, burnished by the morning light nudging in
through the window.

'She's beautiful,' said Matilda.

'She's a girl,' Katherine juddered out, her voice
muffled by the pillow. Her fingers plucked at the
fine linen, agitated. 'John wanted a boy. You'll
have to go and tell him, Matilda. Don't let him in
here. I can't face him. I can't!' Tears of desperation flowed down Katherine's face as she turned
towards Matilda, her expression distraught.

Matilda crouched down by the bed, stroked back
her sister's sweat-streaked hair. 'You'll feel better
soon,' she said. 'When you've fed your daughter,
when you've had a bath…'

'No, I won't.' Katherine's response was clipped,
bitter. 'John wanted a boy! I wanted a boy! You'll
have to tell him, Matilda. Tell John that he has a
daughter and see what he does!' Her voice rose
shrilly, tinged with a tremulous note of hysteria.
Against the bedlinens, Katherine's face was milk-
white, pallid, her lips cracked and dry.

Matilda grasped her sister's hand; the fingers

were limp, cold. 'I think you are exhausted, Katherine. I'll go down and ask the servants to bring up some broth. You need your strength.'

'Find John,' Katherine whispered, her eyes half closing. 'Oh, Lord, I wish I had died along with the child. God knows what he's going to do to me.'

'He will do nothing to you, Katherine,' Matilda replied briskly, frowning at her sister's dramatic words. 'I'll go and find him now.' She moved over to a low table by the window. Pouring water from a jug into an earthenware bowl, she rinsed her hands in the cool liquid and splashed her face. Submerging a linen washcloth, she wrung out the drops from the material, smoothing it across the back of her neck, across her throat. She longed for a bath, a change of clothes. Drying her hands, she snared the eye of another of Katherine's ladies, hovering by the huddled, weeping form of her mistress in her bed. The lady tilted her head sideways, mouth twisted into a wry smile, indicating her surprise at Katherine's behaviour, her reaction to the birth.

Matilda shrugged her shoulders. Tiredness swamped her, robbing her brain of logical thought. She was at a loss to explain Katherine's strange, despairing mood. At a loss as to the method by which she could persuade Katherine to accept her daughter. All she wanted to do was to leave this place, to go home to Lilleshall and sleep. But first, she had to find John.

The great hall was deserted, except for two men-servants working industriously along each trestle table. One piled the detritus from the night before onto a wooden tray whilst the other followed him, scrubbing vigorously at the stained wooden planks. Pewter tankards lay on their sides, both on the tables and across the flagstones; half-chewed meat bones and lumps of bread spread haphazardly across the tables. Dogs trotted about, sniffing hungrily, seeking out a stray crust here, a discarded bit of fat there, their paws making little sound on the mead-soaked straw that covered the grey flagstones.

As she hovered in the doorway, Matilda's stomach heaved at the stench of stale alcohol in the air, the smell of greasy meat and rank straw. Pressing one hand against her belly, she wondered if Henry and his men had found the guest accommodation last night—in her haste to help Katherine upstairs, she had forgotten to give the servants any orders. She hoped John had remembered to tell the servants to make up the truckle beds in the guest tower. Not that they would have been there for very long. Judging by the mess they had made, she suspected they had been taking advantage of John's hospitality until the small hours of the morning.

Seeing her on the high dais, both servants stopped what they were doing, bowing respectfully.

'Any news, my lady?' asked one of them, in the process of carrying a heavily laden tray in the direction of the kitchens.

Matilda nodded. 'Yes, but your lord has to be the first to know. Do you know where he might be?'

'I'm here.' A guttural voice cut across her question, assailed her. From the opposite end of the high dais, John approached from the garderobe, adjusting the leg of his hose, before flapping his tunic down over his thighs. Matilda turned her gaze away in distaste, pert nose wrinkling.

John threw himself into his chair, eyes bleary, bloodshot. 'Christ, my head!' He leaned forwards suddenly, thumping one clenched fist against his forehead. 'It's like hammers in there!' With one hand pressed against his lined brow, he wrenched his thick neck towards Matilda. 'Haven't you got any of those powders you women take?'

Matilda frowned. Why did he not ask about Katherine? Had John drunk so much that he had forgotten that his wife had been labouring away half the night?

'Well?' he barked, unsmiling. His beady eyes roved over her, narrowing on her slim waist in the rose-coloured gown, staring critically at her silky chestnut hair. She had removed her circlet and veil at some point in the night and her hair was only held upright by the few pins driven into the plaited coils above each ear. One of the coils was beginning to work loose; she could feel the slipping hair across her ear.

'I can fetch you some in a moment, if you wish...' she began hesitantly.

'Fetch me some now!' John thumped his fist heavily on the table.

Matilda stepped forwards, her spirit quailing at John's slurred tones. A frozen lump began to form in the centre of her stomach. She stretched out one hand towards his shoulder, intending to touch him, but she changed her mind as his bloodshot eyes constricted, half closing, and his skin suffused with a dull red colour, obscuring the normal unhealthy grey pallor of his face.

'Do it now!' he barked again at her.

'John!' She raised her voice above his, cutting off his speech. 'Have you forgotten what was happening last night? Katherine was in labour, don't you remember?'

He groaned, lifting one hand to his forehead, slumping back in his chair. 'Tell me, then.'

Matilda took a deep breath, feeling the hiss of air slide into her lungs. 'You have a beautiful daughter, John, a beautiful, healthy baby.' She clasped her hands together in front of her stomach, as if the physical barrier could ward off John's next words, the inevitable blow.

But John was staring at the wine-splattered table-cloth, seemingly fixated by it. She wondered if he had heard her. How much alcohol had he consumed last night? He could barely prop himself upright beside the table; his eyes roamed all over the place, unfocused.

'John?' she prompted. 'Did you hear me?'

He stood up so abruptly that she took a couple of steps backwards. He had half raised his fist, as if he were going to hit her for bringing the news. The news that he had no wish to hear.

John's eyes bulged dangerously, but his arm dropped to his side. He swayed.

'You have a daughter, John,' Matilda repeated, more loudly this time, forcing herself not to flinch in his presence. She would not, could not, be scared of this man, like her sister was. Such a pathetic figure was someone to be pitied, not frightened of. Once this was over, she could go home, back to the routines of her own life. If only John would hurry up and acknowledge the information she was telling him, then she could leave. She stood within a scant foot of his wobbling, unbalanced figure, his sour breath wafting over her.

'I heard what you said, sister-in-law.' John ground the words out. 'But you're not telling me what I want to hear.'

Matilda's shoulders sagged. Why was he making this so difficult? 'Why don't you go up and see her?' she suggested, smoothing her palms down the front of her skirts, noting the small flecks of blood adhering to the silk.

'Why don't I go up and see her?' he bellowed back at her, facing her now. Flecks of spittle landed on her face and she wiped them away with the back of her hand, disgusted. 'Why don't I go up and see her?' John planted his hands on his hips, leaning forwards so his face hovered inches from Matilda's. 'Because I have no wish to see my little runt of a daughter, Matilda. A daughter is no good to me. I can't pass on this castle, these lands, all my wealth to a stupid daughter! Don't you understand, you foolish mare! A daughter is no use at all. I want a son. I only want a son!' His straggling grey hair fell forwards across his pleated forehead and he swept it back again, in irritation.

All *our* wealth, corrected Matilda silently. This castle had belonged to their mother before Katherine's marriage and John made no secret of wanting to own all the property and land belonging to the two sisters.

'I will have a son, Matilda! Mark my words. And if my own wife won't provide one, then I'll have to use other means!' He was strutting about before her with rage, a few steps one way, before turning, taking a few steps the other way, like an outraged bantam cock.

Matilda scarcely heard his words, almost staggering back under the weight of her fatigue. Why was no one happy about this birth except for her? She had successfully managed to turn the baby, encouraged those squalling limbs to emerge into the world. She had watched her niece take her first breath, outraged and indignant, her flesh pinking up quickly in the cloth across her lap. To her, the whole occasion had been so wonderful, so special, but everyone around her seemed intent on taking the joy out of the situation.

She turned to go, a sense of wretchedness tugging at her heart. Her long skirts pursued her, slithering across the dusty wooden floor. She would go and bid farewell to her sister, and then leave.

'Wait!' John seized her arm, his grip pinching into her soft flesh.

She arched her gaze back to him, outraged, pulling at his grip. 'John! Let go of me. What do you think you're doing?'

'Did you hear what I said?'

'No, not really. You're obviously not happy.' She frowned down at the pudgy fingers digging into her upper arm. 'Would you let go of me, please?' Her voice wobbled treacherously, the confidence suddenly leaching from her tone.

'I will have a son by any means possible, I said.'

'Fine, it's no concern of mine,' Matilda replied. Let him find some willing whore on whom to father a bastard son, so the line of succession could be maintained.

'You, Matilda. I will beget a child by you. You share your sister's lineage. You will come into a sizeable fortune on your mother's death. My child, my son, shall be your son.'

Shock ricocheted through her; her knees sagged. She stared into his sweaty, pallid face. 'Have you truly lost your wits?' she said, all the time tugging at her arm. John couldn't be serious, could he? She glanced around the great hall, searching for help; the two servants from earlier had disappeared.

'Come with me, now!' He began to drag her across the high dais, towards the side door.

'No, I shan't go with you! I won't! You can't do this!' She yanked at her arm, desperately trying to escape his hold. He was stronger than his portly stature implied. 'John, you can't do this!' They had reached the curtained doorway. Yanking her arm down with a strong tug, she managed to break his hold, to turn away. But he seized the back of her dress, spun her round with such force that her head thumped against the wall.

His hand closed around her neck, his elbow rammed into her shoulder, pinning her against the damp plaster 'You will do this, Matilda, whether you like it or not. And we can do it here, in full view of the servants, with your skirts thrown over your head like a common whore, or we can do it in the privacy of my chambers. Your choice.'

His breath was foetid, rancid with old wine. She closed her eyes, fear running through her like icy liquid, sapping the strength from her limbs, diluting her fighting spirit. Hot tears sprang beneath her eyelids. Was this how her life was going to be? Her innocence seized by her greedy brother-in-law because he wanted a son to inherit? Was this it?

* * *

For the second time that morning, Gilan strode across the cobbled courtyard and into the stables. The horses had been fed and the stable lads were busy running around following his earlier orders: to fit bridles and saddles in readiness for the journey ahead. He lifted his chin to the rafted ceiling of the stables, indicating the floor above, where Henry's soldiers had been housed on simple truckle beds for the night. 'Any sign? Any sounds at all?' he asked one small boy, who darted past him, his arm loaded down with leather bridles.

'Not a peep, my lord.' A cheeky grin flashed out from the boy's grimy face before he scampered on his way again.

Gilan sighed. Scooping a handful of oats out of the wooden tub by the open doorway, he moved over to his own horse, who snorted at his approach, jerking his head up in welcome. 'Here,' he said, holding out his palm, feeling the animal's warm push of breath, the soft muzzle against his skin. He patted the long nose and sighed again, a restlessness coursing through his veins. He was ready to go, to leave this place and head north. But Henry and his soldiers were not. Having drunk so much the night before, they remained in the depths of a deep alcohol-laced sleep and presumably would not rouse for another few hours.

Gilan had woken early, gradually surfacing to full consciousness by listening to the birds twittering outside his window. Before climbing into the generous four-poster bed the night before, he had thrown open the glazed panel, finding the air in the chamber thick, oppressive with heat. His saddlebags containing his clothes had already been delivered to his room, sitting in a neat pile in front of an oak coffer. There was a jug of water and an earthenware bowl for washing. Linen towels had been provided, folded neatly on the chest, a new bar of lavender soap placed on top.

It had taken him a long time to go to sleep, his mind alert, picking over the details of his journey with the puzzling Matilda. The ride across the mood-soaked countryside. Her mother, isolated, detached from society within a priory. Idly, he wondered who was looking after *her*? Was anyone responsible for her? A father, maybe? She had said she had a brother, but had been surprisingly vague as to his whereabouts. Maybe she had a poor, long-suffering husband locked up somewhere—it really wouldn't surprise him. But then, she had been evasive in the extreme on his questioning.

A pair of blue eyes, the colour of forget-me-nots,

danced across his mind, imperious, taunting. He
wondered what she was doing now, this woman
who refused to behave as she was supposed to.
Very early in the morning, before dawn, he had
heard the cry of a newborn and had felt an in-
sane desire to leap out of bed and go to her, to
offer praise for her skill as a midwife. Instead, he
had bunched his fists down by his bare thighs and
stayed rigidly in his bed. He had been able to help
her when she needed help, despite the fact that she
didn't want him to, and that was that. His role was
to support Henry, to aid him in his campaign to
overthrow King Richard, and he would do well to
keep such thoughts at the forefront of his mind.

He would go and see how Henry was faring,
try to wake him. Brushing a length of straw from
the blue linen of his tunic, he marched back to
the main castle across the cobbled courtyard. The
morning sun touched the glazed windows at the
front, firing the glass to molten gold. Leaping
up the main steps, two at a time, he moved through
the main arch and up the stairs to the great hall.
He blinked once or twice, his eyes adjusting to
the shadowed gloom. Servants rustled through the
freshly laid straw on the flagstones, setting out the
pewter ware and long serving platters in anticipation of the midday meal. The smell of roasting

meat filtered along the vaulted corridor from the kitchens. His mouth watered.

He placed one hand on the door of the spiral staircase that led to Henry's chamber in the south-west turret, intending to push it open.

A scream. A woman's scream broke through the silence of the hall. Then another, and another.

Gilan's head whipped around, instantly seeking the source, his hair blazing, a flame in the dim chamber. He turned, moving back into the centre of the hall. 'Who is that? What is going on?' he rapped out to the servants, who stood rigid, like statues, rooted to the spot with fear.

'Who is that?' he roared again, louder this time, grabbing one servant's shoulder and shaking him. Tension gripped his solar plexus, pulling the muscles taut in anticipation of a fight—did he know already?

One of the servants raised a shaking hand, pointed over to a corner of the high dais, then ducked his gaze, not wanting to become involved.

Gilan sprinted across the flagstones, vaulting up onto the dais, then charged through the curtained archway set in the far corner. He fought through the muffling woven curtains, becoming impatient, almost ripping them off the thin iron rail in his efforts to push through. The screams had stopped; he moved into darkness, the fierceness of his breath thumping in his ears. His leather soles made no sound across the uneven floor; he trailed his fingers against the gritty stone wall to guide him along the passageway.

He thought he heard breathing, a stifled sob.

Then suddenly, barrelling out of nowhere, out of the darkness, a slight weight cannoned into him, fists pummelling at his chest, raining blows on his face, his head. He caught the sift of polished hair, the faintest smell of lavender, and grasped easily at the flailing arms.

It was her. Matilda.

Chapter Eight

He pinioned her hands against his chest. Twisting and writhing in his easy hold, she reared back, eyes unfocused, wide with terror, heels skittering against the floor.

'Matilda, stop! It's me, Gilan.'

The low, iron-threaded tone shot through the frantic pounding of her brain, the relentless waves of panic. Gilan? What was he doing here? Hadn't he and Henry left hours ago?

Against his light hold around her wrists, her body slumped with a shuddering sob. Up close, he could see the pearly luminescence of her face, the glimmer of tears on her long eyelashes, sparkles of light. A pulse beating frantically at her neck.

'Let me through, please,' she gasped, breath stumbling over the words. Wriggling one hand free, she clutched at her bodice, the fabric bunched beneath her fingers, her knuckles straining white.

Her face was ashen, a red mark circling the fragile bones of her neck.

'What's happened to you?' he demanded. 'Is it your sister?' As she swayed before him, his hands moved to tighten around her upper arms, thumbs pressing into the soft curve of muscle, holding her upright. The front of her gown had been ripped downwards, a gash of tattered, trailing threads, of sagging cloth that revealed the silky white slope of one breast.

'Gilan, please!' she said urgently, turning her head to check that the corridor behind her was empty, that no one pursued her. 'Let me through! I cannot stay here!' She hopped from one foot to another, her whole body jittery with nerves, her eyes huge with fear.

'Who did this?' he demanded, silvery eyes glittering dangerously in the half-light, searching her face for answers.

She shook her head desperately, panic clogging her lungs, shoving ineffectually at him, trying to push him aside. 'Gilan, I have to go… He'll be after me in a moment.' In the tight confines of the corridor he smelled the sweet fragrance of her hair, the clean scent of her skin. 'It won't be long before…' Her hand fluttered in front of her mouth, agitated.

'It won't be long before…what?' he asked, tilting his head on one side in question, his jawline square—cut, rugged.

'Before he comes around,' she whispered. 'I hit him over the head with a candlestick, a heavy one. It was the only thing I could do!' Her voice rose unsteadily. 'Oh Lord, maybe I've killed him!'

'Looks like he deserved it,' Gilan replied, his voice rough, hoarse. 'Who was it?'

'It was John,' Matilda murmured, her eyes half closing in despair. 'The man who is married to my sister.' She pursed her lips together, trying to stop the constant chattering of her teeth. 'How could he have done this to me?'

'What did he do? Did he actually…?'

'No, no.' She shook her head hurriedly, not wanting to hear the awful words. 'Nothing like that! I managed to stop him, before…before…' Tears splashed down her cheeks and on to his sleeve, marking the blue material with dark, spreading droplets.

Thank God. Gilan sent up a silent prayer. 'Where is he?' A cold, sliding anger whipped through his veins.

'In there.' With a pale, quivering hand, Matilda indicated a door farther down the corridor.

'Stay here, whilst I check,' Gilan commanded. He released his hold so suddenly that she lurched backwards, staggering against the lumpy wall, knocking her shoulder. A debilitating feebleness tugged the strength from her knees; her legs took on the consistency of wet rope, useless. She couldn't seem to stop shaking.

In an instant, Gilan was in front of her again, his face grim, set in harsh, unsmiling lines. She forced herself to raise her lolling head, pressing her hands against the wall for support.

'Is he dead?' Matilda jerked her chin up, trying to suppress the fresh rush of tears that threatened to spill over her bottom lashes. The buttons on Gilan's blue tunic were undone at the high neck and the edges of his collar flapped outwards, revealing the tanned, corded column of his neck, the flash of white shirt beneath. He seemed so calm, so capable. The urge to sink into his arms, to let him take care of this whole miserable mess, threatened to overwhelm her.

'No, unfortunately, he is still very much alive,' Gilan ground out. He should have run the bastard through with his sword for what he had done. 'But he'll have a devil of a bruise on his forehead from where you whacked him with that candlestick.' He smiled grimly. 'You have a good aim.'

Her mind wavered, refusing to calm, to settle. Despite what John had attempted, she was relieved she hadn't killed him. He was still married to her sister, after all. The man was soaked through with alcohol, that was the reason; when he sobered up, she was in no doubt that he would be mortified by what he had tried to do.

'I think he's really quite drunk,' Matilda managed to stutter out. 'I don't think he really knew what he was doing.'

'Are you actually defending him?' growled Gilan. 'God in Heaven. The man tried to rape you! He should be thrown in a dungeon for what he just tried to do.'

Matilda squirmed beneath his harsh words, her breath emerging in shallow, panicky gasps. Her head felt light, as if it were slowly detaching from her body, moving to a safer place, a place where she wouldn't have to deal with the horrible reality of what had happened to her. She had fought for her life in that damp antechamber, fought for her innocence. She had succeeded. But now, as the surging adrenaline leaked from her body, so her strength drained, too. The desire to sit down, to rest, swept over her, swamped her body like a gigantic wave of fatigue. She wanted to slip down where she stood, knees buckling beneath her, skirts pooling across the flagstones. Her legs shook uncontrollably; her heart skipped and danced. The wall gave her some support—in fact, it was her only support. She wondered if she could actually walk.

Gilan watched the scant colour drain from her cheeks, saw her fists bunch, mouth twist in determination as she hung on to what little strength she had remaining.

'Let's go,' he said. Without waiting for her reply, he scooped one arm around her back, easing her away from the wall, the other hand holding on to her forearm, supporting her wilting frame.

'I...' Her protest sounded pathetic, ineffectual.

'You can thank me later,' he said, wedging her tightly into his solid flank and marching her swiftly through the curtain and into the brightness of the great hall. Her slender frame crumpled against him gratefully, cleaving to his muscled strength, her mind unable to think straight, unable to grasp any viable argument as to why he shouldn't be doing this. She hated herself for this frailty, but at this precise moment, she had not one ounce of energy left to fight him.

Half carrying her, her slippered feet barely skimming the ground, he paused only for a moment, in the entrance hall. 'To your sister's chambers?' He quirked one dark eyebrow at her in question, his thick arm braced against her spine, a diagonal line of warmth burning through the stuff of her dress.

'No!' she blurted out in terror. She was not strong enough to face her sister yet, to tell Katherine what her husband had done, why her gown was in tatters. 'No, I must go home. To Lilleshall.'

Despite the growing heat of the day, an icy numbness seemed to take over her body as Gilan lifted her up onto her grey mare, hastily saddled by one of the stable lads. Her movements felt awkward, juddery, her muscles unresponsive. All she wanted to do was vanish into a dark corner somewhere and cry. She clutched helplessly at her ruined dress, her stomach churning with fear and loathing, flicking constant anxious glances back at the main door to the castle.

'He'll be out for a long while yet,' said Gilan, noting the direction of her gaze. How different the maid was from the night before; all her bright confidence, her bossiness, knocked out of her, like the stuffing knocked out of a child's toy. She was so quiet, the softness of her cheeks streaked with tears, her eyes the colour of a winter sea, sad and worried.

'I can't seem to stop shaking,' Matilda whispered, taking a deep, rickety breath. She covered her eyes with one hand, smearing at her tears. 'I wouldn't have got out of there on my own. Thank God you were there. Thank you.'

He reached up and pulled her hand away, wrapping her icy fingers into the warm fold of his palm. 'It's over now,' he said. Something shifted, lurched deep within him, and he frowned at the unusual sensation, dragging his eyes away from her forlorn figure. He felt sorry for her, that was all, sorry for the maid's predicament. He didn't deserve her gratitude; he would have done the same for anybody, any woman. He marched across to his horse. Rooting around in his saddlebag, he drew out a length of scarlet cloth—a short cloak that he wore occasionally.

'Here,' he said, wrapping the fine wool around her shoulders, fastening the cloak with a sturdy silver brooch on her left shoulder. She jumped as his roughened knuckles grazed the bare flesh at her collarbone, a startled flush seeping across her cheeks.

'Sorry,' he murmured, dropping his hands immediately.

Ducking her head, she studied the wispy fall of her horse's mane with studied attention. 'I could have done that.' The colour swept across her face, deepened.

'I doubt it.' His tone was sharp, practical.

The faintest pink stained her lips, the colour of a fading rose, understated, fleeting. They were slightly parted and he could see the tip of her tongue, set between neat white teeth. Unexpected desire, a heady jolt, knifed through him and he clutched at her bridle, willing his heart to stop racing.

'Are you ready?' he muttered between gritted teeth.

Slowly, very slowly, beneath the cover of his cloak, she unpeeled her hand from the ruined fabric and looped the reins around her fingers. 'Only if you promise to stop manhandling me! I've had enough of that for one day. I am perfectly capable of dressing myself. I don't need you to do it for me!' Her eyes bore down on him fiercely, a vivid blue. Pulling herself upright in the saddle, she adjusted his cloak with a brisk, irritated tug. It was as if his touch on her skin had knocked her awake, plucked her from the strange exhaustion into which she had fallen.

Relief flooded through him and he smiled, one edge of his finely etched mouth quirking upwards. Tamping down on the unwanted desire churning in his belly, he swung into the saddle, leather creaking with the movement. His gaze travelled over her flushed face, the challenge of her violet eyes.

'Thank God! I wondered when the waspish tone would return. I thought it had deserted you for ever.' Turning away, he yanked on his reins, and kicked his horse in the direction of the bailey gatehouse.

They followed the stony track that straggled up the limestone escarpment, out of the valley where Neen Castle was situated, the constant chirruping of crickets in the coarse grass beside the path filling the balmy air with sound. Matilda led the way, her knees digging into the soft flanks of the grey mare, urging the animal up, up to the open plateau, to the place where the lilac-blue bowl of the sky met the pale bleached grass of the land. Her horse's hooves clicked and slid on the difficult combination of loose gravel and polished rock and she leaned forwards in the saddle, balancing the upward trajectory of the horse with her own weight.

With every step she made away from Neen, away from John, the fear and panic that crushed her chest began to recede, to ease. She was glad the path was single track and that Gilan was behind her; it gave her a time to think, a breathing space in which to gather her shocked and scattered wits. But, reluctant as she was to admit it, she was glad Gilan was there. John's behaviour had frightened her, really frightened her; for although she had never particularly liked her sister's husband, she had always believed herself to be safe around him. Katherine's home had always been like another home to her, a place of comfort and security. But now, all that had changed.

Matilda's stomach looped with worry; she had rushed away from Neen without any thought or consideration for her sister and her new baby. Katherine's wan, exhausted face swam before her eyes and she prayed that John would be kind to her. Would she ever tell her sister what he had done? How he had almost betrayed his own wife with her sister? She doubted it.

Her horse gained the top of the escarpment, above the bushes of yellow gorse, above the sweeping slopes of lilac flowers alive with blue butterflies. Here, the landscape changed to one of spare, raw beauty: open grassland, studded with a few craggy hawthorns, bent over with the almost permanent onslaught of the wind. The gusting breeze caught at Gilan's cloak that she wore and she grabbed at the flying hem, wedging it firmly beneath her hips. Beneath the scarlet material, the cool air teased the ripped lace of her chemise and her cheeks flamed anew. She glanced down quickly, but, no, there was nothing: all she could see was the wonderful expanse of scarlet cloth, completely covering her naked flesh.

'Is it much farther?' Gilan's horse had gained the level, and he drew alongside her mare.

'No.' She shook her head hastily, conscious that the wind had begun to pick at the loose strands of her hair, blowing it across her face. 'We need to go along the top here and then drop down into the woodland. Lilleshall is in the next valley.' Annoyingly, she was unable to tuck the wayward strands behind her ear, for if she lifted her hands above her waist then the cloak would open and reveal her nakedness. It made her feel vulnerable, exposed beneath his intimidating gaze. She cleared her throat. 'Gilan, look, I'm grateful for you coming with me, but I'll be fine from now on.' Matilda fixed him with what she hoped was a breezy, confident smile. 'I'm sure you have better things to be getting on with.'

'I don't.'

'Really?' She sounded so crestfallen, he almost laughed aloud. Why, he had never met another woman like her: this continual rejection of any help, or support; her stupid, stubborn bravado.

He shrugged his shoulders. 'Henry and his soldiers are still snoring the day away. They had quite a celebration last night, as you know.' A trailing strand of glossy hair wrapped around her cheek, stuck across her mouth. His fingers itched to touch, to pull it away. Her hair would feel like silken thread against his skin.

'There's no need for you to stay on my account,' she responded, frowning steadfastly at the copse of small oaks on the horizon, marking the place where the pathway left the plateau and began to descend into the valley. She tilted her head, allowing the wind to catch at her wayward hair, to tug it from her lips.

'Is it just me, or do you behave like this towards most men?'

'What do you mean?' She whipped her head around, eyes the colour of a stormy sea.

'I mean,' he replied mildly, 'that you seem so determined to do everything on your own the whole time. Determined to prove that you can do anything a man can do. You never seem to want to accept any help, even when you're in trouble.' His voice was calm, threaded with steel.

She squirmed uncomfortably under his softening gaze, focused sternly on the silver discs that decorated his leather reins, sparkling in the sunshine. The childish temptation to kick her horse on faster, to gallop away from his questions, surged through her. She resisted the urge, allowing her horse to match the slighter faster walking pace of his destrier, conscious of his booted foot a few inches away from her own. 'I don't,' she admitted. 'I don't want any help from men. It's hardly surprising, is it, after what has just happened.'

He inclined his head, the sun glinting on his blond hair, touched with gilt in the strong light. 'You were like it before then,' he continued. 'The night you went to fetch your mother…you were about to ride out on your own.'

Above them, a buzzard soared, higher and higher on the rising warm air, great feathered wings outstretched as it wheeled and circled, ringed yellow eye trained on the ground, searching for prey.

Matilda sighed, hunkered down in the saddle. 'I don't expect any help from anyone.' Gilan could not, must not, know that she lived alone. If the news reached John, then he would stop at nothing to try and take over Lilleshall…and, after this morning's performance, possibly her, as well. She rubbed at her eyes, trying to scrub away the itchy exhaustion

'So you've never married?'

She thought of her sister and how her ways had been curbed by her husband, how her whole life was spent in the chase to provide a male heir for John, how he made her completely miserable. 'No, and I've no intention of marrying, either,' she pronounced firmly, the stiff breeze on the top of the plateau chasing crimson into her cheeks.

'Not all men are like John,' Gilan replied, as if reading her thoughts. 'What he did to you was unforgivable.' The loose glossy strands of her hair wove around her head, lifting and dancing in the balmy air.

'He was upset, annoyed that Katherine had given him a daughter and not a son,' she said forlornly, staring down at her fingers curled around the worn leather bridle, remembering the sweet, squalling bundle she had delivered. 'Nobody seemed happy with the birth, not Katherine, nor John.'

Gilan's horse stumbled on a clod of tussocky grass, causing his knee to bump into the curve of Matilda's hip. She frowned up at him, a warning glance as if to ward him away, but he didn't seem to notice. 'You're making excuses for him, again,' he said, a muscle quirking in the shadow beneath his high cheekbone. 'Don't fool yourself that he wouldn't try something like that again even if he were sober. If he wants a male heir, Matilda, then surely he will do anything in his power to get one, even if that means ruining his own—'

'Stop!' she cried out at him, lifting her hand from the reins to push at the air between them, to halt his words. Fear etched at her chest, clutching at her ribs, her stomach, a rigid grip. 'Stop talking like this! I don't want to hear it. He was drunk. He was not himself. Once he sobers up he will love the baby and so will Katherine!'

Gilan shook his head at her unwillingness to hear the truth, to acknowledge it, his horse slowing to a stop as his hands slackened on the reins. He leaned forwards in the saddle, adjusting his position, shifting his long legs against the horse's flanks. 'It will happen again if you go back there, Matilda. And next time he might succeed.'

Although his words were low, measured, they slammed into her with a force that left her shocked, bringing back the full, nightmarish reality of John's attack—the foul breath smothering her, the stubby hands grasping lecherously at her bodice. How she had struggled, pleading, fighting to escape, to save her innocence. And now this man, this horrible man, was telling her it might happen again?

'How dare you talk to me like this? Surely, I know my own brother-in-law better than you do.' Her voice rose, a shrill note. Without thinking, she lunged across the narrow space between them, between the two horses, her hands flying out to his face to hit out at him and stop his loathsome speech. Tears sprung from her eyes, falling haphazardly across her cheeks. With the violent movement, the scarlet cloak blew out and back from her body, revealing the bare skin of her chest, the rounded top curve of her breast peeking through the tattered shreds of her gown.

Immediately aware of the expanse of bare, creamy flesh below the leaping pulse in her throat, Gilan forced himself to keep his eyes on her face. He seized her fluttering hands, cool fingers snaring her wrists. 'Matilda, stop! I'm sorry if I've upset you.'

'Well, you have!' she screeched at him between sobs, her arms held upright in his firm grip. 'Don't talk about things you have no idea about! John never pays me the least bit of attention normally—I'm telling you, he was drunk and annoyed and that's all there is to this!'

Her face was so close, he could smell the perfume lifting from her skin, her peerless skin that glowed like the inside of a shell. Confused and angry, her forget-me-not eyes shimmered up at him, tilting up at the corners like those of a cat, he thought. Tears clung to her dark eyelashes, diamond drops. His blood thickened, gathering. His heart thudded treacherously in his chest, matching the quickening race of his pulse. He should push her away now, back away. His mind loosened, conscious thought deserting him. Logic fled.

He tipped his head down, his mouth touching hers.

He told himself it would be the briefest kiss, a kiss of comfort, of reassurance, a kiss to stop her agitated sobbing, her fear. But the moment his mouth met hers, he knew it was not to be. Her lips were silky soft, like delicate feathers, and he groaned, a precarious heat rising in his body. Desire, an intolerable yearning, scorched through him, a blazing trail of fire, pushing him, urging him on. His hands fell from her wrists and lifted to cup the sides of her face, big thumbs buried in the slipping velvet of her hair.

Wrists released, Matilda bunched her hands, pushing them up against the implacable wall of his chest, intending to shove him away. She had watched the iron glitter of his eyes darken almost to black, and even in the midst of her tirade had known what he had been about to do. As his hands framed her face, warming her tear-soaked cheeks, his mouth playing along the fragile seam of her mouth, her mind told her to back away as her body clamoured for more. More of him.

Warmth curled, deep in her belly; his mouth on her mouth, strong and insistent. Hungry. Blood hammered around her veins, picking up speed. Unwittingly, she sagged against him, her mouth opening beneath his in a surprised gasp of delight, hand splaying against the fine blue wool of his tunic, cleaving to the hard, ridged muscles beneath. Beneath her palm, his heart beat solidly, thudding against her skin. His tongue delved, and an unbearable sensation of longing gripped her, like a thousand butterflies let loose in her stomach, dancing, driving her higher...to what? She had no idea.

High above them, the circling buzzard cried, a low, mournful sound that penetrated the sensual fug of her brain, the liquid softening of her body, driving a sense of sanity back into her brain. What in Heaven's name did she think she was doing? Throwing herself into Gilan's kiss like a wanton doxy, her bosom on show for all to see! She twisted her head to the side, wrenching her lips away, lifting the back of her hand to scrub savagely at her mouth. Her breath emerged in short truncated bursts, punched from her lungs. A warm sensation, dark and melting, swirled in her belly, whispering a promise of how things might have been.

'Mother of Mary,' she bawled at him, reeling back in her saddle, tugging the sides of his cloak angrily over her chest. 'Why did you do that?' Her breath scuffled, fought for evenness, for balance.

He reared back from her, jerking so violently on the reins that his horse threw up its head, then paced round in a circle, away from Matilda. What on earth had possessed him to do such a thing? His mind was empty; he simply couldn't think of the words to explain his actions. She had been there, so close to him, so beautiful, that the physical side of him had taken over, damn it, ridden roughshod over his self-restraint, punched through his thread-bare resistance. The chit stirred feelings within him that he hadn't felt for a long, long time, and certainly not since his brother's death—the resulting grief had been enough to cap any desire. But now?

He cleared his throat. 'You looked so miserable, so sad, sitting there.'

'So you kissed me because you felt sorry for me!' she lashed back at him. 'I was fine until you started talking about John, about what happened! Your words made me miserable, and then you thought you'd try and make amends? With a kiss?' A betraying flush flooded her cheeks, moving down the graceful column of her neck.

He shrugged his shoulders. Self-loathing filled his heart; he was not proud of what he had done. Better for her to believe he was an uncouth soldier, someone who treated such things lightly. 'It was just a kiss, Matilda.' His voice ground into her, hurtful, mocking.

It was just a kiss, Matilda, she repeated his words to herself sternly. She shrank down in the saddle, huddled into his cloak. Her heart folded in on itself, rapidly covering up the delicious, rippling sensations that coursed through her slight frame. She wanted to hide away from him, to flee that glittering silver stare that pierced her hard-won confidence, to escape the tantalising curve of his lips. He could not see what he had done to her, must never know what feelings he had engendered deep within her belly, for obviously such a kiss meant nothing to him. He would laugh in her face, mock her, and she would look a fool.

Her heart closed up in shame.

Chapter Nine

Lilleshall Manor seemed to float on a puddle of hazy air as Matilda, followed by Gilan, approached the gatehouse, horses' hooves crunching over the dusty gravel. The pleasing jumble of buildings, built of a coarse, purple-hued stone, was reflected in the vast moat that surrounded the manor. Dragonflies played across the water's surface, pausing briefly in one spot, before scooting off in another direction, gauzy wings rainbow-transparent in the golden light. Swallows, wings like knife blades, screamed fast and furious up above, occasionally dipping down to skim the pond, catching up unsuspecting flies.

Matilda tapped her heels to the mare's sides, steering her across the small bridge crossing a narrow part of the moat, and halted in front of the gatehouse. Muscular ropes of glossy ivy clung to the front of the building, thick, suckering tendrils reaching up and around the narrow pair of arched windows on the second floor, glossy, heart-shaped leaves stirring briefly in the still air. Through the generous span of the arched gateway, she could see the cobbled path lined with lavender bushes, bees and butterflies quivering above the pale violet flower heads.

Her heart dipped in sadness. How many times had she seen her father and mother emerge from that shadowed doorway, laughing and smiling up in greeting, her mother's skirts brushing against the lavender and sending a burst of delicious fragrance up into the air? She remembered her brother, Thomas, clambering onto his first pony, and Katherine, too, in front of this very gatehouse, and her younger self in her mother's arms, watching them. Like another lifetime.

Gilan's horse snorted behind her and she hitched round in the saddle. 'This is it,' she said bluntly. 'This is my home.' She tried to keep her tone neutral, detached. The rest of their journey had continued in stark, frozen silence; a silence which she suspected affected her far more than it affected him. Her shoulders ached from the effort of keeping herself staunchly turned away from him; she had no wish to look at him, for to look at him was to see that devastating mouth and remind herself of his kiss, that kiss that had plundered the very depths of her soul and left her rigid with longing.

With a slow gaze, Gilan surveyed the diminutive gatehouse, the mirrored moat and the cluster of rambling white roses that scampered across one of the outside walls. 'Very pretty,' he pronounced. One look at her closed features told him she would not forgive him easily for his kiss. He had transgressed a boundary, trampled in a place where he should never have gone. No matter. The taste of her lips had been enchanting, wonderful, a touch that he would remember for a long time; he could easily weather Matilda's annoyance. After today, he would never see her again. Henry would demand his company on the quest to find Richard, and after that? After that he would have to go home and face his parents. His heart shivered with regret.

Matilda shifted uncomfortably on the top of her horse. She supposed she ought to thank him for his help, his escort home. 'Would you like a drink…or something?' she asked, grudgingly, hoping, praying that he would decline. She had no wish to invite him into her home, for him to see the details of how she lived, to possibly work out her solitary living arrangements and condemn her, judge her, for them.

Gilan paused. He should go back. Henry would be expecting him, no doubt ranting as to his whereabouts at this very moment. But Matilda intrigued him, both the woman and her situation. This was her house, her home, holding more clues as to her wayward personality, to her bold behaviour. Besides, the place seemed curiously deserted; no servants had run out at their arrival, which was customary, and he hadn't seen a stable lad. Yet, at first glance, the manor appeared well kept, the stonework maintained, the courtyard gardens tended. Someone must be working here.

He would stay, just for a while, to make sure there was someone else here to protect her. He strongly suspected that John would not allow his sister-in-law to emerge unscathed from this morning's incident. He wouldn't be surprised if John rode over to Lilleshall himself to punish Matilda for what she had done to him that morning. 'I could do with something to eat,' Gilan said. He swung one leg over the rump of his stallion, jumped to the dry earth, chalky pink dust flying up to coat his leather boots.

'Oh!' Her eyes widened, startled. 'I thought you

would want to go back? Surely the duke will be up and about by now?'

He patted his horse's neck, amused by her ungracious behaviour. He supposed he deserved it. 'No, I don't think so.'

'You'd better tie your horse up there, then.' Matilda indicated an iron ring set deep in the ivy 'One of the grooms will fetch the horses, make sure they are fed and watered. The stables are over there.' She nodded across to a couple of low-roofed barns.

'Outside the castle walls,' he noted, looping the reins around the ring. 'Aren't you worried that someone might steal your horses?'

Matilda shook her head. 'No, nothing like that really happens around here.' Nibbling unconsciously at her bottom lip, she kicked one slipper loose of the stirrup to bring her leg over the horse's neck, then wondered how on earth she was going to dismount without her flesh being exposed. Checking covertly that Gilan's head was turned away before she slid down the horse's side, she plunged to the ground without using her hands for balance. Her feet hit the ground, hard, the shock waves from the impact ricocheting up her calves. But the cloak remained intact.

'Come in then,' she said testily, barely pausing

as she swept past him to enter the gatehouse, her skirts brushing against the overhanging clumps of lavender, and up to the front door. She had left her horse untied, standing patiently, so Gilan fastened the reins around the iron loop and followed her in.

The hallway was empty. No servant came out to greet them, no voices called in the distance. Gilan could hear nothing other than the soft whinny of his own horse from the other side of the gatehouse, the constant drone of bees as they worked their way across the lavender.

'Where is everybody?' he asked, blinking. After the strong sunlight outside, the passageway was dark, and he waited for his eyes to adjust to the dim interior. Shapes began to emerge: a low carved chest set upon the flagstone floor, the gloss of dark-oak panelling running the length of the passageway to another door at the far end. A heavily embroidered curtain pulled back across a generous opening to his right, and he glimpsed the serrated ceiling rafters of a great hall, white plastered walls, and rich, sumptuous tapestries.

'We'll have to fend for ourselves today,' Matilda explained, clutching the cloak even more tightly around her shoulders. 'Everyone will be out in the fields, bringing in the harvest.' She led the way into the kitchen, to the left of the hallway. Again, the place was deserted, cold. No fire burned in the grate and the long trestle table used for food preparation was scrubbed clean. Pots and pans hung on the whitewashed walls, wooden spoons and other cooking implements were stacked neatly in earthenware pots along a shelf.

Gilan's stomach growled noisily as he looked around the bare kitchen. 'Are you telling me that even the cook has gone to gather in the harvest?'

'Everyone,' replied Matilda firmly. In truth, she could only afford to pay two servants at the moment to live in the house with her and she had instructed both of them to help with the harvest whilst she was away with Katherine. She walked over to a cupboard set in the wall at one end of the kitchen, clicked up the latch and sighed with relief as she viewed the shelves stacked with food. There would be enough here to offer Gilan: hunks of cheese, a round of bread, possibly only a day old, and a ham, hanging on an iron hook at the back.

'What about your brother?' he asked suddenly, remembering Henry asking her the question on the previous evening. 'Is he out there, too?'

His words stabbed into her—how much could she tell him and remain safe?

'Of course!' She laughed quickly to cover the

lie, but the sound bounced around the cavernous space, brittle, hollow.

Gilan frowned. 'Surely such a role would be beneath his status?'

Matilda hitched one shoulder towards her ear. 'He enjoys it.' A rosy stain crept across her cheeks. 'Now, if you'll excuse me, I must change. Help yourself to any food.'

Before he could answer her, she had ducked away into the passageway, a flash of pink skirts against the plastered wall, drab white, and he stood in the middle of the kitchen, listening to the whisper of her dress on the flagstones until the sound died away.

Cheeks flaming, she scuttled along the passageway. Did he realise she was lying about her brother? Had he heard the false tone in her voice? She had seen the searching look in his grey eyes as she spoke; he seemed a little too interested in her answers. She doubted he was the sort of man to rush back and tell John the precise nature of her living arrangements for he had helped her, not once, but twice now. Even so, the fewer people who knew about how she lived, the better.

Pushing through the curtained doorway, she strode across the great hall. The high-ceiling chamber had a damp, unlived-in feel, for she barely used this room now, living and working mainly in the kitchen. The spiral staircase was set in a circular tower at the far end; she raced up the steps, gaining her own bedchamber on the first floor.

Once inside, she slammed the door shut quickly, heart pounding, and leaned back against the panels, as if she could keep the world out simply by using her body weight. Why did she even think Gilan was interested in her and the way she lived anyway? He had made that perfectly clear after…after he had kissed her. Almost in wonder, she lifted one finger to her lips, the flesh still tingling in the aftermath of his mouth against hers. How could she, an innocent in the ways of men, have known a kiss could be so? Her only experience of men was what she had witnessed of her sister's marriage, and John's despicable behaviour this morning. And yet, John had hardly touched her compared to…compared to this. She dropped her fingers, angry, shamed by her own behaviour with Gilan, and tipped her head back against the wooden door panel.

She was so tired. Tilting her head down, she stared longingly at her bed, her beautiful four-poster bed with its serge hangings embroidered in thick colourful crewel work by her mother. The mattress was stuffed with sweet-smelling straw, the sheets were of bleached linen, the blankets woven out of the wool from the sheep on the estate. Her mother's busy fingers had spun and woven the wool herself, thought Matilda, remembering the constant click of the loom from her childhood. A coverlet of fur was flung across the bottom of the bed, to be used on the coldest nights. How blissful it would be to throw herself full length onto the bed and crawl into that downy fur.

But, no, she must stay awake, she told herself sternly. Once Gilan was on his way, she would go out into the fields and help with the harvest. Her servants, and the rest of the peasants on the estate, had been toiling away for days, under the instruction of her bailiff, and she wanted to see what progress had been made. The forecast had been for an excellent harvest this year; yet she knew that this hot weather would break soon, crumble down into heavy rain and storms, flattening the crops.

Lifting both hands, she fiddled with the clasp of Gilan's brooch, cradling the heavy silver in her palm once it was released. The jewels set in the elaborately wrought silver winked and sparkled; she set it carefully on the coffer at the end of the bed. The cloak dropped from her shoulders, pooled to the floor, and she bent down, folding it carefully, smoothing her hands across the expensive wool, before placing it next to the brooch in a neat pile. His clothes spoke of a noble rank, she thought, and it was obvious that Henry, cousin to King Richard, held him in high regard. Who was he? Who was this Gilan, she wondered, this man who had sprung to help her out of nowhere?

Slithering out of the wrecked gown, she bunched the shimmering fabric between her hands and threw it into a corner of the room. Katherine's favourite gown, loaned for the evening's feasting. Guilt cut through her, a pang of loss and anxiety at the image of her sister alone, defenceless against that boor of a husband. Dare she go back and find out how Katherine fared? Facing John's wrath after what he had done, after what *she* had done to him, sent an arrow of fear piercing through her. She couldn't do it—not yet, anyway. She would send a messenger over to Neen instead.

She switched her gaze sharply away from the gown, the fabric crumpled against the plastered wall. She never wanted to see that dress again. She would ask the servants to burn it on the kitchen fire when they came in from the fields. Her fingers stumbled, clumsy over the long rows of buttons securing the fitted sleeves of her underdress, but at last she managed to undo them, along with the laces holding the material into her waist.

Clad only in her linen shift, her stockings and slippers, Matilda rummaged around in the oak coffer beneath the window, pulling out a floppy-necked working gown made of practical fawn linen, with a surcoat to match. She closed the lid. Through the wobbly glass panes of the window, small figures bent over the ripe wheat in the golden fields, sickle blades flashing as they worked methodically along the rows. The women stacked the crop into sheaves behind them. Impatience swung through her—what was she doing, idling away in here? She needed to be out there, helping them.

Stuffing the dress over her head, the fabric whispered over her polished skin, the hem dropping to the floor. She adjusted the ties, pulling the fabric into her neat waist. The surcoat, which acted more like an apron, had no sleeves and hung loosely from her shoulders, sides open to her hips, from which point the seams were joined like a normal gown. It meant she could bend and stretch her arms with more movement, ideal for working in the fields, or in the kitchens.

Legs suddenly weary, she plopped on the edge of the bed, fingers raising to check her hair. Her circlet and veil lay abandoned in Katherine's chamber; in the rush to leave Neen, she had travelled with her hair uncovered. She hadn't realised how many hairpins had been lost out of the coils on each side of her head; she would have to redo them. Yanking out the last of the pins, she allowed each braid to fall down into her lap. Undoing the leather laces that secured the ends, she sifted her fingers through the loosening hair, half closing her eyes at the wonderful sensation. The pads of her fingers moved up through the silky tresses, lifting the hair away from her heated scalp, and she tipped her head back, enjoying the cool air, delicious against her skin. She would plait her hair into one simple braid and wear a wimple, she decided, a long length of linen that wrapped around her head and protected her face and scalp from the strong sun. Her mother's scolding tones echoed in her head, chastising her for spending too long in the open air, pointing out with long fingers the freckles sprinkled across Matilda's cheeks and nose. She sighed heavily, yawning after her sleepless night. The air in the chamber was soporific. Maybe she should open a window.

Sitting at the trestle table in the kitchen, sword placed on the scrubbed wood beside him, Gilan pushed his plate away. He had eaten well and now stretched his legs out under the table, calf muscles cramping slightly, then releasing with the movement. He massaged the heel of his hand into the puckered skin of his scar. Raising his arms above his head, he released the taut muscles in his shoulders, ligaments shifting. Draining the last drops of mead from the flagon he had discovered lurking at the back of the cupboard, he set the vessel down, noting that the ray of sunlight streaming in through the south window had moved, now picking out a row of pewter plates in the corner, grey and gleaming. A lone fly bumped lazily along the inside of the kitchen window, a glazed, narrow aperture set up high in the plastered wall. First it went one way, then the other, before its wings became snared in a spider's web, where it buzzed furiously.

Where was she? Surely it shouldn't take her this long to change her clothes? That is, of course, if she were planning to return to bid him farewell. Maybe she had decided to sit in her bedchamber, expecting him to leave when he had finished eating. She was probably hoping that he would do this, so horrified was the look on her face when he announced that he would stay for something to eat. He grinned to himself. It would be far simpler if he picked up his sword, strode out of the gatehouse and climbed on his horse, never to see her again, but for some peculiar reason, he had to make sure there was someone here to protect her, before he rode off again.

He climbed over the rickety bench, fashioned from one plank of wood, and sheathed his sword, adjusting the leather strap around his hips. Tipping his head on one side, he listened for the sound of her footsteps, or the faintest swish of her skirts. But all he could hear was the insistent croak of a jackdaw echoing down the cavernous chimney and, through the open front door, the constant murmur of bees, busy outside in the lavender.

Crossing the hallway, he entered the great hall, his eye running in appreciation over the sumptuous furnishings: the large tapestries covering the walls, the gold-embellished banners hanging from iron poles jutting out into the space above his head. No expense had been spared in the decoration of this room, he thought. Matilda's family, her brother, must be fairly wealthy in order to create such a beautiful home. Yet the fireplace was empty, even of spent ash, which suggested that the fire had not been lit in some time, and the smell of the room was damp, unused. He frowned, for every moment longer he spent in Matilda's company, the more questions he felt he needed to ask her. The woman was a complete enigma.

Bounding up the spiral staircase which he found at the far end of the great hall, he gained the first floor, convinced now that Matilda sat stubbornly in her chamber, waiting for him to leave. Nearly all the doors of the chambers upstairs sat open, revealing clean, comfortable rooms flooded with light from the glazed windows. Wooden floorboards, dimpled and worn from use, shone out, strewn with bright rugs woven from heavy wool. The bed curtains were embroidered: colourful, detailed scenes depicting all manner of birds and flowers, all executed in perfect, minute stitches. Furs and blankets were stacked high on each bed, the bleached linen sheets crisp and glowing.

Only one door in the corridor was closed.

He knocked, knuckles rapping sharply against the solid wood. 'Matilda?' he called. Irritation trickled through him, a thread of annoyance that the chit continued to thwart him. Why, he would be gone soon, and then she would never have to deal with him again! He knew he was a fool for kissing her, but she had seemed so….so…what? His mind dug down for viable reasons, but he could find no excuse for what he had done, for that unexpected surge of desire had welled up like a storm unleashed at the sight of her beautiful, windswept face, out there on the plateau. It had seized him by the throat, overpowered his ironclad self-restraint, swept normal boundaries away. No wonder she had scuttled away to her chamber at the earliest opportunity; especially after what had happened with her brother-in-law. He was no better than John, a lout, and a lecherous lout at that. He should feel thoroughly ashamed, guilty about what he had done.

But he didn't. The touch of her lips had made him feel alive, nudging the numb, wooden lump that was his heart and melting the frozen beat of his blood. Something stirred, deep in his belly, the remnants of their kiss lingering like a promise.

He shoved the feeling away; he would do well to remember his true purpose in this country, which was not to fall for the first woman who caught his eye. She acted like a lodestone on his pared-down feelings, poking and prodding at his damaged heart. He must stop this ridiculous behaviour; the chit was safe now, home—he had done his duty. All he needed to do now was to take his leave of her and be gone.

'Matilda!' he called. A hint of steel threaded his voice.

Silence.

A rising exasperation, coupled with a growing realisation that he must leave this place, leave *her* before he did any more damage to her innocent nature, drove him to click up the latch and shove into her chamber.

He stopped, suddenly.

Matilda lay sprawled across the bed, her slender build pillowed by a rippling pelt, one cheek, flushed, turned into the soft fur. Her legs hung over the edge of the bed, delicate ankles and small feet encased in stockings, exposed. Her slippers had fallen off, discarded on the floor, the soles upturned, scuffed and dirty from the journey. And from the top of her head to the curve of her hips, her hair flowed like a glorious waterfall, glossy like chestnuts, smooth as polished stone.

Her hair.

His heart seized and he clasped his hands together in front of him, almost as if to prevent them springing forwards and plunging them deep into that luscious mass. The tresses followed the curving line of her body, the outline of her breast pushing against the rough material of her gown, the indent of her small waist, the jutting, sensuous curve of her hip. His heart skittered erratically, zigzagging out of control, his fingers itching to remove his sword, to tear off his tunic and leggings, to press his bare skin against hers, to make sweet, delicious love to her.

He groaned, tearing his eyes away from her pale cheeks, her skirts rucked up around her knees. Christ, what was the matter with him? He was behaving like some callow youth, heart rising and plummeting all over the place, his senses scattered, whipped by an unseen, unpredictable wind, unable to douse the climbing flames of his desire.

Rearing back from the bed, ignoring the clamouring in his body, he flung himself into a seat at the side of the room, the spindly chair rocking back violently under the force of the movement. He thrust his head down into his hands, forearms resting on his knees. He should let her sleep. She was exhausted: deep violet shadows marked the space below her closed eyes, like bruising thumbprints. She would have been awake all night during her sister's labour, and that, coupled with the shock of her brother-in-law's assault, would have taken its toll.

But he couldn't stay here all day, watching her sleep. That would be torture.

Leaping out of the chair, Gilan strode over to the bed, willing himself to remain immune to her, shoring up the fragile remains of his self-restraint. He had spent the better part of two years fighting in the Baltic, surviving through the bitter winters, up to his knees in freezing mud, had watched his own brother die in his arms. It would take more, much more than the exquisite beauty of one small, feisty woman to break through the stony crust of his heart.

Chapter Ten

It was a perfect summer's day. Not a single wisp of white cloud marred the sky. The strong sunlight warmed her cheeks and the curve of her neck as Matilda raised her arms to gather in the linen sheet, spread out across a low laurel bush to dry. Drawing the hemmed edges together, she folded the fragrant, clean-smelling material against her chest, inhaling the wonderful fresh, dry fragrance of the sun-baked sheet. From somewhere, far away, she could hear a masculine voice calling her, shouting her name over and over. It was her brother. *Thomas!* she thought, her mind befuddled and hazy, but then, no, how could that be? Thomas was not here…

'Matilda!'

Layers of blissful unconsciousness peeled back, the straggling threads of a wonderful dream fleeing back to the deeper recesses of her mind. She chased after them, trying to snare their flying trails; she had no wish to wake up...

'Matilda!' The rude, strident voice bellowed in her ear once more. 'For God's sake, will you wake up?' Hands cupped her shoulders, bounced her gently against the mattress, shaking her mind to a vague sense of clarity.

Her eyes popped open. A blue tunic stretched over broad shoulders loomed before her unfocused vision, muscles bulking out the cloth, pulling it taut. Too close!

'You! What are you doing here? What are you doing in my bedchamber?' Her voice cut across the narrow, intimate space between them. Heart thumping erratically, she struggled against the bed-clothes to sit up, up and away from him, pushing errant wisps of hair back from her heated face. Gilan thrust himself upright, standing at the side of the bed. His height, the shock of his blond hair, all seemed incongruous, out of place in the dimin-utive dimensions of her bedchamber, the muted colours. He seemed too dazzling, too fierce, his brawny build dominating the space, overwhelm-ing, as if vanquishing the very air.

'You shouldn't be here!' she hissed at him. 'Why didn't you wait for me downstairs?'

Gilan's laugh was harsh, truncated. 'Because I would have waited all day.'

Her hair clung to her neck, a curving curtain of shining dark chestnut caressing creamy alabaster skin. A tiny pulse beat frantically in the slender column of her neck. He swallowed, mouth dry, snapping his gaze away from her exposed calves encased in flimsy stockings, away from the luscious bloom of her face, refreshed from sleep. He cleared his throat and held out his hands, as if to apologise for his curt statement. 'I'm sorry, Matilda, you fell asleep.' His voice was softer now. 'I had to wake you. Henry will be expecting me.'

'Yes, of course,' she replied, trying to exert some sort of control over her erratic breathing. 'I'm surprised you haven't left already.'

He tilted his head, frowning, a small deep line creasing the space between his dark blond eyebrows. 'It crossed my mind.' His eye travelled over her rough outfit; the expensive gown of fine silk with its low neckline had been replaced by what were essentially peasants' garments: a fitted gown of linen, topped by an apronlike gown fashioned from old, worn-out material.

'You've changed your clothes,' he remarked, bluntly.

Matilda tugged industriously at her hemline,

which seemed to have rucked up around her knees, acutely conscious of his shrewd perusal. 'At least I managed to do something before I fell asleep. I'm going out into the fields, to help,' she added.

'You?' A look of faint amusement crossed his carved features.

'Everyone needs to pull their weight at harvest time. It could rain at any moment and rain would rot the grain where it stands. We have to take advantage of this good weather. I don't want my whole crop ruined.'

He couldn't resist a slow smile at her knowledgeable tone. 'You make it sound like you own the place, as if the crop belongs to you.'

It does, she thought. *At least, it does now, with Thomas away.* 'To my family,' she said hastily, 'the crop belongs to my family.'

'Ah, yes,' he murmured, 'your family. Your sister, I have met. And as your mother is in a nunnery, I'm assuming your father…'

'Is dead,' she supplied, shortly. 'He died of the plague two winters ago.' Hopping off the bed, Matilda dragged her fingers through the length of her hair, plaiting it quickly, efficiently. Gilan watched her deft fingers, in, out, over, under, until she reached the curling end, tying the glossy strands with a leather lace. He pulled his eyes away, feeling a tremendous sense of loss as her beautiful hair was tucked away neatly, and scrutinised the polished floorboards beneath his feet for a moment before turning back to her.

'So that leaves your brother,' he said, 'whom I am anxious to meet before I depart.'

'Anxious to…why?' she blurted out, hands stalling in the process of wrapping the linen wimple around her head.

'Because I want to make certain you are safe before I take my leave,' he said.

'He's in the fields, I told you that!'

'Forgive me, Matilda, but I don't believe you.'

She glared at him, eyes sparking blue fire. 'It's the truth!'

'Then, take me to him.'

Tying the ends of her wimple into a loose knot below her chin, Matilda thought rapidly. How long could she keep up the lie that Thomas was actually here on the estate, whereas in truth, he was miles away, campaigning at the king's side? Maybe she could convince one of the servants to pretend…

She shrugged her shoulders, attempting to appear unconcerned, unmoved by his insistence, plumping back down on the mattress to pull on a pair of calf-length boots, the leather scuffed and pitted from use. They would serve her better in the fields than her flimsy slippers with their thin, soft soles. 'I don't know why you're so concerned about me,' she grumbled, standing up and flicking the bunching gathers out of her skirts with brisk efficiency. The linen cloth wrapped around her hair in soft folds, the pale fawn colour emphasising the hectic colour in her cheeks, the challenging glint in her eyes. She stuck her pert nose in the air, haughtily, awaiting his answer. 'You scarce know me, you only met me yesterday. I'm nothing, a nobody to you.'

No, Gilan thought, *you're wrong. You are most definitely a somebody. A sweet, vivacious somebody who, by a tremendous fluke of fortune, has burst into my life and kicked up the ash-cold embers of my hard, embittered heart, stirring them to life.*

'Take me to your brother and then I will be gone,' he said firmly, his features set in stony lines. She scowled at him briefly, as if judging how much to argue, how much to protest, before whisking away to lift the latch and open the door.

He followed her down the spiral staircase, watching the slipping hemline of her serviceable gown trail after her, the seductive sway of her hips. Despite the ample proportions of her surcoat, the open-cut armholes displayed the fitted underdress, the lacings drawn in tight to her neat waist. *What would it be like,* he thought, *to span that waist with his hands, to splay his palm across the bare flesh of her belly?* Desire shivered through him, a ripple of expectation.

Going through into the kitchens, she dragged open a narrow door beside the fireplace that led to the rear of the castle. She stopped suddenly, so rapidly that he almost ran into the back of her, the span of his chest almost colliding with her neat, graceful shoulders. 'Did you find enough to eat?' she asked, blue eyes shimmering up at him, huge violet pools of light. Her tone sounded so unconcerned, so indifferent about his well-being that his lips twitched. Her mind was most definitely on other things; it was almost as if he could see her brain working at top speed behind her smooth, pale forehead, trying to think of a way to outwit him. He knew she was lying. He doubted there was anyone living in the castle with her at all, bar one or two elderly servants.

He nodded. 'I did. Thank you.' How long would she try to string him along with this ridiculous charade?

Matilda led the way outside, into the glare, the breezy air nipping at her skirts, blowing them sideways. The air was alive with birds, swallows screaming long threads of sound, knifing this way and that through the hot air, black blades against vibrant blue. Higher up, where the white cloud had been reduced to a few lacy wisps by the sun, a buzzard wheeled and soared, chased by thuggish black crows. Crickets chirruped continually in the long grass by the side of the path, the bending seed-heads brushing against their clothes as they passed.

Opening a gate in a high wall, shoving at the wooden planks, Matilda marched into a substantial, well-kept vegetable garden, with clipped laurel bushes at one end used for drying the washing. At the far end, the garden opened on to a rutted track that ran between the scrubby hedgerows of the fields. Up ahead, where the blue of the sky lightened to a colourless vibration on the horizon, she could see the figures of her own servants working. But how could she reach them, warn them about Gilan and ask someone to pretend to be her brother, without him being by her side to hear it?

Matilda paused, pursing her lips together in grim resignation, acutely conscious of the tall man at her side. This was idiotic. She would continue no longer with this stupid pretence. She stopped, pulling her wimple forwards to shade her eyes from the harsh sunlight, and turned towards him.

'Gilan...' She cleared her throat.

He paused midstride, squinting down at her.

Sweat prickled his scalp; he stuck one hand through his hair, sifting the blond strands, enabling a breath of air to cool the skin. Even wearing only a shirt and tunic, with trousers of thin wool, the intense heat of the afternoon pressed down on him, thick and sultry. His feet boiled in his calf-length leather boots.

'Gilan, I need to tell you something.'

His eyes pierced through her like silver daggers; she had his attention. Binding her arms across her chest, the loose sleeves of her gown fell back; the flesh creased on her forearms with the ferocity of the movement. Behind her, a long trailing bramble snaked out from the hedge, threatening to snag her head cloth. Green, unripe berries clustered along its length.

'He's not here, is he? Your brother isn't here.' His voice was stern but not unkind.

Sighing with resignation, she traced the firm outline of his lips with her gaze, the surprising upward tilt at each side of his mouth which lightened the hard, sculptured lines of his face. Had he known all along? She nodded, dumbly, head lowered, unclasping her arms to fiddle with the double strings of her girdle, the fraying tassles bouncing against the folds of her dress. 'No, he's not.' She arched her head up at him, eyes flashing, as if expecting him to argue with her, to remonstrate and tell her what a fool she was.

Above them, swallows sliced and danced through the balmy air, diving suddenly, screeching.

'Go on, then,' she said into the lengthening silence. The linen cloth around her hair cast shade across the top half of her face, the sprinkle of freckles across her pert nose. Her eyes blazed out from the darkness.

'Go on then…what?' His shaggy blond eyebrows drew together.

'Tell me what a fool I am for living here alone, for keeping the whole thing going. John doesn't know that I'm on my own at Lilleshall, did you realise? He thinks my mother is here, still in charge—as a widow, she has that right by law. But she has given up, Gilan, she went to pieces when my father died—well, you saw what she was like. If John finds out that I am here on my own, I would be in that nunnery with my mother as fast as this—' she snapped her fingers in front of his face '—and, with Thomas away, he would appoint himself as my legal guardian. He is desperate to get his hands on this place…' she glanced around briefly, taking in the vast sweep of fertile fields burgeoning with ripening crops '…and I am desperate not to let him. He cannot know that I am here alone.'

She turned away suddenly, head bowed, clapping a shocked hand across her mouth. She had said too much, her mouth running away with her like some old fishwife! What must Gilan think of her? He had no interest in her domestic minutiae, and here she was, pouring out the gory details. Where had her pride gone, her own self-restraint? She hoisted her shoulders up, stuck her chin in the air. 'But of course, this is no concern of yours. You don't want to know all of this.'

But he did. He wanted to know everything about her. Matilda intrigued him, made him curious, questioning. Here was a woman who had fought the odds, defied convention by running her own estate, with no male guardian to help her. He couldn't imagine many women, any other woman, in fact, taking on such work, such responsibility. That she had managed to do such a thing for so long was incredible and brave; her intelligence and quick wit had served her well, giving her the means to hoodwink her powerful brother-in-law. He hated to think what John would do when he found out what Matilda had been up to, but he surely would; it was only a matter of time.

'You're not a fool, Matilda,' Gilan said slowly. Her linen wimple had begun to slip back from her forehead; his fingers itched to bring it forwards, to shield her delicate skin from the hot, burning sun. 'But you are vulnerable.'

'Everything was fine until…until…' She closed her eyes, unwilling to recall the events of the morning…

'…until John attacked you,' Gilan supplied.

She nodded shakily, chest gripping with a renewed surge of fear. 'He thinks my mother is here, so he never bothers to come to Lilleshall, but now—' her voice rose tremulously '—now, he might come here after all.' A huge wave of loss, of vulnerability, swept over her. Everything that she had built up on the estate over the past years, the energy she had expended, all could be taken away by a single point of law: the fact that women had no right to own property, unless they were a widow. 'Katherine knows, but she also knows how important Lilleshall is to our family. She had no wish for John to seize it.' She chewed idly at a knuckle. 'Oh Lord, I hope she's all right. I hated leaving her like that, in the state she was in…'

'You had no choice after what happened with John, Matilda.' Gilan watched the anxiety play across her exquisite features, the desolation. The urge to sweep her into his arms and tell her that all would be well swept through him so strongly that he almost lied. But that would make him the fool. Who was he to offer her comfort, security? He couldn't even protect his own brother, let alone a maid he had met only yesterday!

'Where is Thomas now?' Gilan asked calmly, a slender muscle quirking in his cheek. 'Is he nearby? Can he come home?'

Hoisting her sagging shoulders upwards, she shifted miserably, from one foot to another, shaking her head. 'Thomas is with the king,' she whispered, the coarse fabric of her wimple sliding back to reveal curling damp wisps on her hairline, 'which, seeing as you ride with Henry, Duke of Lancaster, makes us, makes me, your enemy.'

He lifted one eyebrow, grey eyes glinting. 'Hardly,' he replied. 'Henry has no quarrel with the English people. After all, he is one himself. But Richard has confiscated all of Henry's estates and lands, in what seems purely a fit of jealousy. That's why we've come back to England—to track down the king and force him to return what Henry is rightfully owed.'

The meaning of his words, and their importance, percolated through Matilda's brain. Hope, a sinuous, gathering thread, trickled through her. 'And where are you and Henry going to find King Richard?' Beneath her subdued demeanour, her heart began to race.

He frowned. 'The messages we have received indicate that Richard is heading towards Wales on a ship from Ireland and is aiming to land on the north coast…which is where we should be…now.' He cast an irritated look at the sun, beginning to slide down from its zenith.

'And do you think he will be there?' she asked eagerly, despair dropping away from her like a cloak. Her mind worked furiously, a vague, haphazard plan forming in her mind. Maybe, just maybe, Gilan had provided her with the answer to her problems. 'How certain can you be that Richard will be there?' She reached out instinctively, laid one hand on his arm, roped muscle iron-hard beneath her fingers.

His eyes flicked down; she snatched her hand away, cheeks crimson. She hadn't known what she was doing; if she wasn't careful, her eagerness would betray the progression of her thoughts. But Gilan peered down at her anyway, pewter eyes dark with suspicion. With the sun behind him, the shadows beneath his cheekbones seemed more pronounced, giving him a lean, predatory look. 'Why are you so interested? Surely you have more pressing problems to think about?'

'Because this is it!' Matilda blurted out. Why shouldn't he know her plans? He had wanted to make sure she was safe before he left—surely this way was the safest she could be? 'You have given me the answer. I can't stay here, obviously, because John will likely come after me at some point, and then who knows what might happen.' She shuddered with revulsion, clasping her hands together in front of her. 'But Thomas is the key. I need him to be here, but I haven't known how to contact him for this past year. Nobody knew where he was. But now I do,' she spoke happily, hopping from one foot to the other with excitement, 'because he's with King Richard, and you know where King Richard is.'

Gilan groaned. He thrust his chin up to the sky, his burnished lashes closing momentarily, spiky against the sunburn of his cheek. 'Please don't say what I think you are about to say, Matilda.'

'I want to come with you.'

He glared down at the perfect oval of her face, so full of hope, so full of determination, the downy hairs beneath her earlobe catching the sunlight, silky soft. He was about to ask her if she were mad, but for some strange reason, he found he knew her character well enough to know that she was completely serious—the question would be wasted on her. Her chin thrust up stubbornly into the air, tilted slightly, her arms laced defensively across her bosom as if to deflect any refusal he was about to deliver.

Which he was.

'It's out of the question,' he said, firmly. A woman on campaign! He could almost hear Henry laughing into his boots from here.

'But, I wouldn't be any trouble. Gilan, please! I can ride and I can shoot. You know I can look after myself. No one would even notice me.'

His heart flipped over, a treacherous squeezing of desire. His eyes roved over her sweet, delicate features, the full rosebud mouth he had so recently kissed, the neat indent of her waist. He thought of Henry's men, some of them rough and uncouth, desperate for a bit of female comfort after the long arduous winter. 'Oh, but I think they would.' The hoarseness of his voice surprised him.

'I would dress in boy's clothes...'

Why, it was as if she hadn't heard his words! 'Matilda, stop!' he said, placing his hands firmly on top of her shoulders as if trying to clamp down on her crazy ideas. 'I've told you, it's out of the question...'

'...and I haven't got anyone to look after me here!' She raised her voice, hating his cool, modulated tones, his reasoning. The warmth from his fingertips flooded through her, delight knifing direct to her heart, but she was determined to ignore it. She would ignore it. 'John will come after me, and that will be that—'

'Don't try to make me feel guilty for not taking you,' he interrupted. But even as he said the words, a vast sense of remorse swept over him. Who would take care of her? Who would look out for her when John came hammering on the castle door, coming to finish what he'd started?

From the shimmer on the horizon, a tall figure straightened up from the line of workers moving steadily across the wheat field and squinted over to the two figures on the track. The vague outline broke away from the pack, striding through the cut wheat, stubble grating on the threadbare wool of his trousers. Shoving open the flimsy field gate, he stepped up on to the dusty track, heading towards Matilda and Gilan.

'My lady!' the man called out as he approached the pair. 'My lady Matilda, you are back!' He raised a muscled arm in greeting.

Gilan chucked a swift glance over the man: thickset and burly, with grizzled grey hair and fierce, intelligent eyes. His whiskery cheeks were tanned, leathery; his hands scratched and calloused.

'Good day, Ansel.' Matilda flicked a brief smile at her bailiff, annoyed that he had chosen this moment to appear. Surely she had only needed a few more minutes with Gilan, to make him feel bad enough about her situation to take her along with him?

'Good day to you, my lady.' Ansel bowed deeply from the waist. 'And to you, my lord.' He peered at Gilan through narrowed eyes, gimlet sharp.

'Er, yes, this is Gilan de Cormeilles,' Matilda stuttered over his name. 'He...he escorted me home from Neen. And this is Ansel, my bailiff,' she added by way of explanation to Gilan.

Ansel bowed towards Gilan, who inclined his head, watching the interchange between Matilda and her bailiff with interest.

'I trust all is well at Neen?' Ansel asked. 'Has Lady Katherine had her baby?'

'She has.' Matilda bit down hard on her bottom lip, unwilling to go into details. 'And everything is fine,' she added with an edge of finality, to stop Ansel asking any more questions. The less she remembered about that horrible night at Neen, the better.

'Everything is going well here, mistress, as you can see.' Ansel swept his arm back across the fields. 'The weather has been kind to us this year.'

Matilda nodded. 'Did you manage to fix that cart?'

'The wheel was completely warped, but the blacksmith has fitted a new rim. It's running much better now. The hay is almost stacked up to the roof of the new barn—'

'Do you live in the village?' Gilan interrupted, noting the sturdy set of the man's shoulders.

Slightly puzzled, Ansel smiled, revealing a row of blackened teeth, some missing. 'No, my lord, we all live in the manor...'

Matilda's heart sank; she knew what Gilan was doing. He couldn't wait to shove the responsibility of her plight into someone else's hands—it was plain to see.

'How many of you?'

'Why, I'm not sure...about fifty of us, I suppose?'

'How many men?'

'Too many!' Ansel laughed. 'No, I jest, there's probably about fifteen women.'

Gilan nodded, satisfied, and turned to Matilda. 'Nobody to look after you, eh?' He raised his eyebrows. 'First you do your level best to rid yourself of me, and then, once you realise I could be useful to you, you beg me to take you with me!'

'I—'

'No, enough now. You will be safe here with your

bailiff. He looks like he could take on anyone in a fight, even your brother-in-law.'

'But—'

'I said, "enough," Matilda. Keep yourself away from John, hide out at your mother's nunnery if you have to, and keep yourself safe. When we meet up with the king, I promise to seek out your brother and send him home.' Face set in harsh, grim lines, he bowed smartly from the waist, a brief, perfunctory movement towards herself and Ansel.

Then he turned on his heel and walked away.

Matilda stared after Gilan, his back ramrod straight and rigid, as he strode back down the track, long legs kicking up the grey dust, his bright head shining in the sun, like the halo of an angel. A huge knot of disappointment, of sadness, gathered slowly in her chest, beneath her ribs, coagulating and spreading. She couldn't explain it, couldn't fathom this extreme feeling of desertion that swept over her, driving deep through her solar plexus. She would never see him again. This handsome stranger who had barrelled into her life with such dramatic intensity, who had touched his lips to hers and pressed a lingering mark on her soul, like a brand upon her heart. She closed her eyes, fighting to dispel the evocative image, willing her heart to close up over the bitter loss. She would do well to shove the romantic images from her mind and concentrate on her own self-preservation. This man was useful to her, nothing else. He was riding to a place where her brother was, but she knew Thomas would only come home if she went to him and begged him to return, to do his duty by the estate. She turned to her bailiff, who was surveying the whole proceedings with a bemused smile on his face.

'Where's your son, Ansel? I need to borrow some clothes.'

Chapter Eleven

'Thank the Lord we are away from that place,' Henry remarked to Gilan as he followed the knot of his soldiers along the banks of a small, slow-moving stream. Two knights led the way, holding flapping banners aloft, the horses slowing to a walk as they negotiated the deep dried-up ruts of the track. 'I swear I shall never have another drink as long as I live.' Lifting one hand into a fist, he scrubbed furiously at his forehead, trying to alleviate the thick, pulsing headache that cracked his skull, driving needles into the back of his eyes. His tongue seemed too big for his mouth, dry and fusty, cleaving uncomfortably to the roof of his mouth. He shifted around in the saddle, barely able to hold his body upright, and fixed Gilan with a curious look. Reddish-blue blotches sat in deep pockets beneath the duke's bloodshot eyes, his jawline coated in a rusty fuzz of unshaven beard. 'I couldn't find you anywhere when I finally made it out to the stables. Where did you go?'

The stream meandered along the flat, wide bottom of a valley; shallow slopes stretched up from its base, the upper levels topped with groups of trees: spreading oaks, ashes heavy with bunches of green seeds that would soon turn to brown as the summer ended. The grass was lush on the sides of the valley, grazed by russet-brown cows, their strong teeth ripping at the fertile growth. The sunlight touched everything with a hazy, golden light; the armour, the heavy helmets and breastplates of the escort knights shone, sparking fire, but Henry had decided he couldn't bear the weight and was clad in only tunic and leggings, as was Gilan.

'I was making myself useful,' Gilan replied, vaguely. A sear of…what? A sense of betrayal, maybe, flooded his veins, making him want to turn back, to defend Matilda against her lout of a brother-in-law. As he had ridden away, he had convinced himself that she would be safe, tucked up in the manor house with her bailiff, Ansel, and his men to ward off any attack. But doubt plagued him and he questioned his thoughts constantly, wondering, wishing he could have stayed a while, wishing that maybe, just maybe, he should have let her come along with Henry, to find her brother. At least that way, he would have known she was safe. But who was he to think he was any better than the next man to protect her? He had let his own brother die—Matilda was probably better off without him.

'Useful? How?' Henry rapped out. The headache rapped incessantly on his skull.

'Lady Matilda needed to return home. I escorted her.'

Henry peered at him, brows drawn close. 'She's a pretty piece. I envy you. You must have had a pleasant morning.'

Gilan shifted uncomfortably in the saddle, unwilling to divulge his own uncouth behaviour. The treacherous dip of his head. Matilda's upturned mouth, plush as a feather cushion, so trusting, so innocent, troubled his conscience. Lord, surely he was no better than her brother-in-law, taking advantage of her like that!

'It was fine,' he replied, his tone curt. 'There was no one else to take her.' He hunched sideways to avoid the overhanging branches of a rowan tree, growing out at an odd angle from the edge of the field. Bunched between the serrated leaves, clustering red berries, a herald of autumn, brushed across the top of his tunic, vivid orange-red against the blue.

Henry shrugged his shoulders, grinning broadly.

Gilan's explanation was tenuous; there was always somebody around on a big estate who could escort a lady homewards; he wouldn't have considered Lord John's household to be any different. Why would Lady Matilda let a complete stranger take her home, when she was surrounded by her family? Leaning over, he punched Gilan's shoulders, a friendly, jostling contact. 'Have you taken a shine to the lady, Gilan? After all these months, I must say, it's good to see.'

Henry had looked on, aghast, as Pierre had died in Gilan's arms, almost obscured by whirling flakes of snow. Clutching his brother, Gilan had howled, cried up to the Heavens, cursing God, the universe, but above all, himself, for what had happened. The broken bits of the scaling ladder scattered around them, and still, the flaming arrows had rained down from the battlements. Eventually Henry had managed to drag his friend away. Such grief had been terrible to see. He had witnessed first-hand the effect Pierre's death had wrought upon the other man—months in which Gilan had moved around like a shadow. Nothing seemed to matter to him; he had hurled himself into battle as if he wanted to die, wanting to join his brother. But now, now he seemed changed, easier, with a brightness around him that Henry had not seen for a long time.

'It's not like that.' Warmth coiled in Gilan's belly.

'No, of course not.' Henry smirked. 'I must say, I was quite taken with her myself.'

Gilan sighed, hitching forwards in his saddle. 'For God's sake, Henry, if you must know, her brother-in-law attacked her. I had to get her out of there. She could hardly speak, let alone stand! Anyone else would have done the same.'

'My God, I had no idea!' Henry's coarse red hair glimmered like rusty iron. 'Why on earth would he do such a thing?'

'Because he's a bastard, of the highest order,' Gilan ground out. 'He is desperate for a male heir. After his wife delivered a daughter last night, he was not happy.'

'So he thought he'd try the sister,' Henry supplied. He shuffled around in his saddle, reaching for his leather water bottle. Pulling the stopper, he took a long, deep swig.

'Precisely.'

How long would it take John to muster the men he needed to attack Lilleshall? Gilan wondered. Did the manor house have a portcullis, or a thick set of gates they could close against attack? Why couldn't he remember? Because he'd been fixated on the seductive sway of her hips as she'd led the way into the house, that's why, damn it! She would do better to leave the manor entirely and hide out in the village or, better still, the nunnery with her mother. But that would mean she would have to hide for ever, or at least until she was past child-bearing age. And with her away from Lilleshall, John would simply commandeer the place for himself.

'Gilan! Did you hear me?'

'Sorry.' His thoughts bounced chaotically around his skull. Every step his horse took away from Matilda seemed to scour at his conscience, send a fresh leap of guilt through his veins. He should never have left her. Henry didn't need him; he had enough soldiers to protect him, enough soldiers to contest Richard when they finally caught up with the king. He should go back.

'Things like this happen in families all over the country, Gilan. She's not your concern now.' Henry touched his heels to his destrier, encouraging the animal to start the long, slow climb from the valley bottom to the top of the ridge, where the stunted hawthorns clung to the skyline like a fence of broken bones. His bridle jangled as he picked up speed, moving in front of Gilan to negotiate the path that snaked through the whispering grass. 'You have more important things to deal with.'

The icy water of Henry's speech sloshed over him. His mouth tightened to a straight, stern line, compressed. Providing a beautiful, wilful distraction, Matilda's plight had driven all thoughts of Pierre from his mind, of the obligation to his parents who awaited his return, his explanation of events, to them, and to his brother's wife, Isabelle. He had sent them only one letter, dashed off hurriedly for the messenger in his thick, unruly scrawl, providing them with the barest of facts about Pierre's death, promising that he would tell them everything in more detail when he returned home. When he returned home. Which, at the moment, he was doing everything in his power to avoid.

Up ahead, the lead soldiers had stopped on the top of the ridge, their horses surrounded by a froth of yellow gorse. Henry's horse gained the ridge, closely followed by Gilan. The stiff breeze fanned the tails of the horses, sending them flying sideways, like a drift of pale seaweed.

'We're not certain of our direction, my lord.'

The landscape was curious. They had reached an upland plateau, expecting to gain far-reaching views, yet all they could see were more ridges of grassland stretching away from them, expanding in all directions, cut through with lumps of limestone outcrop, casually scattered, as if by a giant hand. Black-faced sheep roamed free, cropping the coarser grass, trailing amongst the rounded clusters of oak and sycamore, the lumps and bumps of prehistoric mounds. The sun was sinking slowly now, casting long shadows across the land; soon, it would be necessary for them to find shelter for the night.

Henry frowned, hunching around to look at Gilan.

Gilan shook his head. 'I've no idea, Henry. This part of the country is a mystery to me.'

'Then, we need to find ourselves a guide. On the morrow. Now, let's find some shelter.'

Matilda prided herself on her navigation skills. Where most of her female contemporaries had no idea how to travel from one place to another and were content to sit dumbly in a litter, or be led on a docile palfrey, she would instead take an active interest in a route. The clues were everywhere in the landscape: church spires on the horizon would take you to the next village or town, or a knot of trees on a prominent hillock would signpost the main route west, or east, for example. With a knowledge of the sun's position in the sky, taught to her by her father, and taking note of the way the shadows fell on the ground, it was relatively easy to work out one's direction.

At least that was what she told herself, now, trotting gamely in a vague north-westerly direction. Ansel had remonstrated with her, of course, about going, but she had overridden his concerns, demanding that his son lend her some clothes, insisting that a horse be made ready. She had been cantankerous and irritable, she thought now, regretting her earlier bossy behaviour, but she had been anxious not to waste any time.

For, if she wasted time, then she might miss Gilan, might miss Henry and his men riding towards Wales. By her reckoning, if she rode in a diagonal line north-west, and they followed the only route north from Neen, she would not miss them. Her plan would be to find them on the road, and follow them, at a discreet distance. She didn't think the north coast of Wales was far away, maybe a couple of hours' ride, but she couldn't be sure. Henry and Gilan would lead her straight to King Richard…and by association, her brother, and they would be none the wiser.

Dressed in itchy woollen trousers, folded over several times at the waist and secured with a makeshift belt made of rope, a linen shirt and an ill-fitting tunic, laced up to the throat, she was able to maintain a reasonably fast pace through the forests that lay to the north-west of her home. A hood, with its scalloped edge resting over her shoulders, covered the glossy brightness of her hair and kept her face in shadow. She had wound the plait around and around into a simple coil at the back of her head, now hidden by the hood. Without her bow and arrow, she felt vulnerable; no doubt her weapon of protection still lay at the bottom of the river where she had first met Gilan.

Emerging from the rustling forest, the smooth bark of the tree trunks glowing in the setting sun, she kicked her heels into her horse to climb up on to the limestone plateau, the only ridge of high ground that sat between her home and the huge river that divided England from Wales. It stretched from her sister's home at Neen all the way to the remains of an old settlement at Uphill, on the coast.

She gained the level ground through a scrubby copse of larch and holly, her horse picking a fastidious path through fallen branches, rotten and bare of leaves, and thin twigs, fragile, desiccated, poking up to scratch against the horse's legs. Lichen, pale green, frilled vigorously on the sickly wood. There was little water on the plateau, she remembered her father saying, which was why no one had made a home up here in this bleak, desolate land. The falling rain dropped straight through the limestone surface, forming hollows and fissures within the porous rock.

Drawing on the reins, Matilda screwed her eyes up, scanning the bulbous pockets of yellow gorse, the solitary hawthorns.

Her lungs stilled, breath trapping in her throat.

There. Silhouetted against a sky striped with the colours of the setting sun, a riot of pinkish-red, suffused with an almost transparent yellow, Henry and his soldiers huddled in a group on the far edge of the plateau, plate armour reflecting the dying sunlight, banners flapping, narrow triangles of fabric, the gold of Henry's coat of arms emblazoned on each one. One blue tunic covering a tall frame, straight-backed, set a little apart from the main group. Gilan.

Her heart plummeted, constricting with a looping panic. Instinctively, she nudged her horse into the scant shadows of the copse from which she had just left, seeking invisibility within the rickety trees. This was what she wanted, wasn't it? To find Henry and his men, to track them to her brother? Her situation at home was untenable and this was the only solution. So why did she feel so scared?

It was him. Of course, it was him.

What would he do, if he discovered she had de-fied him? She shook her head sharply, dispelling any further thought. No. It would not do to dwell on something that might never happen. It made her fearful, and when fear arrived, fault would follow. She could not afford to make any mistakes; her whole future was a stake and she was not about to let the man with diamond eyes ruin her only chance of a solution.

'Someone is following us,' Gilan said quietly.

They had ridden for what seemed like hours across the endless, unrelenting ground, but at last, they seemed to have reached the end, to a point where the view opened up, spectacularly. The land-scape dropped away, flattening out into low-lying marshland, cut by man-made drainage channels set into a grid system. And there, in the distance, the shining line of the river that they would have to cross. The track they were following began to descend; first, through a band of short, wind-blasted oaks, then as the sides of the valley rose up, huge cliffs of vertical limestone appeared.

'Who?' Henry bent round in his saddle, but the curve and steepness of the track obscured whoever it was that followed them.

'I'm not sure, I only glimpsed him. One man, on horseback.'

'Could be anyone.'

'Or someone,' Gilan said. 'It's almost dark. Who would be travelling at this hour? You're vulnerable, Henry, and Richard's supporters are everywhere. It pays to be cautious.'

'Well, I'm glad I have you to watch my back,' Henry said.

Gilan glanced up at the craggy limestone that towered over them as they descended into the gorge, casting swathes of shade as the sun inched downwards. Scrappy hawthorns poked out from the vertiginous rock face, clinging on wherever they could find a hold—spiky, angular branches reaching out like crooked fingers against the strip of sky above.

'You go on ahead and take the soldiers with you,' Gilan said. 'Find somewhere farther down to spend the night.' His eyes gleamed with silvery intent.

'But what are you going to do?' Henry's eyes narrowed.

Gilan jumped down from his destrier. 'Surprise him.' He grinned, but the smile did not reach the hard glitter of his eyes. He led his horse beyond the next outcrop of rock, making sure he was well hidden from the track, securing the reins.

He waited until Henry and his men had disappeared, then began to climb the rock face with the speed and agility of a much smaller man. Using the long, roping muscles in his arms, he levered himself up, strong legs powering him over the steep, slippery rock, slick with damp. Ferns sprung out from angled crevices, bright green in the dusky light; his hands reached up and sought gaps into which he could dig his fingers and pull himself higher. About twelve feet from the ground, he found the perfect spot: a flat ledge dotted with loose scree and shallow depressions that provided him with an ideal hiding place from which to pounce on their follower. And he was certain the rider was following them. What other person would take their haphazard route across the countryside? Haphazard only because Henry and his men were unsure of their direction. And yet the rider had dogged their tails, turning when they turned, doubling back when they doubled back. He grinned to himself, splaying his big body across the ledge, lying flat and stealthy, unmoving, like an animal awaiting its prey.

He didn't have to wait long.

The shadows were lengthening quickly now, creeping inexorably across the tall fingers of rock, across the jagged vertical chasms; a shadowy twilight filled the valley. Trees and shrubs sank into the greying background, edges blurring slowly, the fine details of branches and leaves vanishing as the light fell. And, from the top of the gorge, the distinct clip-clopping of a horse on the loose scree.

He raised his head, the thick blond strands of his hair riffling in the breeze. The rest of his body was still, poised, ready to spring down.

The rider negotiated the uneven track slowly, carefully, a pale silhouette. The neat forelegs of the horse flashed white as they moved against the dark rock.

Gilan shifted, a tiny movement. His right knee was damp; water had seeped through his woollen trousers from one of the shallow depressions in the rock. As the horse and rider drew level with him, he propelled himself forwards, leaped out and down with blood-curdling roar, slamming into the shoulders and flanks of the rider and falling with him in a tight bundle to the stony ground, twisting his body in one sinuous movement to sit heavily astride his victim, who lay face down on the track.

'Who are you?' he bellowed down at the inert body. 'Why do you follow us?'

Stunned by the force of the attack, Matilda lay prone, her forehead ground into gritty damp stones, her mind scrabbling to comprehend what had just happened. One minute she had been riding along easily, believing she was reasonably safe, and the next, why, it was like the Devil himself had burst out of nowhere!

But she was in no doubt as to the identity of this devil.

Her unconscious mind had known almost immediately: the flash of gilt hair, the heft of a big body, the short cloak flying out like wings, the press of solid thigh muscles snug against her own backside. In the darkness she flushed with shame at the intimacy of the contact and the rapidly accelerating beat of her heart. What was he doing here? Why had he not stuck with the others?

'Who are you?' Gilan demanded once more.

She shifted her head to one side, one ear grazing against the stony ground. 'For God's sake, it's me!' she managed to gulp out frantically, sucking in air in order to speak. Her voice sounded like the pathetic mewl of a kitten. Had he even heard her? She tried to wriggle beneath him, to no avail. His superior weight was simply too heavy for her, the rocklike muscles of his inner thighs clamped hard around her hips. Her mouth went dry at the closeness of his body and she immediately chastised herself. How could she even think of such things, when she was stuck fast beneath this monster of a man?

He lifted her shoulders off the ground, shook her roughly. 'I can't hear you,' he said. His voice held a taunting, menacing tone.

'Gilan! Get…off…me! Now!' she yelled.

That voice. *Her* voice. The sweet tone plucked at something deep within him, screwing it round like a piece of wet rag between two meaty fists. A wave of pure disbelief swept over him. Knees punched cruelly into his captive's slender flanks, as he stared down, incredulous, at the slim back clad in a padded tunic, at the head covered by a coarse, woollen hood.

He ripped the hood back.

Shiny, glossy strands, wound into a bun at the nape of her neck, mocked him. Her neat head, the delicate set of her shoulders.

Damnation!

He scrambled back, away, on to his feet. 'What in hell's teeth are you doing here?' he bellowed down, glaring at the prone form sprawled beneath him. To his surprise, his voice wavered. *My God, I could have killed her,* he thought. It was only a matter of luck that he hadn't chosen to jump out with a knife in his hand.

'Get up,' he said, sternly, compressing his lips into a forbidding line.

Her heart fluttered at his steely tone. She had an overwhelming desire to suddenly keep lying there, face down in the dirt, until he had gone away.

'Come on,' he said. One hand spread across her shoulder, rolling her over. She sat up, a little woozily, legs outstretched. Her head swam and the back of her shoulders ached where he had slammed into her. Her cheek was impregnated with grit and she brushed at the tiny granules, dislodging them. Drawing her knees up, she tilted her face up towards her captor.

He stood above her, long legs planted a pace apart, arms folded high across his muscle-bound chest. In the twilight his eyes shone down like diamond chips. 'I thought I told you to stay put,' he growled. The bulky fabric of the hood she wore billowed in soft gathers at the base of her neck, revealing the delicate creamy column of her throat. He wanted to verbally lash out at her, be angry at her foolishness, yet all he could feel was a tremendous sense of relief. She was here and she was safe. For now.

'And wait like a sitting duck for John to turn up and attack me again!' she flashed back at him. 'Not likely!'

'You're lucky I didn't run you through with my sword,' he said. 'I could have killed you!'

She lifted slim shoulders towards her ears. 'It was a chance I was willing to take. I didn't think you'd see me following you.'

He frowned down at her. 'Either you're extremely brave or extremely foolish,' he said. 'And right now I can't work out which one it is. Surely your bailiff, Ansel, would have given you protection at your manor? John wouldn't have been allowed to come near you.' His words sounded hollow, unconvincing, even to his own ears.

She shook her head. 'But it's not solving the problem in the long term, is it? Ansel can't watch me every hour of every day. He has other work to do and John is sneaky—he would have found a way to get to me, somehow. Finding my brother is the only solution, believe me. I'm sorry, Gilan, I know you don't like this, but you are my only hope. You have to let me come with you.'

Chapter Twelve

Like a pall of dense grey smoke, cloud clumped on the horizon, then edged across the limpid sky above, obscuring the silver arc of the moon. To the west, brilliant streaks of the dying sun dimmed suddenly, then veiled and, at the bottom of the towering cliffs of the gorge, the light darkened.

'Matilda, you have to go home,' Gilan said. A single raindrop touched his face, a cold pinprick. 'Where Henry is going…where I am going, is no place for a woman.' Was it his imagination or did he hear the note of resignation in his voice?

'But—' Matilda protested, attempting to decipher the contours of his face. All she could see in the growing blackness was the decisive flash of his eyes, the glimmer of his hair.

'Besides, it's unheard of, a woman travelling with a group of men who aren't related to her, or part of her household.' He cut across her answer, his tone deliberately stern. 'I told you all this before.'

Edging closer to her horse, she clutched on to the bridle beneath the animal's chin, as if to give herself the extra strength she needed to argue with him. 'But, Gilan, I'll stay dressed as I am!' As if to emphasise the point, she yanked her hood more securely over the velvet fall of her hair. 'No one would ever guess I was a woman.'

Somewhere, high above them, an owl hooted, calling to its mate, a haunting, lonely sound.

A jolt of desire scythed through him. *I'd know,* he thought. The woollen leggings fitted snugly to her shapely calves; the tantalising curve of her bosom pressed against the voluminous tunic. And it wasn't just her figure beneath the clothes, he thought, it was everything about her: the graceful, efficient way she walked, the fragile curve of her jawline, the exquisite smoothness of her skin peeking out from beneath the hood.

'They wouldn't guess, would they?' she asked.

He would be a fool if he agreed to this. It was wrong, all so wrong. Women weren't supposed to roam about the countryside dressed as the opposite sex; they were soft, vulnerable creatures who needed to stay within the relative safety of their castle walls. But Matilda's home wasn't safe and now she was pursuing the only solution open to her in order to rectify that situation. Most women would have probably resigned themselves to their fate long ago, had they found themselves in a similar position, but not Matilda. She was so different and he could only approve of her tenacity and determination. She had defied him, but strangely, he applauded her defiance, admired her. Her obtuse, stubborn behaviour had burrowed deep within him, sneaking beneath the ironclad coating that surrounded his heart and coaxing it back to life.

He sighed, sticking one foot into his stirrup and swinging up into the saddle, tanned fingers wrapping around the rubbed leather of his reins. 'No, I suppose they wouldn't guess,' he said finally, looking down into her expectant face. This was wrong, all so wrong. She should be tucked up in a cosy manor somewhere, a doting husband looking at her fondly, a trio of children playing at her feet. A slew of rain chased between them, spattered against his cloak; drops of rain glittered on her cheek. 'I will pass you off as a guide—do you know where the crossing is over the river into Wales?'

'Er…yes, why of course I do!' she blurted out inanely, a surge of joy coursing through her at his tepid agreement, squashing down the flicker of doubt that rose up momentarily. She had been over the crossing once, with her father, and that had been several years ago. But surely the memory would come back to her once they neared the river.

'Mount up, then,' he ordered her. 'I want to catch up with Henry before this rain becomes any heavier.' He glanced at the rolling black clouds above their heads.

She sprung into her saddle with all the agility of an acrobat, her face bright with hope. 'Thank you, Gilan,' she said, wriggling her hips in the saddle to adjust her seat. 'I know this wasn't an easy decision for you, but I promise you, I won't let you down. I'll be safe enough, you'll see.'

Raindrops sluicing down his skin, trickling down beneath the collar of his tunic, he dug his heels into the muscled flanks of his horse, doubt clagging his throat, a sour taste. She would be safe from Henry and his soldiers, he would make sure of that, but would she be safe from him? Tugging his eyes from the plush curve of her upper lip, a traitorous leap of memory surged through him and he turned his face into the strengthening rain, praying for self-restraint.

The rain continued to batter down. As the pair rode down the gorge, Matilda's horse plodding docilely after Gilan's springing destrier, the raindrops hammered down relentlessly. Soon, the intensity of the downpour made it difficult even to see a few feet in front of them; it was lucky that they only had one path to follow.

Matilda bowed her head, very much aware of how fortunate she was that Gilan had agreed to take her along. She wasn't entirely sure what had persuaded him in the end; he had been so adamant at Lilleshall that she should stay at the castle and he was certainly not the sort of person to give in to feminine wheedling. Blinking up through rain-soaked lashes, the water stinging her eyes, she studied his figure riding up ahead: immense shoulders, powerful back, sitting easily in the saddle, and his bright golden hair, pale and luminous, shining out through the greyish gloom. What had made him change his mind? Despite her own assurances, she knew she would be an encumbrance to him, but then, what choice did he have? Miles from anywhere, there was no one apart from him to take her home and make her stay there, and his duty lay with Henry. He hadn't time to take her home and then double-back. Thank the Lord he had caught her at this point and not at the start of the journey when he would have surely marched her homewards by the scruff of her neck.

The water had begun to seep through the thin

wool of her hood and crawl uncomfortably down her neck. She wiggled in the saddle, the coarse wool of her leggings damp, itching against the delicate skin of her thighs. 'Gilan!' she called out. 'Can we find some shelter? This rain isn't going to stop.'

He drew on the reins, reluctantly, shifting his hips round to face her. Matilda sat on her horse, every part of her dripping, saturated with water: her faded hood, her long, spiky eyelashes, her clumsy boots. Behind her, frothing rivulets of water tumbled down the sides of the gorge, gathering momentum, carrying small rocks in their bouncing streams. Such a gorge, with its loose, fissured rock, would be notorious for landslips; it wouldn't be long before a large boulder came down those sides, dislodged by the force of the rain. He didn't want to be around when that happened.

'How much farther until we are out of here?' he shouted at her.

'Not long.' She raised her voice against the clattering rain. This part of the land was familiar to her, at least. With her family, she had travelled on a regular basis through the gorge to visit an elderly aunt of her mother's, on an estate nearer to the sea. Swiftly, she quelled the pang of nostalgia that rose within her; no, it would not do to dwell on those halcyon days when her father had been alive, when her brother was her constant companion. Those days were over, they could never be brought back.

'Matilda!' Gilan yelled at her. A look of pure, intense sadness crossed her face and tugged at something deep within him.

'Sorry,' she mumbled, throwing him a wan smile, kicking her horse so that she drew alongside him. 'There's a group of caves at the end of the escarpment, on the face of the cliff. We can shelter there.'

Gilan nodded silently, his face shining with rain, the water highlighting the carved beauty of his cheekbones. He held on to his reins, indicating that Matilda should lead the way, gritting his teeth as her knee brushed his as she moved past him.

They emerged from the narrow path of the gorge some moments later. The land opened out before them in a sodden vista of flat plains and drainage channels, the rain moving across the flat countryside like a fine-needled curtain. Gilan screwed his eyes up, searching for a flash of red and gold, a sign of Henry, but found none.

'This way,' Matilda said breathlessly, steering her horse up to the right, through an area of low scrub and gorse. Beyond he could see several dark fissures marking the limestone at ground level: caves, and lots of them. She paused in front of the largest gap in the rock face: a triangular opening, as tall as a man and as wide as a barn door. Her horse lowered its head, then stretched its neck to try to reach a sparse crop of grass spurting out of the rocky ground. Hesitating, Matilda observed the cave in dismay, the full reality of the situation into which she had so willingly thrown herself suddenly taking shape before her with sharp intensity.

What had she done?

A horrible, debilitating realisation tugged at her brain. She had been so pleased with herself, so happy that Gilan had agreed to take her along with him, that she had failed to consider even the most basic details of the journey. As the rain continued to pour down around her, she sat ramrod straight on her horse, frowning intently. Her hands froze around the reins, courage failing with every breath. She was about to share this cave, this very small space, with a man she barely knew. A man she had met only yesterday. A man whose devastating presence sent reason flying, a man whose unexpected kiss had made her senses reel, a kiss that she now could not forget.

Behind her, Gilan jumped down from his horse. 'What are you waiting for?' he said, the rain funnelling down over his hair, dripping off the ends of his ears. As she stared down into his silver eyes, her heart squeezed, gripped by longing, a yearning that she couldn't explain, couldn't even begin to understand. Her chest quivered with fearful excitement. Suddenly the prospect of dealing with her brother-in-law didn't seem so bad at all.

She cleared her throat. 'Er…look, maybe we should keep riding after all, at least then you can find Henry. We'll waste too much time if we shelter here.'

Hanging the reins of his destrier over a rock, Gilan threw her a sideways look, frowning. 'Henry would have no intention of riding in this weather,' he said. 'Believe me, he would have sought shelter far sooner than we have. We'll find him easily in the morning, he won't be far ahead.'

'Then, why can't we see him? Why can't we find him?' She swept one hand across the vast plains, disconcerted by the edge of shrill desperation in her voice.

He frowned, coming towards her and placing one hand on her horse's neck. 'Why are you so concerned? It will be much more difficult for you to maintain your disguise once we find him. At least you only have me to contend with at the moment.'

And that was precisely the problem, she thought. Alone with him, she felt decidedly unsafe from her own desires. Shifting miserably in her saddle, cold water seeping through her thin tunic down the length of her spine, she tucked her chin down into the damp folds of her hood, avoiding the drilling power of his gaze. 'I think maybe you were right, Gilan,' she managed to splutter out. 'I've made a mistake. I should go home.'

The hot brilliance of his eyes swept over her, openly mocking. 'You're changing your mind?' he said, incredulous. 'After all that effort you've put into persuading me to take you along? You decided to change your mind now? Why?'

She flinched slightly as his words rapped into her. How could she tell him? How could she tell him that being this close to him sent her whole body into a flutter of excitement, of anticipation? Even now, with his hand on her horse's neck, close to the curve of her knee, her senses ran amok, scatting wildly, shredding her train of thought, her calm composure. His presence turned her into someone she had never been, the type of woman she feared, a woman who was out of control, a slave to emotion, to feeling.

'I...er, well...' She shrugged her shoulders, eyeing the mouth of the cave warily. 'I thought it was better if we carried on, that's all.' Even to her own ears, her excuse sounded lame.

'That's not it. You were the one who suggested we find shelter,' he pointed out, raising one eyebrow, watching the shudders rack her slender frame. 'And you're freezing. It's madness not to stop now. Why do you suddenly want to carry on? To go home?' He tilted his head to one side, a quizzical look on his face.

She pursed her lips, and sighed. 'If you must know, I'm not in the habit of doing things like this.'

He smiled, teeth flashing white in the gloom. 'Which bit? Riding around the countryside dressed as a boy, or sleeping in a cave with a man you hardly know?'

Sleeping in a cave with a man you hardly know. His words pressed down into her; a flush of hot embarrassment coursed through her limbs. 'The...the last one,' she muttered, closing her eyes in shame. Oh God, why had he made her admit such a thing?

'Oh, don't worry,' he answered, reaching up and encircling her waist with strong hands. Before she even had time to squeak a protest, he had lifted her down, keeping one hand on her upper arm to steady her as he propelled her towards the dry innards of the cave. 'I'll keep well away. You're safe from me.'

Turning away from her, he returned to his horse, unbuckling the saddlebags slung on to the rump of the animal, the lie scorching through his conscience, a flare of brilliant light. But if he had any respect for Matilda, or any sense of civility at all, then he would listen to the voice of self-restraint in his head and keep his distance.

'You stay here whilst I try to find some dry wood.' He pushed Maltilda into the dark confines of the cave, shoving his saddlebags to one side. 'You might want to take off those wet things,' he added, casting a critical eye across her thin, sodden clothes, her hood drooping forlornly around her pale face. Already she was shivering, a bluish cast to the skin around her mouth. Ripping open one of the saddlebags, he rummaged around and extracted a woollen blanket. 'Here,' he said, shoving it at her crossed arms, 'you can wrap yourself in this when you're done.'

His words blazed a trail across her raw senses. Undress? Was he completely mad? It was bad enough that she was alone in a cave with him, but to be naked and alone in a cave with him—that was sheer foolhardiness. She lifted one finger to her mouth, touched her bottom lip, experimentally. His devastating kiss still lingered there, luscious and full-blown; she would do well to remember what he was capable of. She wrapped herself tightly in his blanket.

He returned some moments later, grinning, clutching a bundle of sticks. His sudden smile lit up his face, made him appear younger, more boyish somehow. 'I found a dead tree that had fallen into one of the other caves. There's enough wood to keep a fire going all night.'

'Great,' she replied tonelessly, standing back in the shadows, desperately wriggling her icy toes to try to regain some feeling in them. How stupid she had been to not wear woollen stockings beneath her leggings; in her haste to leave Lilleshall, she had shoved her bare feet into the rough boots without a second thought.

Gilan crouched down at the cave entrance, placing a pile of dry leaves and sticks on the rocky ground. Extracting a flint from the leather pouch that hung from his belt, he struck a spark, immediately coddling it within the leaves, feeding the small flame until it grew and seized on the dry wood criss-crossed around it.

'There,' he said, satisfied as the flames reached higher. 'I'll go and fetch the bigger branches now.' He jerked his head up at her, taking in her appearance in one swift glance: the lumpy boots poking out of the bottom of his blanket, the bulk of her hood pushed back across her shoulders in an effort to hide it. 'It will give you time to change out of those wet things.'

'They're almost dry,' she protested, clutching her

hands across her stomach awkwardly. 'It's hardly worth my while.'

In the flickering shadows of the cave, his eyes sparkled with diamond fire. 'Matilda, either you remove your clothes, or I will do it for you. I've seen men twice your size cut down with the cold and suffer with it. I'm not doing this to deliberately thwart you, I'm telling you to do it for your own good. '

And with that he lowered his head beneath the low stone lintel across the opening, and disappeared.

Watching his receding back, Matilda clamped her lips together mutinously. Typical! Dispensing orders as if she were one of his foot soldiers, not some noble lady! And then the outrageous threat that he would remove her clothes if she refused to do it! As if he would do such a thing! She watched the flames, her hands clutched around the edges of his blanket, not wanting to think, not wanting to move. Exhaustion made her brain swim; her eyes smarted with tiredness.

The heat from the flames rose up, touched her face like a balm. She sighed, closing her eyes briefly. It seemed a long time since she had delivered Katherine's daughter, a long time since she had had any sleep. And yet, the thought of any sleep at all with Gilan in the cave seemed outrageous, laughable, somehow. Sinking to her knees before the dancing flames, she picked up a stray stick, poking at the innards of the fire to send up a shower of sparks, aware of the tension stringing through her body, the wet garments sticking uncomfortably to her flesh.

The cave entrance flickered with the fire's lambent glow as Gilan dragged the heavy branch up through the gorse. The horses were quiet, chomping steadily on a small patch of skimpy grass growing to one side of the cave. Leaving the branch, he went over and made sure their reins were tied securely.

Confident that he had allowed Matilda enough time to change, he approached the cave once more, coming to an abrupt halt at the entrance. On her knees before the fire, Matilda was staring into the flames, her expression wistful, dreamlike. Her delicate hands rested in her lap, palms upturned, vulnerable, like limpid flowers. Fanning down over her flushed cheeks, her eyelashes drooped with fatigue, glossy spikes like black velvet feathers.

Breath punched from his lungs.

Stalled in the cave entrance, he gritted his teeth, struggling for control. Desire coiled, deep and treacherous, a slow ripening of lust. Where was the self-restraint that was so customary to his character, the thread of logic, of sanity that would pull him back, away from temptation? He was a soldier, a commander in Henry's army, relied on by others for his strength of resolve, his clear head in the dire extremes of battle. How was it that this single, wayward maid could affect him so? He lifted one hand, surprised to see it was shaking, and pushed dripping hair away from his forehead.

'Matilda?' he called out quietly, startling her from her reverie.

'What…?' She glanced up at him as he stepped towards her, his cloak sparkling with raindrops.

'You were miles away.' A smile played at the edge of his mouth, a dimple creasing his cheek.

'I…er, yes, sorry.' Her eyes shimmered like sapphires in the juddering flames. 'I was thinking about Katherine, about my family when we were all together at Lilleshall…' Her voice drifted away on a forlorn note. She jerked her head towards him, tracking upwards along his honed, tough body to meet his eyes, a rueful smile pinned on her mouth. 'Foolish thoughts.' She shrugged her shoulders. 'Stupid, really.'

His heart creased. 'No, no, not stupid.' He hunkered down beside her, the material of his trousers stretching taut against his big thigh muscles. She averted her eyes, staring resolutely into the fire. With his body so close to her, her stomach looped crazily; she could smell the fresh air on his skin, vibrant, invigorating. 'You're fighting for your livelihood, Matilda, to save all that is dear to you...'

She caught the note of empathy in his voice, was surprised by it. 'Do you have family?'

'Yes, I do,' he said, picking up the stick she had discarded, throwing it into the flames. 'They live farther north from here, in the castle where I was born. My parents and my sister-in-law, Isabelle.'

'So you have a brother, then.' Her eyes shone over him, brilliant pools of cerulean light.

The air in the cave stilled, suddenly.

Pain flashed across his face, his eyes hollowing out to solid discs of silver. He bounced to his feet abruptly, almost knocking his head against a low overhang of protruding rock. Shocked by the violence of his movement, Matilda struggled to her feet, clutching Gilan's blanket about her, arms laced tightly across her body, a defence.

'Gilan?' she whispered. 'What is it?'

Wind gusted against the mouth of the cave, sending a squall of rain scurrying inwards. Droplets splattered in the fire, hissing, thin trails of steam rising upwards. He clung to the sympathy bound in her earnest perusal, the concern, and wondered what she would do if he told her what had happened, how he had caused his brother's death. Would she be able to show such kindness towards him then?

His voice, when it came, was wretched, scoured with grief. 'My brother...is dead.' With his words, the familiar black guilt washed through him, yet it was muted somehow, thinned, like an echo gradually fading into the distance.

Matilda blanched at his guttural tone, the hoarse syllables. 'Oh, Gilan, I'm so sorry.' She reached out instinctively, her fingers splaying across his sleeve.

He pulled his arm down, roughly, away from her soft touch and turned away, hauling in the larger pieces of wood from the cave entrance and throwing them haphazardly on the fire. He didn't want her sympathy; he wasn't worthy of it. Instead, his eye focused critically on the wet splotches soaking through the light-coloured wool of his blanket, and his mind seized upon her transgression, her refusal to change her clothes as a way out of this conversation, an excuse to deflect any further questions.

Reaching across, he snatched the blanket away.

Her hands flailed outwards, trying to snare the flying edges. 'What are you doing? That blanket is keeping me warm!' The swift change in his behaviour appalled her, the harsh breaking of any sort of connection between them. She wanted time to digest his speech, to sift through his few scant words that gave her a glimmer of insight into this man who stood before her. But he wasn't going to let her.

'I told you to take off those wet things.' He scowled down at her.

'Otherwise you would take them off for me,' she chanted back at him, jeering faintly with her head tilted on one side, a taunting smile deepening the shadows beneath her cheekbones.

'Do you think I wouldn't do it?' His response was terse.

'As if you would do such a thing!' she blurted back at him. Her smile vanished as his eyes darkened, predatory, unwavering.

Oh, Lord, he did mean to do it, she thought, interpreting the determined look in his eyes. Panic jolted through her veins. 'You wouldn't dare!' she squeaked, shuffling back in a futile effort to escape him.

'I'm used to having my orders followed.' He reached out and began to pluck at the lacings on the front of her tunic. He knew he was behaving like a boor, but this made it easier to deal with her, to maintain some distance between them. Unlaced, her tunic gaped open at the neck, revealing the startling white of her damp chemise pressed stickily against her skin. His gaze touched on the upward thrust of her breasts, nestled pinkly beneath the gauzy material. Hell's teeth! What had he got himself into? This situation was difficult enough, without him wanting to throw her to the ground and make long sweet love to her.

'I'll do it,' she flashed back hotly, smacking his hand away, tugging the hood angrily over her head and throwing it to the ground. 'Go out, or turn your back at least, if you have an ounce of civility about you!'

He stood up, releasing a stiff, clenched breath. His whole body, the muscles, the ligaments, all seemed strung out with tension, rigid. Thank God, he thought. Thank God she had said she would do it herself. He pushed out into the night air, his body compressed with longing. How on earth was he going to spend a whole night in the cave with her?

He pressed his spine up against the rock face, in the lee of the escarpment. Waited.

The rain continued to pour down, pattering on the gorse bushes surrounding the cave, gushing down the rocky sides. If it hadn't been wet, he would have slept outside.

'You can come in now,' she called out to him, her voice bristling with annoyance.

He peeked around the rocky edge. Matilda stood in the centre of the cave, arms folded resolutely across her bosom, his blanket wrapped very firmly around her slight figure. Bare feet poked out from beneath the trailing hem. Clothes were strewn about her, as if she had torn them off in a fury, her boots lying on their sides, flung into the back of the cave.

He picked a spot as far away from her as possible and slung himself down against the ragged rock, raising his eyebrows towards her trembling, statuelike figure positioned like a sentry in the middle of the cave. 'I would try to get some rest now, if you can,' he suggested equably. 'We have a long day tomorrow.'

'Fine!' Glaring at him, Matilda lunged towards the opposite side of the cave. Lying down, she turned her back staunchly towards him, shuffling against the hard, uncomfortable ground.

The fire burned brightly between them, the leaping flames highlighting her small bare toes and slender ankles poking out from beneath the blanket: smooth, perfect skin, like alabaster. *What would it be like to tug that blanket upwards,* he thought, *to run his hand across the tempting curve of her hip, up, up, and hear her sigh with desire at his touch?* The temptation to lie alongside her, to bend his body around her slim back, to...

Stop, now!

Grimacing, he unbuckled his belt, detaching his sword and flinging both down on the rocks beside him. Drawing one knee up, he tilted his head and shoulders back against the stone, closing his eyes and willed himself to think of anything else but the woman lying a few feet away from him.

It was going to be a long night.

Chapter Thirteen

Matilda had no idea what time it was when she awoke, but she had a very clear idea of what had awoken her. A hoarse cry, a man's shout, echoed upwards into the high confines of the cave, drowning out the gentle crackling of the fire like a sear of pain. Confused, she opened her eyes, blinking up into rosy glow that bathed the rocky interior. A sharp lump of stone stuck into her left hip; pins and needles raced along her forearm on which she had rested her head and she flexed her fingers, trying to dispel the uncomfortable feeling.

Sitting up, her eyes flew to Gilan, on the other side of the cave. Was it he who had called out? Awoken her? He had fallen asleep sitting upright, his head and shoulders tilted back to rest against the rock, one arm crooked, resting on an upraised knee. The jewelled hilt of his sword lay gleaming on the ground next to him, topped with the blue bundle of his tunic. Beneath the thin stuff of his white shirt, the extraordinary breadth of his shoulders was revealed, the bunched muscles on his chest. The lacings at the neck had come adrift, splaying the linen; the column of his neck was banded by two thick cords of muscle, deepening the hollow of his throat. His chiselled features seemed softer in sleep, the tough curve of his upper lip slanting up at the corners like a smile. *Those lips were on mine,* she thought, the breath surging from her lungs, her innards gripped by molten quicksilver at the memory. She lowered her eyes, ashamed by her furtive perusal.

And then he howled.

Aghast at the horrible sound, Matilda jerked her chin up; Gilan's head thrashed from side to side on the rock, his hands flying out, fingers outstretched as if he were trying to grab hold of something. In the light of the fire his hair shone like gold filaments. 'No! No!' he shouted. 'Pierre!'

Matilda leapt across the cave, spurred on by his hollow cry, the pure sound of desperation, of loss that seized him with an invisible grip. The blanket fell away, a gathering jumble of folds lapping against the ground. Reaching down, she grabbed instinctively at his floundering hands, snaring his wrists. 'Gilan, wake up! You're dreaming!'

To her horror, still in sleep, he wrenched free of her loose grip, rearing up to manacle her shoulders and twist her down beneath him. She landed on her back with a hefty thud, momentarily stunned. 'Stop!' she yelled at him, as his hands pressed her wrists back either side of her head, his chest heavy against her breasts, the solid muscle of his legs tangled with the bare flesh of her shins. 'Wake up, Gilan!' she gasped up into the handsome face mere inches from her own. 'Please, wake up now!'

Shuddering back to consciousness, he opened his eyes, torso heaving with rapid breaths. Matilda lay beneath him, her body squashed by his superior weight, eyes enormous, fearful, shining with tears.

'What have I done? What in Christ's name has happened?' he managed to gasp out, his mind clearing, chasing back the threads of nightmare. Dear God, had he raped her?

'Nothing, you have done nothing.' The look of sheer horror in his eyes made her hasten to reassure him. 'You were dreaming, Gilan, shouting out.' He was so close to her that the fringes of his hair tickled her forehead. Through the flimsy layers of cloth that separated their naked flesh, his heat pounded against her. The honed, ridged muscle of his torso fitted snugly against the concave scoop of her belly. Warmth flooded her body. She had never, ever, been like this with a man—who could have known that this was what it felt like? Darts of exquisite delight quivered in her stomach, excitement building.

She swallowed quickly, her mouth dry. Inch upon delicious inch of unyielding muscle pressed into the length of her body, making her aware of every part of him, the hardness of him. Her face flamed, a flush extending down her throat. A wildness prickled through her, a surging sweeping sensation. Mother of Mary! What was happening to her? She should tell him to move.

No words came.

Strange feelings plucked and squeezed in the deep pit of her belly, newborn, flaring, gripping at her innards, then building, building with sweet fire, a dangerous, heady sensation. As if by their own volition, her hands left the loose hold of his fingers, rose to his shoulders, cupping the solid muscle. Beneath the gauzy shirt, his skin burned.

She sighed, her breath fractured with desire.

The ragged sound echoed against his ear, the seductive flutter of her breath stirring his hair. His mind hazed with need, lust seizing him, striking through his limbs like hot, molten metal, like liquid fire.

Her eyes darkened, the colour of vast oceans,

endless seas. He lowered his head, a fraction of movement, lips grazing her mouth, feather-light. A tumult of awareness burst through her, a sound tearing deep from her lungs, uneven, demanding, wanting more.

He groaned, his body grinding down against her taut stomach, burying into the pillowed cradle of her hips. His mouth tore at hers, frenzied, devouring, driving sensation after sensation through her, lightning strikes of pure ecstasy. The reason why he was here, why she was here—all turned to dust, sifting like fine sand through his fingers, blowing away on an unseen wind, to nothing. Nothing mattered but the woman beneath him, her hot silky skin, the plushness of her mouth. The frantic beat of her heart against his own.

Her arms ran haphazardly along his shoulders and up the thick cord of his neck, fingers clutching wildly into his hair, its rough silk. Her senses ricocheted, clamoured for more, more, as if she were crazy or delirious, or both. She would not stop him now; she could not. It was too late; her body had taken hold of her practical brain, her self-restraint, casting it aside like a heap of old clothes on the side of a forgotten path. Her feet skipped, danced on the edge of an abyss, flirting with danger; with a jolt of shock, she realised she wanted to jump in, feet first.

He should lift his head and roll off her, now. It was the last thing he wanted to do. The suppleness of her body beneath him had driven the final remnants of his nightmare back, back into the depths of his brain. Lord, she was so soft. Beneath the circle of his fingers, her pulse jumped erratically in her wrist; her breath raced against his cheek. She was not immune to him, her body was responding to his, whether she liked it or not. His mouth roamed over hers, tongue flicking against the closed press of her lips. Her mouth opened beneath his like a flower to the sun and he dived in, tasting the inner sweetness. Like a man possessed, he drank deep of the elixir of her beauty, ravenous, a man deprived of a woman's touch, devoid of human emotion.

Devoid of human emotion. The thought shuddered through him, an icy blade slicing through the fountain of heady desire that consumed him. He had forgotten who he was; the sensual press of her body, her mouth, had made him forget. This wasn't how it was supposed to be. Matilda was worth more than this, far more than a rough, urgent coupling in some damp, remote cave. And she was worth far more than him, too. He was a black-hearted oaf, a loutish soldier, no better than Matilda's brother-in-law. He was no good for her.

Tearing his mouth away, breathing heavily, he wound thick legs around her naked calves, then twisted, his arms clasped about her waist, until he lay on his back and Matilda's supple weight draped across him, her thighs pinned to his thighs, her belly slipping across the flat muscle-bound expanse of his. She lifted her head, expression stunned at the abrupt change in position, eyes huge, liquid with unspent desire, shimmering layers of sapphire, questioning him.

He released his breath: one long tattered gasp, the hint of a groan. 'Matilda, forgive me. We have to stop. This should never have happened.'

No! No! she wanted to scream at him, sprawled inelegantly across his taut, honed chest. She gripped his shoulders, seeking support, seeking to brake the headlong rush of blood through her heart.

'You should have stopped me,' he said quietly. His breathing evened.

How could she have done that when she hadn't even the resources to stop herself? She stared down at him in disbelief: bereft, rejected. She wanted to pummel his chest, hit out with small fists at his sturdy frame and demand that he finish what he had started. But that would be the way of a harlot, of a woman with no morals, no self-control. She had never been like that. At least, she had never been like that until now. Until him.

Shame slapped her in the face, flooding her skin. She reared away from him, sliding sideways from his lap, propelling herself up to stand on shaking legs that barely promised to support her, vulnerable, humiliated. 'I'm sorry. You were having a nightmare. I didn't know how to wake you.' Her voice was clipped, wooden. Uncertain, her hands fluttered up to her face, tucking non-existent hair behind her ears, then crossed awkwardly across her chest, pressing the flimsy stuff of her chemise against her torso. Her belly lurched under his perusal, at the memory of how he had made her feel; her lips stung from the vibrancy of his kiss.

He sat up abruptly, stuffed one hand through his hair, sending the blond strands awry. How like her to be the one to say sorry. 'No, Matilda, it's me who should be apologising.' He threw her a rueful smile. 'In my…dream, I thought someone was attacking me at first, but then…well, I could claim I didn't know what I was doing…' he spread his palms aloft as if in apology '…but that would be a lie.' His eyes blazed into her, liquid pewter. 'I knew exactly what I was doing.'

Then why did you stop? she wanted to scream at

him, chewing unconsciously at her bottom lip. His words trailed over her like a heated brand. Her face flamed and she stumbled back, bare heels scuffing the spent ash around the fire, embarrassed by his speech. Already she missed his touch, his hands roaming possessively across her limbs. There could only be one reason why he had stopped: he had found her lacking. She trawled her mind for the various criticisms that her siblings had levelled at her over the years: short, thin, her breasts too small. What man could possibly be attracted to her, let alone one with eyes that sparkled like diamonds?

'I suppose it's better you found out now,' she managed to croak out, turning briskly away from him. She lifted the fallen blanket, shook out the creased folds with unnecessary violence.

'Found out what?' he asked, his gaze sliding across the shadowy curve of her hips beneath the flimsy chemise.

She eyed him with a hostile glare, one shoulder raised towards him, a defensive gesture. One of her braids had come adrift, looping down over her shoulder and across her breast. His eye followed the burnished rope, stopping at the curling end on her waist, secured with a leather lace. Matilda cleared her throat. 'Found out what a disappointment I would be, when it comes to...' She hesitated, struggling to find the words.

He frowned and sat forwards, resting his forearms lightly across his knees, mouth turned up in a half smile. 'What are you trying to say, Matilda?'

Her tongue felt like a clod of earth, stiff and awkward in her mouth. Why had she even started to embark on such an intimate subject with him?

'It doesn't matter,' she said. A hectic flush lined the top of her cheeks, crawled down her slim neck. The fact that he had witnessed her shameless behaviour was mortifying, especially now that he had pushed her away. Her heart closed up with humiliation.

'I think it does,' he replied.

An involuntary shudder tore at her chest; she bit down hard on her lip to stop the flood of tears from welling up. She jerked her chin up, faced him squarely. 'You stopped because I am...because I would be a disappointment,' she blurted out in a rush, clapping her hands over her face.

Never.

Astounded by her words, he sat dumbfounded for a moment. How could one woman be so completely mistaken? Surely she had been aware of his reaction to her? She made his body sing, pushed the grim threads of his nightmare back to the dim recesses of his mind; it had taken every ounce of his strength to break the kiss, to stop things going any further. And it was for her, all for her. By stopping, he was protecting her, protecting her from who he really was, a murderer, someone who had failed to protect his own brother, who had contributed to his death. This way he could safeguard her innocence for another man, a husband who would be worthy of her.

Sparkling in the glow of the fire, a tear slipped out between her fingers, running over her knuckles, across the back of her hand to her fragile wrist. Guilt scythed through him. He should go over to her now, peel those fingers away from her face and comfort her, but how could he trust himself after what had happened only moments ago? Even in this dim light, the delectable curve of her breasts was visible beneath the single layer of fabric that covered her nakedness, the slim indent of her waist. Desire snared him anew and he tore his eyes away, focused on the fire, the pile of wood, even his sword lying beside him, anything but her. From now on, he would have to maintain a distance, for both their sakes.

As she peeked through her fingers at him, Matilda's heart compressed, squeezed—a pinched, frozen knot. Gilan's expression was rigid, blank, his eyes averted, staring down at the hilt of his sword. He couldn't even look at her! If she had wanted any confirmation of his rejection, then there it was, pinned to the carved features of his face. Turning away from him, she sank to the floor, a raft of misery engulfing her, and wrapped his blanket around her body, her movements stiff and angry. How dare he! How dare he make her feel like this, like a reckless whore!

He gazed at the inflexible line of her back faced towards him like a barricade, her rounded hip jutting upwards as she balled her body up on the ground, and sighed. Why couldn't he keep his hands away from her? Her beauty drew his touch, his kiss, time and time again, like a moth to a flame. It was better this way. Better for her to think he didn't care. She might be hurting now, but in the long term, it would be easier if she hated him. He could not, would not touch her again. For that would give her hope and hope was something he could not give. Not now. Not ever.

It was early when she woke again, head groggy as she sat up and slowly stretched her aching limbs. The rocky ground had pressed sharply into her left hip overnight, making it sore. Gilan was not there. Grabbing her clothes, thankfully now dry, Matilda dressed quickly, her movements brisk, rapid. Her hair had come adrift in the night, pins dislodging with her fretful sleep. They now lay scattered around, bright silver sparkles across the floor of the cave. She scrambled to pick them up, anxious to sort her hair out before Gilan returned.

As she crawled around on her hands and knees, picking up the hairpins, the stony ground grinding into her shins, a huge sense of doubt flooded over her. How could she continue this journey with Gilan after what had happened last night? Even now, the memory of his hands running confidently across her spine and down over her hips brought a flush to her cheeks, a heady rush to her heart. What a fool she was for begging him to take her along with him; how utterly pathetic and desperate she must have looked in his eyes. But what other option did she have? To go back to Lilleshall would be to accept whatever fate John had lined up for her, so continuing on this journey, however uncomfortable the relationship between her and Gilan, was her only option.

Sitting back on her heels, she plaited her hair roughly, dredging deep for any ounce of determination, of courage. It was as if he had grasped every last piece of her self-confidence and wrung it out of her like a wet cloth. She sighed, the influx

of breath shuddering her chest. How had it come
to this? That she, level-headed, practical Matilda,
could feel such overwhelming desire? She had truly
believed she could go through life without the need
for a man's touch, yet the slightest brush of Gilan's
fingers twisted her belly to such a frenzied knot
of excitement that she wanted to yell out with delight. Her emotions teetered between wanting to
cry and wanting to laugh—for the very man who
drove her flesh to such delicious heights was the
same man who cast her aside, leaving her wanting more. Much more. Her heart closed up with
sadness.

She secured the end of her plaits with leather
laces. A shadow fell across the mouth of the cave,
blocking the meagre sunlight. Gilan.

'Here,' he said, handing a bread roll across to
Matilda. 'You'd better eat something before we
start riding again. I suspect Henry has lodged in
the next town, so we'll start soon and catch him up.'
Between them, the fire smoked fitfully, ashy embers piled around the one branch that still burned.

My God, he acted as if nothing had happened
between them! Matilda stared at the bread roll, not
trusting the steadiness of her hand if she reached
out to take it. 'I'm fine...thank you,' she croaked,
keeping her eyes fixed firmly on the ground. She

had no wish to see the pity within his gaze as he looked down at her. Instead she fiddled with the braids pooling in her lap.

Gilan eyed her bowed head, her studied avoidance. 'Look,' he said eventually, withdrawing the bread. 'Last night was a mistake. My mistake. I behaved like a lout and took advantage of you. But please don't let your opinion of me cloud your good judgement. You need to eat if you're going to keep up with me all day.'

'I'll keep up with you anyway!' she flashed back at him, folding her arms huffily. Why did he have to refer to last night? Embarrassment rafted through her; she wanted to crawl beneath the nearest stone, to hide. But the emptiness in her stomach began to nibble away at her spine; her mouth watered at the smell of the bread.

'This isn't a game, Matilda.' Gilan hunkered down beside the fire, opposite her. 'Henry and I are going up north to challenge the king. It will not be pretty.' He placed the bread back down on an open cloth beside him. Matilda could see a lump of cheese, a couple of apples. The cheese looked fresh, crumbly.

'I do know that,' she replied, her eyes fixed on the tempting pile of food beside him. 'Maybe I will have something, after all.' She dropped the hairpins into a spiky pile beside her and held out her hand.

'And try to be a little more grateful.' His sudden grin startled her as he handed her a bread roll and a slice of cheese. 'Don't forget that I'm doing you a massive favour by taking you with me. I will leave you in the next town if you don't behave.'

She shrugged her shoulders, the lace of her chemise scratching the delicate skin of her throat. 'I'll do what you tell me. Within reason.' Eyes of periwinkle-blue flicked over him, defiant.

He stood up, raised his eyebrows in exaggerated surprise. 'That remains to be seen, Matilda.' Shifting his saddlebags across his shoulders, he stamped the fire out with one large booted foot. Sparks flew out from the base of his leather sole. 'I'll meet you outside.'

Matilda wound her plaits into a tight little knot at the back of her head, securing the hair with as many hairpins as she could find. The cool metal tips slid against her scalp as she drove them in. With each hairpin fixed into place, her mind began to settle, to shift down from the emotional turmoil of the previous night, to be replaced by a renewed sense of confidence, of fortitude. The worst was over. They had spoken. Once her hair was finished to her satisfaction, she pulled the voluminous hood over her head, adjusting the scalloped hem so that it lay flat on her shoulders. There, that should do.

Gilan was lifting a leather saddle onto his horse, shoulder muscles bunching tightly with the movement. Her own horse was nearer the cave, plucking at the wispy grass. Spying her saddle propped up against the rock face, Matilda strode over and picked it up, manhandling the heavy leather up against her chest to balance herself. She turned, intending to hoist it on to the mare's back.

Adjusting the leather straps beneath his destrier's belly, Gilan straightened up and glanced back to the cave mouth to see if Matilda had emerged. His mouth almost dropped open. There she was, dressed in her rough boy's garments, carrying the weighty saddle between her slim arms. The breadth of the saddle, glossy chestnut leather, all but obscured her upper body, the stirrups dangling down and knocking heavily against her knees.

'Here, let me.' He marched over, his hands already outstretched to take the saddle from her.

She frowned at him, the curving arch of her brows drawing together. 'I'm almost there, Gilan. Don't worry.'

He stopped short, watching her puff slightly with

the effort of carrying the unwieldy load. 'That saddle is far too heavy for you.'

She eyed him squarely, eyes blazing blue fire, her mouth set in a terse, faintly amused line. 'I can do it, Gilan. I'm used to doing it, anyhow. And besides, how would it look in front of Henry, if the young squire you've found to guide you all can't even saddle his own horse?'

His hands fell to his sides. She had a point. But he hated to see her struggling under such a cumbersome weight; his fingers itched to help, to move in and relieve her of the load. He watched her shove the saddle up onto the back of the mare and flip the stirrups down, expertly fixing the straps beneath the horse's stomach.

'See? I told you I could do it.' Pivoting on her heels when she had finished, hands on her hips, she faced him triumphantly. 'Not bad for a girl.'

'Not bad at all,' he agreed grudgingly, amazed at her skill. 'You're stronger than you look.'

She flushed under his close perusal. But the chill breeze rising from the plateau below brushed her skin, quickly cooling the flags of colour in her cheeks. 'I've had to learn to fend for myself,' she said, annoyed by the waver of hesitation in her voice. 'Since my father died, and my brother left to fight with the King, everyone on the estate had to do their bit. Including me.'

'Surely you could have kept a stable lad on?' Gilan asked.

'What, have a lad kicking around all day on the off chance that I might need someone to saddle my horse, when he could have been putting a full day's work in on the fields?' She frowned at him, openly mocking. 'Where have you been, Gilan? I couldn't afford such luxury.' Sticking her toe into the stirrup, she swung herself up into the saddle, her movements precise, elegant, leaning down to pat the mare's neck.

Where had he been? Away, away from this land on Henry's endless, futile crusades. He had spent hardly any time at his estates in Cormeilles in the past year. But he had another home, too, where his parents lived. A home to which, at the moment, he was reluctant to go back. For to go back meant he would have to tell his parents everything, to his parents and Pierre's wife, Isabelle. He would have to relive the details of that horrible day.

Caught up in his own personal nightmare with no thought to how others lived their lives, Matilda made him feel cloth-headed, doltish, too self-interested to care for others. How difficult it must have been for her to pick up the reins of the estate and make the land return an income. With no male guidance, she had acknowledged the difficult situation and battled through, aided only by her own wit and intelligence. The amount of strength and courage bundled up in that svelte lean body was worth ten thousand of him, with his superior physical strength. No wonder she was so stubborn, so headstrong.

She'd had to be.

Chapter Fourteen

For most of that bright morning, Gilan and Matilda made steady progress north, galloping fast over the flat plain of land. A grid of straight ditches drained the earth, shining ribbons beneath the blaze of sun; the generous drove ways that bordered these channels made for easy riding. Soon the church spire and towering walls of a small town came into view on the horizon, shimmering in the noon heat like a mirage, floating on air.

Gilan pulled on the reins, gradually slowing, flexing his thigh muscles against the animal's flanks to turn the destrier round into a loose circle in front of Matilda, a healthy glow reddening the tops of his high cheekbones. Golden strands of hair feathered down over his tanned forehead.

'What is that place?' he called out to Matilda as she galloped up to him, her lungs bursting with exertion. She believed herself to be a competent, quick horsewoman, but Gilan was far superior and much, much faster. He scarcely looked around to see if she was with him, making it clear that if she failed to keep up, she would be left behind.

Hauling on the reins, she scrunched up her eyes. 'I think...yes, it's Brinsea,' she said.

'Been there before?' he asked mildly. He bunched his hands on the horse's neck, leaning forwards in the saddle to ease his muscles, awaiting her answer.

Her heart fluttered; she forced herself to concentrate on his tunic lacings rather than the handsome lines of his face. Remember, remember, the words chanted through her head, he doesn't want you here, all you are is an encumbrance to him. She cleared her throat. 'Yes, a few times. It's a good-sized town, with a couple of inns. It's on the main route north,' she added.

'Then that's where Henry will be,' he said, his eyes on the road in front. 'Let's keep going so we can catch him before he leaves the town.'

A wave of fatigue shuddered through her. Suddenly the short distance between her and the town, not above a mile, seemed interminable. Exhaustion sapped the energy from her arms and legs.

'You go,' she suggested. 'I'll catch you up. It's not a big town. I'll find you.'

Gilan threw her a teasing smile. 'What's the matter? Can't you keep up with me?'

'No, I can't!' She jerked her chin up, eyes flashing sapphire. 'I thought I was quite good at riding...' She trailed off.

He assessed her wryly. He had ridden too fast, too hard for her, treating her like one of his soldiers, when she most obviously was not. 'I'm sorry, Matilda, you should have called out to me, called out for me to slow down...' he watched as she drew her spine up straight, saw the shine of determination in her eyes '...so why didn't you?'

Matilda shook her head. The movement dislodged the voluminous brim of her hood, causing it to slip back. 'If I slowed up, you would have left me behind.'

'No, I said I would help you,' he replied firmly. 'I'm not about to abandon you in the middle of nowhere. You need to learn to accept help, to rely on others.'

'Why?' she questioned. 'When everyone I ask will only help if there is something to be gained for themselves, except—' She stopped suddenly, her words vanishing into the balmy air.

Except you. Gilan had asked for nothing in return for his aid.

'Except?' he prompted.

'Except nothing,' she replied. 'I'm not sure what I'm trying to say.'

'Not everyone in this world is as bad as you make out, Matilda. You have to learn to trust people.'

'I'm trusting you, aren't I?' She pushed the words back at him. 'You might have arranged for my brother-in-law, John, to meet us in Brinsea, to haul me back home. I'm trusting you not to do that. Isn't that enough?'

Gilan's heart knocked against his chest at her quiet response. *Yes,* he thought. *It's enough that you trust me, even though I am not worthy of such trust.* Without thinking, he lifted his hand and pulled her hood forwards so the cloth shadowed her fine features. Her hair, the colour of rain-soaked bark, was silk against his fingers. 'You need to keep your face covered, Matilda, otherwise the game will be up.' His eyes flared over her, metallic silver.

Beneath his wrinkled tunic sleeve, she could see the corded muscles in his wrist as he drew his hand away, the riffle of short blond hairs along his forearm. Wrenching her gaze away, she moved her horse alongside his, falling into a slow pace along the drove way.

'Your voice, too.'

'My voice?'

He grinned down at her. 'It's far too shrill at the moment. You'll have to lower it.'

'I will. But there's no point lowering it with you, is there? You know who I am.'

Yes, I do, he thought, thinking of that delicious body pressed against him, the yielding cushion of her limbs tangled with the hard muscle of his legs. Even now, dressed as she was in the disguise of her boy's clothes, her slim legs encased in fitted leggings, his body responded as if she were naked. He focused grimly at the horizon—why, in Heaven's name, why could he not find the power to resist her?

He cleared his throat. 'Try it. Try speaking like a boy.'

'Like this, you mean?' she croaked gruffly, lowering her voice as much as possible.

'You sound like a strangled cat.' He laughed, a smile pinned briefly to his face, laughter lines crinkling out from the corners of his eyes. 'But I suppose it will have to do. Let me do most of the talking. Act dumb. And for God's sake, keep your head covered.'

A sense of relief surged through her at his easy camaraderie, a lightness easing her chest. This would be all right, she told herself. It had to be, because Gilan was her only hope of bringing her brother back home. His outright rejection of her last night had made her even more determined to build her self-restraint; he must never know how the closeness of his body made her blood race, her heart pound. If only, she thought, if only he hadn't shouted out like that; then she would never have gone to him, never would have found herself in such a mortifying situation. But no one with any heart could have resisted such a cry of wretchedness and pain.

She glanced across at the tall figure riding alongside her, his stern profile softened by the sun shining through the gold filaments of his hair. She watched as he kneaded one hand into the top of his thigh, the fawn fabric of his leggings puckering beneath his fingers.

'Why do you do that?' she asked suddenly, breaking the silence between them.

'Do what?' He glanced over at her.

'Rub your leg like that—are you hurt?'

He snatched his hand away. 'No, it's an old wound. It aches sometimes.'

'Where did you get it?'

'Oh, I can't remember,' he replied lightly. 'One of the many battles I've been in.' His hands had clutched towards his lifeless brother as the hot, flaming gobs of tar had rained down around him, one splashing on to his leg, burning through his trousers. He hadn't felt the pain of it until much, much later.

As their horses trotted together over the short, bleached grass, Matilda scrutinised the lean lines of his face, trying to penetrate the reflective surface of his eyes, wanting to read his mind. 'Battles with Henry?' she questioned.

His shoulders slumped forwards, fractionally. 'Yes, always with Henry. We've been friends for years.' He lowered his eyebrows at her, eyes twinkling. 'Why do you ask?'

'Last night...' She hesitated, then, emboldened by his relaxed manner, she plunged forwards with her question. 'Last night, when you were dreaming...you shouted out.'

He frowned. 'I don't remember.'

'You shouted out a name.'

'What name?'

'Pierre.'

The air between them hesitated, paused. Even the swallows that dipped and swung against the blue, shimmering sky seemed slowed, somehow.

His chin reared upwards, diamond eyes pinning her like a rapier.

She swallowed, her throat suddenly devoid of liquid, shaking her head briskly. 'Sorry, I should never have said.' Ducking her gaze, she shuffled her hips uncomfortably in the saddle.

The pewter in his eyes turned to black, a gouged-out, cavernous look. 'Pierre is…was my brother.' Regret smudged the shadowed patches beneath his eyes.

'Last night…' She paused. '…you said…you said he was gone. What happened to him?'

Tension strained his neck muscles as he looked down into her sweet face, the perfect arch of her eyebrows, dark wings above periwinkle-blue eyes. Could he tell her everything? In all those cold, aching months after his death, he had never spoken about Pierre to anyone. But, like yestereve, he noticed how the flare of grief tamped down when he spoke to her about him. 'Pierre was my brother, Matilda, and he died on our last campaign, because of me.' His sombre eyes flicked over her horrified face, before he squeezed his knees against his horse's flanks and rode off towards Brinsea.

The town was small: one church, its spire looming up into the bowl of clear blue sky; ramshackle cottages clustered around a market place, huddled; roofs butted up close to each other, teetering and sagging at different levels. Raucous music rose from the centre, a grinding hurdy-gurdy clashing with the high-pitched screech of a violin. The sound of drunken singing, even at this time of the morning.

The impressive three-arched bridge that led into the town over a shallow river was crammed with people, carts, animals, all pushing their way into town, calling, gesticulating to each other. As if by unspoken agreement, Gilan and Matilda reined their horses in, allowing the animals to drink from the river, waiting for the bulk of the crowd to squeeze their way across the bridge.

'Looks like it's market day,' said Matilda, her voice a bright falsetto. 'The town will be busy.' Peeking over at Gilan's uncompromising stance, she wondered if he would even answer her. He had said nothing since she had asked about his brother. For the hundredth time she wished she had never opened her mouth.

'Gilan?' she ventured. She took a deep breath, searching his implacable profile for some sign of leniency. He stared straight ahead, brows drawn together at the crowds of people gathering to funnel over the bridge into the town centre. This was ridiculous! He would have to speak to her at some point. Irritation flashed through her; she leaned over and grabbed at his rein, shaking it so the bit between the horse's teeth jingled sharply. He turned his head swiftly, his eyes filled with sadness.

'Gilan! Look, I'm sorry about…about your brother. But how was I to know it was something you didn't want to talk about? You were having a really horrible nightmare—was it so unreasonable of me to ask what caused it?'

She held his gaze, refusing to quaver beneath his glittering appraisal. Her words were outspoken, bold, but she didn't care. She had nothing to lose by speaking to him like this; he would be angry, but then he had been angry with her before and she had survived. She watched in surprise as his mouth softened, tilted up into a slight smile.

'You think I'm angry with you for asking, but I'm not, truly.' He crossed his arms across the pommel of the saddle, eased forwards slightly. The thick leather saddle squeaked beneath his weight. 'When you asked about Pierre it was a shock. I didn't re-alise I had shouted out his name last night.' His voice lowered and he hesitated.

'It doesn't matter,' she replied, relief coursing through her. 'I should never have asked. I wanted to establish that you're still speaking to me, that's all.' She released his bridle and straightened up in the saddle, biting her lip with consternation.

His heart cleaved towards her; she thought she

had done the wrong thing by him, gone too far. He could read the worry, the flicker of concern in her face. Little did she know that if there was anyone in the world he could talk to about his brother, it was her. The realisation hit him in the gut like a crossbow bolt. Matilda wouldn't judge, wouldn't condemn; she simply didn't possess such character traits. She would understand. Breath pulled from his lungs, fledging, unsteady.

'Pierre was…' He paused, wondering how to even put into words what had happened out in the Baltic.

'Truly, Gilan, you don't have to tell me.' She hitched forwards in the saddle, touched his forearm with a gesture of reassurance.

He covered her hand with his own. He wanted to tell her. 'Pierre died only about a month ago, on our last campaign to the Baltic. He fell off a scaling ladder trying to break a siege.' He pushed one hand through his hair, separating the thick blond strands. 'I should have been on that ladder, not him.' Remorse thickened his voice, the pitch becoming guttural, low.

'But why?' she asked, tentatively. The desolation in his expression scraped her heart, nipped at her.

'Because Pierre was ill that morning,' he replied tonelessly, 'but I didn't realise, and he…he didn't tell me. Too proud, I suppose, like he always was. And I was too stupid not to see it! I teased him, for Heaven's sake! It was my goading him that forced him up that ladder.' He turned towards her, eyes red-rimmed, bleak. 'If only I could turn back time, Matilda. If only it had been me who had gone up.'

His mouth twisted as he caught the spangle of tears in her eyes. 'No!' he barked at her, grabbing her wrist with strong fingers. 'Don't waste your tears on me! I don't deserve them. His death is my fault.'

'No, it isn't.' Matilda shook her head vehemently, aghast at the bitterness of his tone. 'Surely he was an experienced soldier. Why did he not tell you he was ill, that someone else must go up?'

'Because he was too proud to admit that he was feeling ill. To him, it would be a sign of weakness.' Gilan's shoulders slumped. 'He was always too proud.'

'Then you would have been unable to stop him, even if you had tried,' Matilda said, softly.

Her eyes, periwinkle orbs, were fringed with lush, black lashes. He wished with all his heart that he could believe her, allow her words to act upon him like a balm, absolve his sin. But he knew it was useless. Self-reproach hovered above him, like a great black raven, vicious beak ready to peck at any moment, to jab at him and remind him of what he had done.

'Did you hear me, Gilan?' Suddenly she realised how imperative it was that he believed her. He was not at fault, yet she could see from his expression that the guilt was eating him up inside. 'It is not your fault.'

He smiled grimly. 'No matter how many times you say it, Matilda, it won't scrub away the truth of what happened. Believe me. It won't. It's something I have to live with, for the rest of my life.

Dismounting, leading their horses, they joined the cluster of people crossing the bridge over the slow-flowing river, stinking with effluent, and almost immediately found themselves in the marketplace, lined with colourful stalls. Bolts of cloth—silk, cotton, linen—were stacked up in teetering heaps, groups of women fingering the fabric, testing the fineness before raising their voices to barter with the traders. Rounds of floury bread balanced on a wooden table next to a stall selling kegs of ale. Hawkers pushed through the crowds, carrying aloft huge trays of hot, steaming pies, keeping up a steady chant of sales patter as they walked. It seemed like the world and his wife had descended on Brinsea on that day.

Despite the hubbub around her, all Matilda could

think of was what Gilan had told her. How his brother had died; the relentless, scouring remorse that he carried within him. She wanted to reach out and wind him in her arms, comfort him, but knew such an act was impossible. She watched his big body move with agile grace across the dry, dusty cobbles, looping the bridle with practised efficiency around the post-and-rail fence, and her heart creased with sadness at the thought of the hurt that he carried within.

'Matilda? Are you coming?' He reached out his hand for her bridle.

Shaking herself out of her reverie, she shook her head at him, a warning look in her eyes. 'Gilan, remember! I must do it myself!'

He grinned, his hand dropping away, and patted the side of her mare's head. As she secured her bridle, he flipped a coin to a small boy to keep an eye on their horses, asking directions to the two inns.

'One to the south and one to the north,' he said once he had his answer. 'I'll wager Henry is at the more costly one.' He plunged into the crowd, the heft of his body surging through the tightly packed crowd with ease. Being smaller, Matilda found it difficult to follow him. Realising she was falling back, he reached his arm behind, seizing her fingers. 'Hold on to me,' he growled at her, 'otherwise I'll lose you.'

His fingers were strong, cool around her own as he all but dragged her through the press of people. She followed the heft of his shoulders, muscle-bound beneath the blue tunic, the flare of his golden hair above the crowds, her fingers laced tightly with his. Soon, they were out of the marketplace, plunging down an alleyway and faced with the carved wooden angel hanging across the street that signified the more expensive inn.

Diving into the cobbled courtyard, Gilan stopped, looking up at the two-storey building on either side of him, the stables in front, then banged on the oak door. A short man answered, a stained linen apron covering the girth of his stomach, the dirty hem almost touching the ground. Remembering their linked hands, Matilda swiftly tugged her fingers from Gilan's grip before the innkeeper spotted them, her cheeks flaring with colour.

'Can I help you?' he asked, his tone guttural. The stink of stale ale wafted past him into the yard. Matilda wrinkled her nose up at the acrid smell.

'Is Henry, Duke of Lancaster, here?' asked Gilan. 'He and his men?'

'Who wants to know?'

'I am Gilan, Comte de Cormeilles. I am one of

Henry's commanders. We became separated on our journey north.'

The innkeeper's face broke into a smile, stepping back into the murky depths of the inn. 'Then you are welcome, sire. Your lord is indeed here, breaking his fast.'

At the river's edge, frothy wavelets breaking against the sandy shore, Matilda contemplated the sparkling stretch of water in misery. The frilly oak trees on the opposite bank seemed a great distance away, and, despite the shallowness of the water at the edge, a powerful current churned and whirled in the middle of the river, thick silver ropes of water that would drag a man down in an instant. Farther downstream, mudflats glistened: thick, treacherous mud, a stinking, oozy mixture of soil and sand. Beneath the hot sun, a weird cracking, squeaking sound emerged as the mud slowly dried out, stalked on by long-legged sea birds, picking their way delicately across. Despair flooded through her. Having travelled this way with her father, she had hoped some distinctive landmark would jog her memory, but nothing was familiar.

Despair turned to fear. They were all behind her, horses stationary in the stretch of sand dunes: Henry and his men. Gilan. Waiting for her to point them in the right direction. She chewed anxiously on her bottom lip, watching a flight of geese arrow their way through the brilliant sky, honking loudly. She never believed this bit of the journey would be the most difficult part. When Gilan had led her into the inn, this morning, Henry had barely blinked at her, accepting Gilan's explanation that he had found a guide who would lead them to Wales. Standing in the dim, fuggy confines of the hostelry, the air thick with the smell of stale beer, Matilda had held her breath, waiting for one of the soldiers to denounce her, to rip the hood off her head and expose her femininity. It hadn't happened.

But now, her own memory had failed her, stripping away the one trump card that was the key to finding her brother. If she couldn't remember the way, then they would dismiss her, Gilan insisting that she returned home. Her heart twisted, sadness digging in like a knife blade, surprising her. Was it that, the thought of being away from him, rather than the fact that she couldn't remember the way, that caused such unhappiness to cascade through her body?

'What's the matter?' Dismounting, Gilan had broken away from the group and now stood at her side. His large boots pressed down into the soft, wet sand, creating indents.

She jumped, unnerved by his sudden appearance, the low rumble of his voice. Her heart skipped, jolted at the beauty of his tanned features, the firm line of his mouth tilted up at the corners. 'It's not as easy as it looks,' she answered him vaguely. Her face puckered with worry, fine skin taut across the high, delicate bone of her cheeks.

'We can't cross here, if that's what you were thinking.' Gilan nodded significantly across the deep expanse of water, the swirling force. A white mass of seagulls swirled in the balmy air above the estuary, screeching, indignant, as they wheeled and flapped.

'No!' she snapped at him under her breath. 'I wasn't thinking that at all.'

'Then why have we stopped?' Beneath the fawn-coloured fabric of his trousers, his thighs were lean and strong, the fabric stretching across the bulging muscle.

She sucked in her breath, folding her arms tightly across her chest, as if her limbs' constricting brace could control the reckless knocking of her heart. 'I needed to get my bearings!' Her tone was defensive, shrill.

'Don't screech at me, they'll hear you,' he warned quietly. The breeze from the river whipped at the blond strands of his hair; he pushed them back from his forehead. 'Do you know the way, or not?'

She glanced behind her. The bright surcoats, the shining armour of the soldiers, stood out against the bleached sand of the endless dunes, the stiff dull marram grass that riffled in the wind. The horses' tails fanned behind their shining rumps, feathered, glossy. Henry's horse pawed at the ground, agitated, and she saw one soldier lean across to the other and mutter something under his breath while looking straight at her. Her heart plummeted.

Gilan followed her worried glance. 'We need to keep going,' he said. 'What about if we carry on upriver? Surely there'll be a causeway, or a narrower stretch?'

Her shoulders sagged forwards, confidence draining from her. She longed to lean into the softness of his blue tunic, to cling to his solid chest and draw comfort from this man who had made her heart sing. 'I don't know,' she replied truthfully. 'I'm not sure I can remember the way.' Her wide eyes met his with candour. 'I'm not sure I'm going to be much use to you, after all.'

He traced the downward tilt of her lips, wanting to touch her face, her shoulder, to offer her some small gesture of comfort. But with Henry watching, that was out of the question.

'What, and give up now?' he challenged her instead, voice laced with steel. 'After everything you've risked to get to this point? Riding through the rain and darkness, disguising your true identity with boy's clothes?'

And a night in a cave with you, she thought with a rush. *The biggest thing, the only thing I have risked, is my own heart.*

'You must keep going, Matilda,' he urged, scrutinising her anxious features. 'You have too much to lose if you give up now. We will work out the way together.'

We will work out the way together. She traced the firm outline of his mouth, the full bottom lip so shocking in the lean, carved planes of his face, then raised her eyes to his. 'You mean…even though I'm not sure of the way…you will help me?'

'Close your mouth, Matilda,' he ordered sharply. 'Is my suggestion that much of a surprise? I said I would help you.'

'Yes, but that was when you thought I *knew* the way.'

He laughed, a restrained upward curl to his lips. 'I never believed that you knew the way, Matilda.'

'Then why…?'

Why indeed? The question reverberated in his brain, mocked him. Why did he keep her with him, when it would have been so easy to force her back to her brother-in-law, to employ the cool strength and detachment for which he was so renowned on campaign? Because…he lifted his eyes to the scudding clouds, wispy veils against the blue sky…because, in truth, he had become used to her determined little figure at his side. The inadvertent brush of her knee as they rode, the feel of her small hand in his. The press of her near-naked body against his own. The rigid restraints around his heart shifted a little, eased. He couldn't bear to let her go. Not yet.

Aghast at his own thoughts, he cleared his throat. 'Because you have too much to lose.' He kept his voice deliberately gruff, coarse. 'I am not such a hard-hearted ogre to leave you here, alone, because you have admitted to something that I suspected anyway.'

Relief softened her face. Instinctively, she lifted her hand, intending to touch his shoulder, or his chest, she knew not what, to give him a gesture of her thanks, some recognition of his kindness. Without him, without his help, she would be lost, an unwilling slave to her brother-in-law's outrageous demands. Gilan's protection gave her the freedom to pursue what she felt was the right thing.

As she began to raise her hand, he gave a swift,

almost imperceptible shake of his head. 'Matilda,' he reminded softly, silver eyes drilling into her. 'Do not forget who watches us.'

She whirled her head away, down, studying the hard-packed sand with a frowning gaze, dull colour sifting across her cheeks. Standing close to him, hearing the rough murmur of his voice, every nerve ending in her body bristling alert to his presence, she had forgotten where she was and who she was supposed to be.

Farther north, the river flattened out, became shallower, bisecting into a myriad of interlinking channels. Between the channels, small islands had formed, large patches of flat, dry land. As the banks of the estuary moved closer together, the rolling sand dunes gradually disappeared, along with the briny tang of the sea, replaced by a mixture of deciduous trees along the banks: lacy oaks, beech trees drooping their long trailing branches into the water, and spindly ash. The crossing to the other side was obvious, Matilda noted with relief. A series of rickety wooden bridges spanning the deep channels of water, linked one area of dry land with another, like huge stepping stones.

She led the way, leaning back in the saddle as her mare ambled down from the trees, following a faint track that led to the first bridge. Heat gathered at the back of her neck, beneath her armpits, trickling down the flanks of her torso. The quilted tunic that she wore was more suitable for winter than the thick, oppressive heat of a summer afternoon. It was fashioned from a couple of layers of material with wadding in between. She longed to push the voluminous hood back, longed for the slight breeze to touch her face, to sift through her hair. Dryness scraped her throat and she licked her lips surreptitiously, tasting the salt on her skin. Squeezing her knees into the horse's rounded flank, she encouraged the animal to mount up on the loose horizontal boards of the bridge, to step across, albeit hesitantly.

'I must admit, I had my doubts about you, boy.' As she descended the other side of the bridge, she was dismayed to find Henry pulling alongside her. 'You had us all worried back there—for a moment, I thought you had lost your way.' His flat face assessed her with a terse smile.

The gold embroidery on his surcoat glared in the sunlight, flashing painfully into her eyes. She twitched her gaze away, staring determinedly ahead. 'No, my lord, merely gaining my bearings,' she replied, keeping her voice deep. 'It's some time since I came this way, but I do remember.'

'Good, because I don't want you leading us astray,' Henry said, his bloodshot eyes constricting. 'Into an ambush, for example. There's a fair few people who would rather see me dead than sitting on the throne of England, people who would pay handsomely for the privilege of seeing me strung up. I wouldn't want to think that you'd taken money from anyone like that?' He leaned forwards in his saddle, peering at her closely, trying to read her expression beneath the shadow of her hood. 'Have you?'

Sweat broke out across her brow beneath his close scrutiny. Would Henry recognise her? Remember her as the woman he had shared his dinner with at John's castle? Hopefully he had been too drunk to recall the finer details of the evening. She lifted one hand slowly to bring her hood down more closely around her face. 'No, rest assured, my lord, no one has given me any money.'

The scant width of the next bridge forced Henry to drop back, giving Matilda time to catch her breath. But, a moment later, on a flat stretch of land connecting two of the bridges, Henry was with her again. Her heart sank.

'Then do you know the castle where King Richard is supposed to be?' Henry asked. 'Clancy Castle? I think it's not far?'

Matilda nodded. 'Yes, it's not above two hours ride from here.' She hoped.

'Then we must find a place to stop and rest up for the night,' Henry said. 'Any suggestions?'

'All I know is that there's miles and miles of forest between us and Clancy,' Matilda responded, hoping it was true. Shifting her eye to the horizon, seeing the mass of trees stretching endlessly, she felt reasonably confident that her suggestion was correct.

Henry groaned. 'What, no inn? No manor house? Am I really to sleep out under the stars?' He stalled his horse, waiting for Matilda to negotiate the last bridge, addressing his last question, plaintively, to the lad's scrawny back.

'It's not so bad, Henry, especially in this heat.' Gilan trotted up beside him. 'Why risk the foul interior of a rowdy inn, when you can stretch out beneath the oaks?'

Henry eyed him suspiciously, then switched his gaze back to Matilda, now cantering across the next area of tussocky land towards the final bridge. 'Where did you find our guide, Gilan?'

'Why?'

Henry shrugged his shoulders. 'There's something not quite right about him. He seems so shifty, always pulling that hood down to cover his face.

And his hands! Have you seen them? They look as if they haven't done a day's work in their life. So fine and white!'

'I'll keep an eye on him,' Gilan promised. 'I don't think there's anything to be worried about.' But as he tracked Matilda's slight figure, he realised the clues to her femininity were plain for all to see: the seductive flare of her hips beneath the tight-fitting leggings, visible when her tunic hem flew up at a gallop, and her slim waist beneath the cling of her tunic fabric. It wouldn't be long before Henry figured out what she was, let alone who she was.

'We'll make camp tonight, and keep him with us until we have Richard in our sights,' announced Henry. 'I don't want him running ahead and warning our enemy. There's something about him that I don't trust.'

Chapter Fifteen

Matilda continued to lead the way on the opposite bank, along a muddy trail that followed the river's curve, sometimes dipping down to the water's edge, sometimes rising up into the oak forest and wending its way around the huge trunks. She was confident of her route now: the track was well used, despite there being few travellers on it at this late hour, but her confidence was marred by the fact that Henry was obviously suspicious of her, and watched her closely, attentive to her every move. Even now, he rode immediately behind her, alongside Gilan. Tension pulled at her neck and shoulders and she rolled them forwards, trying to relieve the strain in her muscles. She was so close, so close to finding her brother that she couldn't afford to slip up now. One more night of disguise, one more night and then she would find Thomas. Once she found him, everything would be sorted out.

As the sun dipped slowly in the west, sinking below the branches of the oaks across a translucent sky streaked in a riot of pink and orange, the track opened out into a clearing: a loose semicircle of short grass set back from the river, with a small exposed shoreline of muddy stones extending out from the trees where the horses could drink. The ground was level enough for Henry and his men to sleep comfortably.

'You, boy!' Henry shouted at her, his ruddy face streaked with dust and sweat. He tugged irritably at his surcoat, bunched up beneath his arms. 'Take the horses to the water whilst we set up camp!' Jumping lightly from the saddle, Matilda caught the looping bridles, the leather rough against the softness of her palms as the soldiers thrust them into her hands. Not one man gave her a second glance, merely turning away to release the straps on their saddlebags across the horses' rumps, laughing and joking amongst themselves. Fear raced along her veins as the powerful destriers surrounded her, bundles of pent-up volatility, snorting, pawing the ground, trapping her slight figure within their jostling high-spiritedness. A huge muscled flank barged against her shoulder and she staggered forwards, briefly losing her balance. She straightened, attempting to sort the jumbled reins out with shaking hands.

Then the horses parted and Gilan appeared before her. 'Give me some of those,' he said gruffly. 'There are too many animals here for you to cope with.' His hands covered hers, untangling the bridles from her numb, nerveless fingers.

Her eyelashes fluttered down with relief. She wanted to cry out at his tough presence, the easy way his big shoulders pushed aside the heaving mass of horseflesh. 'But Henry will...'

'Henry doesn't tell me what to do,' he replied shortly. 'And he doesn't question what I do, either.'

Matilda tilted her chin up at him. 'I thought Henry was your lord,' she whispered up at him.

'Nay, he does not command me,' Gilan said. 'He is my friend. I am here of my own free will.' He turned away from her, holding more than half the horses. Matilda followed, the animals' noses nudging eagerly at her spine, keen to reach the water. A slick green algae covered the stones beneath her feet and she slipped, stumbling to keep up with Gilan. At last she stood at his side, securing the very ends of the reins around her wrist so the horses could drop their heads to drink.

'So why are you here at all?' she asked. 'Why fight for a cause that isn't even yours?'

'Because Henry asked for my help,' he explained, staring out across the river, tracking a couple of black-headed moorhens as they bobbed and dipped in the shallows. The lengthening rays of the sun turned the water to a mirror, the quiet surface reflecting every last particle of light, a lustrous ribbon.

'I always knew you had a heart,' Matilda teased lightly, glancing around to make sure the other soldiers, and Henry, were safely high up in the forest, far enough away to not hear their conversation.

His mouth curled upwards at her jest, shadows clouding his face. 'You're wrong, Matilda. I'm not the man you think I am. I'm not kind.' Not after his heart was gouged out on the day his brother died.

'You are,' Matilda contradicted him. 'You've shown me kindness, when no one else would bother to help. With my sister, with this, without you I would...'

His heart squeezed at her simple words. 'Any man with an ounce of chivalry would have done the same.'

She drew her head up, set it squarely on her shoulders. 'No, I don't think so...chivalry means following the rules, but instead you break them and chide convention...'

He threw her a mocking smile. 'Just like you, in

fact,' he finished for her, pushing one hand through his hair, sending the silken strands to one side. 'We're two of a kind, Matilda. Two lost souls. You are fighting for your home and I am fighting for...' He stopped. What had he been about to say? That he was fighting for his sanity, for some semblance of normality in his life again? Love? He stared down at Matilda's vivid face, tilted up towards him, cerulean eyes sparkling out from beneath the shadows of her hood. She seemed to have such faith in him, such belief that he would do the right thing by her.

As his sentence trailed away, she realised how anxious she was to know his answer. Anxious for any further glimmer of insight into his soul, to find the key that would lift the darkness that shifted across the pewter of his eyes, settling his face into cruel, hard lines. The memories surrounding his brother's death plagued him, but he was not responsible—surely he could see that?

'What...?' She cleared her throat to speak, prompted by the terse silence. 'What do you fight for?

Words of explanation deserted him. How to explain the hollowness in his heart, the grief that tore at him day after day? He shook his head. 'It doesn't matter,' he replied, his voice devoid of tone, blank.

It matters to me, she thought, her heart skipping suddenly, the beat increasing with a strange emotion. What went on beneath those hard, chiselled features, what thoughts, what fears? But he wouldn't want to hear such sentiments, or answer her questions. He had made it perfectly clear how he felt about her.

Gilan dragged his eyes from her face, glancing behind him to the low fringe of trees. 'Henry is watching us—' his voice sharpened '—and he's suspicious of you already. Stay with the horses now and I'll send one of the other soldiers to help you.'

For what seemed the hundredth time that night, Matilda jammed her sweating forehead into the crackling pile of leaves, inhaling the rich, earthy scent of the forest floor. A rawness dragged at her closed eyelids; she was tired, exhausted, but sleep continued to evade her. Fervently willing unconsciousness to consume her, she lay on her front, bundled into a smelly horse blanket that one of the soldiers had chucked at her, fists balled beneath her chest.

Everything itched: the rough wool of the tunic tickled the back of her neck, the loose waistband of her trousers rucked up around her hips, digging into her flesh. Heat suffused her body—surely it was hotter tonight than it had been during the day? The thickness of the air pressed down on her hips, her spine, coating her skin with a prickly perspiration. The hood remained firmly tugged over her hair, making her scalp even hotter. Twisting irritably on to her other side, she glared out at the sparkling river, splashing and gurgling across the shallows. She longed to rip the dusty garments from her body and dive into those swirling eddies, feel the delicious lap of water against her fevered skin. With her flesh clean and cool, she would, without a doubt, drop off to sleep.

Set against a velvet-blue backdrop of twinkling stars, the full moon has risen high, bathing the land in a ghostly white sheen, limpid, iridescent. The light was so strong, she was able to pick out the gathered silhouettes of the oak leaves hanging above the water. If only…Matilda licked her lips, swallowing awkwardly, trying to alleviate the parched state of her throat. Maybe if she only went down for a drink, to dip her toes in, to splash her face? That way, if anyone saw her, suspicion would not be aroused. Around her the soldiers slumbered, snoring heavily, having eaten and drunk their fill around the campfire earlier. Throughout the evening, Gilan had deliberately kept his distance from her, conversing late into the evening with Henry on the other side of the fire.

But now, deep in the middle of the night, all was quiet.

Slowly, she wheeled her body away from the tantalising sight of the river, running her gaze over the blanket-rolled lumps of the sleeping soldiers. All appeared to be fast asleep, including the soldier who had been posted on guard that night. He sat, loosely propped up against the gnarled bark of an oak, his head lolling forwards, snoring gently. His mouth sagged open.

Of Gilan, there was no sign. She searched for the hint of golden hair poking out from a blanket, but in the shadows beneath the trees it was difficult to spot him. Mentally, she shrugged her shoulders. What would it matter to him, whether she took a bath, or not? Surely he wouldn't care? As long as she was careful not to be seen, no one would be any the wiser as to her actions.

Rising slowly, she allowed the blanket to drop off her shoulders and fall to the ground. Instead of standing, she crawled on her hands and knees towards the shrubby undergrowth circling the clearing; the dry leaves on the ground crackled beneath the weight of her palms. Breath caught in her lungs, she forced her body to cover the ground quickly and silently until she was shielded by the thicket of brambles and dogrose. Pushing through the snagging branches, still on all fours, she made her way diagonally, down, down towards the metallic wash of water.

A pair of boots appeared before her. Large, salt-stained boots, inches from her nose. Gasping with annoyance, she stopped, sitting back on her heels, and thrust her chin stubbornly into the air, prepared to do battle with whoever it was blocked her way.

Gilan crouched down in front of her, a lopsided smile on his face. 'Going somewhere?' he asked mildly. 'You ought to be more careful, Matilda. I might have been anybody.'

She frowned, thinking he would be angry with her. 'I'm not trying to leave, if that's what you think,' she replied, immediately on the defensive.

'I didn't think that,' he said. 'I know how important it is for you to find your brother.' In the moonlight, his eyes were solid silver.

'I was so hot!' she explained softly. 'This padded tunic, this hood, I feel so constrained by it all! I couldn't sleep and I thought…I thought if I could go down to the water, and dip my toes in, wash my face, I would feel a lot better. I suppose you think it's a ridiculous idea! But no one would see. I was going to make sure I was far enough downriver.'

Balancing lightly on his heels, Gilan laughed. His teeth flashed white in the moonlight, giving him a devilish look. Her heart flipped, skipping a beat, her nostrils inhaling the heady scent of him: rich leather mingling with woodsmoke, and the tangy, clean smell of the river.

'I don't think it's a ridiculous idea. I have done the exact same thing.' His blond hair was saturated, darkened to a tarnished gold, water droplets clinging to the lobes of his ears, flashing like gemstones.

'You went swimming!' The words burst out of her, outraged, jealous.

He chuckled softly at her protest. 'No need to sound so envious.' Lines of water trickled from the ends of his hair across his tunic, glistening thread in the moonlight. 'You were obviously intending to do the same thing.'

'I was,' she gasped, shifting her gaze longingly towards the river, 'but now you're going to stop me.'

He paused, drinking in the beauty of her face, the luscious pink curve of her bottom lip. It would be so easy, so easy to march her back to the camp, to deny her what she so obviously craved. But he couldn't do that. He wanted her to have the wonderful feeling of the cool water against her skin, even if it was only to dip her toes in. 'No, Matilda,

I am not going to stop you.' Shaking his head, he straightened up, holding out his hand. 'But I am going to go with you. I can take you to a safe spot.'

She gaped at him, astounded by his offer. Her heart soared, picking up speed, anticipation rippling. His sinewy fingers hovered in the air between them and she bit her lip, fighting the urge to seize his hand. If she touched him, she knew what would happen. The same familiar lurch in her chest, the slow coil of heat in her loins. The thwarted burn of desire buried deep in a secret place, frustrated, desperate for release. Pretending she hadn't seen his offer of help, she scrambled clumsily to her feet, unaided.

Following his broad back in and out of the trees, she watched the play of muscles across his shoulders as he walked. He must have left his tunic back at the camp, and now wore only his shirt and trousers, thick leather sword belt slung low about his slim hips. The gemstones in the hilt of his sword glinted in the dim light. Breaking out from the shelter of the trees, the moonlight striking his gilded head, he led her on to a small gravelly beach. 'I found this earlier,' he said.

The crystalline surface reflected the round, yellowish globe of the moon. Water slipped and gurgled against the stones along the shoreline, the sound occasionally broken by the isolated screech of an owl, high up in the trees. A breeze had picked up over the water, ruffling the surface like stitches gathering fabric.

'Oh, Lord,' she murmured, 'what a beautiful spot.' Her fingers drifted to her tunic hood and she shoved it back, relishing the balmy air against her cheek.

'Go on, then,' urged Gilan. Her hood gathered in lumpy folds at the nape of her neck, the fabric's coarse weave highlighting the delicate silk of her skin. The urge to reach out and touch her, to run his big thumb along the fine line of her jaw tingled at his fingers.

She hugged her arms about her body, skipping from one foot to the other like an excited child. 'What will you do?'

'I'll sit here, on the bank. Keep watch.' He stuck his thumbs into his sword belt with an ironclad determination. He needed to keep his hands to himself.

'You need to turn your back.' She placed two hands on her hips, glared at him fiercely, then realised the foolishness of her maidenly outrage. It wouldn't matter if he saw her stark naked; he had no interest in her that way. Misery bit at her heart.

He lifted his eyebrows. 'I thought you said you only wanted to dip your toes in.'

No, she wanted to swim! She wanted to rip off these horrible clothes and immerse herself completely! But if she told him that, he would certainly stop her for fear of being seen by Henry.

'I…I might take this tunic off, wash my neck and shoulders,' she hedged, blushing, 'and I can't have you watching if I do that.'

'Fair enough,' he said. 'But make it quick. I'll stand back in the trees over there.' Striding briskly away, back to the place where large branches overhung the beach, he propped his right flank against the large trunk of an oak tree, staring out towards the direction from which they had come.

As soon as his back was turned, Matilda grabbed the hem of her tunic and pulled upwards, yanking the hated fabric from her slight figure. Kicking off the unwieldy boots, she released the belt on her trousers, the fabric pooling around her bare feet. Clad only in her short chemise, she made her way tentatively out into the river, little stones sharp against her bare heels. The water rose against her body as she waded in, until she was up to her waist, her chemise billowing out like a white wave around her hips. She closed her eyes at the sheer pleasure, a whisper of delight springing from her lips at the breeze against her heated face, the tantalising slip of water against her flesh.

Uncaring now, she tore at the pins and leather laces binding her hair, releasing the tight braids. She would keep the pins and laces safe, clutched in one fist. Her hair fanned down around her, silky, the glossy ends floating momentarily upon the surface of the water before she sank, down, down, submerging completely. She rose up again, water streaming from her shoulders, hair like dark ropes plastered across her bosom and stomach, and laughed aloud with pure joy, the sound tinkling out merrily across the water.

Steadfastly keeping his eyes averted, Gilan scowled. Although they were some way from Henry's camp, Matilda ought to be more careful. Sound travelled farther and faster across water, especially at night when the land was quiet. He could hear her splashing about now—what the hell was she doing? Surely it didn't take this long to wash her face and neck?

He would steal a quick glance. She should almost be finished by now and with any luck would have her tunic firmly back in place.

Moonlight glistened across the water, the whole surface milk-white satin. His eye skirted back and forth, from the point where the shallow water lapped the shore to the middle of the river. Heart plummeting, he broke from the tree, running forwards. He couldn't see her! Boots crunching heavily across the sparse gravel, he reached the pile of clothes.

All her clothes—boots, leggings, tunic!

His chin jolted up and she was there, a few yards out, her neat head carving a path through the still water—*Dear God!* he thought. *She's swimming!*

'Matilda!' he hissed across to her, resisting the temptation to wade in fully clothed and pull her out himself. 'Get out! Now!'

She twisted her head round and saw him standing next to her clothes. Fear laced through her. 'What is it?' she called out, tentatively, not wanting her voice to be heard by anyone else but him. Treading water, she searched the beach behind him, thinking someone had discovered them.

'Get out of there!' he growled at her. Little witch! Wash her face and neck indeed! No doubt she'd been planning this all along.

Hearing the urgency in his voice, she panicked. Someone must be coming! Diving forwards, she swam strongly until her knees bumped against the bottom. Staggering upwards, she clambered to her feet, glancing hurriedly past Gilan's tall figure. Was someone coming? Water streamed down from her hair, filling her eyes and nose, making it difficult to see.

Riveted to the spot, Gilan realised he had made a terrible mistake. Defences crumbled, flicked away like smoking ash on a lazy breeze.

Matilda rose out of the water like a siren of the sea, some enchanted water nymph intent on casting her spell. Bundles of thick, luscious hair straggled like seaweed across her shoulders, sticking to the slim indent of her waist, following the tempting curve of her hips. Sagging with water, the neckline of her chemise dipped downwards, revealing the shadowed cleft between her breasts. Her nipples pressed against the gauzy material, dark round aureoles.

Desire smacked into him with the force of a spear, harassing his blood, blistering his innards with a raging fire. Breath stuck in his throat. Frozen to the spot, he was unable to move, unable to think. All thoughts of Henry and his soldiers, all thoughts of their own safety were chased away by the mesmerising sight of Matilda.

As she moved forwards, water cascaded down from her slight figure. Droplets clung to her pearly white skin, like spangles of light, her thin shift clinging to the rounded push of her bosom, the juncture of her thighs, the long slender line of her legs. An unstoppable heat coursed through Gilan's body, flooding his loins, his chest, a starburst of yearning, as his mind scrabbled desperately for stability, for some hint of self-restraint.

'No...go back!' he croaked, willing his mind to take control. But it seemed his body had set against him, lust surging along his veins like a tide, inexorable, flames licking at his heart. Control unravelled, rolling from his grasp like a ball of string.

Intent on reaching her pile of clothes before she was caught wearing only her undergarments, Matilda failed to hear him, wading purposefully through the shallows. A jagged stone pinched cruelly at the soft underside of one of her feet and she lurched forwards unsteadily, about to fall.

Instinctively Gilan reached out, caught her beneath her forearms. Her sleeves bunched up at her elbows, wet and cloying; her skin beneath the rough pads of his fingers was fine, like gossamer cobweb. At her throat, a pulse knocked hurriedly against gleaming skin. A fresh smell drifted from her, mingling with the sweetness of lavender.

'God in Heaven—' the words punched out of him on a snared breath, his restraint in tatters '—why didn't you go back into the water?' His heart bumped erratically against his chest wall.

'But you told me to come out,' she whispered

hurriedly, conscious that his hands still supported her, warm and tight. 'Are we in any danger?'

You are, he thought. *You are in danger from me.* His tanned fingers clasped around her arms, pressing into her smooth, luscious flesh. A faint voice nagged at the back of his brain: *remove your hands, step away now, step back...*

He smashed down on the warning, not wanting to hear it.

Sparkles of water clung to her long eyelashes, glittering like precious jewels; her eyes were huge, the dark irises reflecting the moonlight, the faintest line of a frown caught on her brow as she peered at him, warily.

With one thumb, he smoothed away the soaking tendril of hair that stuck to her cheek, his fingers moving decisively to cup her chin. 'You should never have gone swimming,' he murmured, his voice unsteady. 'I should never have let you go.' His expression was raw, intense.

'Gilan, what is it? Has something happened?' Pleasure shook her limbs at his touch and she fought the urge to turn her head, to press her lips into the warm palm of his hand.

'Not yet,' he growled. 'Run away now, Matilda, if you know what's good for you.'

'But I don't understand,' she murmured softly,

'Neither Henry or his soldiers are here—who would I be running from?'

'From me,' he ground out. The jewelled granite of his eyes glittered down. 'Do you have any idea what you are doing to me? You stand there in your damp shift, inches away…you need to push me away, now.'

A slow shiver built within her belly. 'I don't want to push you away,' she replied, truthfully.

'Matilda, do you know what you are saying?' His words emerged as a long groan.

She nodded shakily. She knew and she welcomed it. A glorious feeling of pleasure suffused her body.

In reply his arms snaked around her, sinewy ropes jamming her slender frame hard against the long, solid length of him. He dipped his head, warm mouth slanting across hers, roaming against her soft lips. Under the questing play of his mouth, her limbs liquefied, melting into the brawny outline of the man before her. Instinct drove her. Arching her arms upwards, she dug her fingers into the vigorous strands of his hair, smoothing one hand down the powerful cords at the back of his neck, wanting to drag him closer, wanting more of him.

Working his hands up the delicate bones of her spine, he braced his palms on either side of her cheeks, deepening the kiss, his tongue flicking along the fragile line of her mouth, seductive, inquisitive. She gasped as the tumult ricocheted into her and clung desperately to him, rocked by the unstoppable sensations. She dropped her hands to clasp his waist, to winch him closer. The frantic bump of her heart thrilled her, scared her. Beneath his searching hands, Gilan urged her towards a place hitherto unknown to her, a landscape of dark, secret desire, of unbridled passion. A land she yearned to discover.

Together, they sank to the stony beach, Gilan ripping at his clothes, casting them aside, uncaring as to whether they landed in the water or not. The river lapped at their bare toes as they fell on the stones, rolling together. His eyes had darkened to black pools of desire, dangerous and wild, as he crushed her to him, hip to hip, belly to belly. Breath seized in her lungs as the lean, naked length of him folded against her, hard muscle pressing into soft curves.

He pushed at the sopping fabric of her chemise, the ties at her bosom coming adrift easily beneath his fingers, until one creamy shoulder was exposed, shining like the inside of an oyster shell beneath the pearly moonlight. Bending his head, his dampened hair tickling her chin, he dropped a line of kisses along her collarbone, then lower.

Her insides squeezed with delight; she cried aloud, thinking she would die beneath the chaotic feelings striking her skin.

'Gilan...I...' She thought she would explode beneath his touch, the pulsating storm of need, of yearning, amassing forcefully within her. Her diaphragm quivered, then tightened with sweet awareness, excitement flowing like boiling honey within her.

He moved over her. Cascading rivulets of sweet-edged terror pulsed through her at the thrilling proximity of his naked flesh, the scorching brand of his need hard against her thigh. His lips seized hers once more, before she had time to think, to question, roving across her mouth, teasing and tantalising as his hand shifted up beneath the damp hem of her chemise, up, up, along the satiny length of her thigh to the very core of her womanhood.

'Gilan...' she gasped, as his fingers ventured where no man had been before. Reason fled, chased away by his questing hand, as her mind sunk down into a churning whirlpool of passion, her body buffeted by enormous waves of pleasure. Her muscles tensed, her body a taut bowstring about to snap, as he slowly moved into her, easing his way through tender folds. Her hands flared outwards, at the bewildering onslaught, scrabbling for purchase, then clung to his face, holding fast to the fierce glitter of his eyes, her only anchor in the face of the on-coming storm.

He surged into her then, his body overwhelmed by a passion that took him by surprise. The flimsy barrier of her innocence checked him for a moment, before he filled her completely, utterly. Consumed by him, Matilda barely had time to protest against the painful sting of his possession, his gentle movements replacing the mild ache with a swelling, eddying fullness. He moved within her, slowly at first, before gathering momentum, faster and faster. She moved with him, delighting in his increasing rhythm, matching his powerful thrusts with a blissful eagerness of her own. Her eyelids fluttered down, the conscious part of her mind barely functioning as desire rippled through her, breaching all defences, threatening to overtake—nay, overwhelm her! Breath ripped from her lungs, hurried, frantic, as a boiling, surging wave broke the very innards of her flesh. White-hot needles of light exploded in her brain, a chaotic whirlpool, a storm of scattering stars.

She cried out then, as Gilan pounded into her, fingers wound into her hair, and the taut strain-ing skin that held them split with scorching vio-lence, unbridled waves of pleasure hurtling through her body, again and again, leaving her gasping, spent. Reaching his own peak, Gilan threw his head back, shuddering in tandem with the woman beneath him.

'Sweet Mother of God!' he yelled out, as Matilda's fingers dug into his shoulders, and he collapsed on top of her, heavy, sated and alive.

Chapter Sixteen

Washed in the soft, lambent glow of the moon, they lay there, parcelled tight in each other's arms, rapid breath slowly subsiding. The sheen of sweat across their naked flesh gradually dissipated into the balmy air. A sweet, strength-sapping languor stole through their bodies, replacing the reckless rush of blood, the thunderous surge of lovemaking. The river lapped at their bare feet, Matilda's small pink toes resting on Gilan's rough-haired calves.

Waves of fading pleasure licking his flesh, Gilan gazed up at the millions of stars twinkling above his head, amazed, astounded by what had happened between them. Matilda's slender frame rested along his right flank, fitting snugly up against his waist, her head nestled into his neck and one arm flung out across his chest. Her damp hair smelt of the river: vital, invigorating. How could he have known? How could he have predicted that this beautiful, stubborn bundle of femininity could have made him feel so whole, so complete again? He hadn't known such serenity, such calmness since before Pierre's death. Torn apart by grief, his soul had become ragged, threadbare; being with Matilda had begun to stitch the gaping seams together. She had given herself to him, utterly and freely, with no consideration to the consequences, driving him to a point where he had lost control, and lost himself. His mind had emptied, cleared of all past, all memory; all that had mattered in that single moment had been her, Matilda, the woman in his arms. He had forgotten who he was.

Guilt—black, coruscating blame coursed through him. What had he done? Caught up in the diaphanous web of her beauty, he had taken her innocence without thought, plundering the delicious softness of her body, rolling around on the inhospitable ground with her as if they were roughneck peasants. His thoughtless actions had destroyed her future. She was damaged goods now, unfit for marriage.

Eyes closed, Matilda shuffled alongside him, her fingers tangling with the short, blond hairs on his chest. She rubbed her cheek against the flank of his torso, sighing with pleasure. Nobody had told her that being with a man could be like this. Both her mother and her sister had told her it was a case of 'lying back and putting up with it.' Her flesh luxuriated in the flickering aftermath, a beloved ache resonating through her loins, her belly. She wanted to rest there for ever, savouring the sinewy ridge of muscle beneath her forearm, the strong curve of his shoulder against her cheek.

'What are you thinking about?' she whispered hesitantly.

Beneath her fingers, his chest heaved, a deep unsteady breath. 'About how badly I have treated you.'

'Badly?' Placing one palm against his bare torso, she levered herself up, bending her legs sideways. The white chemise, sodden with water, shimmered against her flesh, highlighting every tempting curve of her. 'What do you mean?'

Mouth set in a grim, unsmiling line, Gilan sprang to his feet, yanking on his trousers, struggling with his shirt, his tunic. He bent down to scoop up his leather belt and scabbard, wrenching the leather tongue of his sword belt through the silver buckle, bending it back with unnecessary violence to secure the clasp. A sour taste clung to the roof of his mouth, the taste of self-disgust.

Matilda eyed his blank, dispassionate expression. A horrible sickness slithered through her veins.

A tiny voice chewed at the back of her brain: *you were a disappointment, not good enough.* Was her memory so bad that she failed to recall the night in the cave and how he had responded to her then? Despite what he had said, he had pushed her away, discarded her. And now, here she was again, back for more, like a foolish moth to a stupid flame. Why had she expected him to behave in any other way? She had been warned. Only this time, the stakes had been far, far higher. Thrusting her chin in the air, she bit down hard on the treacherous wobble of her bottom lip, bracing herself for a renewed onslaught of rejection.

A muscle jumped in the side of his jaw. 'I mean,' he replied with icy heaviness, 'that I took something that didn't belong to me, Matilda. Something I should never have taken, however great the temptation.' His eyes flicked over her, angry, hard. 'I took your innocence, took away the one thing that would have ensured you a good marriage, a secure future. Now you have nothing.'

I have the memory of you, she thought with a rush. Sadness gripped her heart. Pinning a bright, overly confident expression on her face, she scrambled to her feet, arms wrapped around her middle as if to protect herself from further assault. 'And I told you before, I have no wish to marry. So what you say is of no consequence.'

He scowled, picking up her clothes and throwing them towards her. The ragged, handwoven fabric jumbled across her toes. 'You say that now, Matilda, but it's a hard life living alone as a single, unmarried woman.'

Shock sliced through her belly. What had she expected? That he would go down on bended knee and ask for her hand in marriage? No, he was not that sort of man. He was a soldier, a fighter, with hidden demons plaguing his conscience; too volatile, too physical to adapt to any sedate domestic routine.

Resolve hardening, she settled her shoulders in a straight line. She would have to be strong. 'I live alone already.' Her voice rose, trembling slightly. 'You make out it's all your fault, Gilan, that we laid together, but I knew what I was doing. You gave me a choice. I could have stepped away.'

'Then why didn't you?' he asked quietly.

Because I love you. Her unspoken words shimmered in the air between them, hung like a promise. She knew it. She had known it almost from the time she had first met him. She was drawn to him. She loved him.

'Because I wanted to know...' she tipped her

head on one side '...to know what it can be like, between a man and a woman.' *And I wanted it to be you.*

He clapped a hand to his forehead. 'My God, Matilda, are you telling me you slept with me out of some misguided sense of *convenience*?'

No, I slept with you because I wanted to.

She shrugged, sticking one foot in her trousers, dragging the unwieldy fabric up her leg. 'Maybe the words came out wrong,' she said, 'but I only want to absolve you of any remorse that you might be feeling on my part. I will be fine, Gilan. Truly. It's fine.' Even to her own ears, her voice rang out with an unnatural, jerky brashness, betraying her true feelings.

'Fine?' he bawled at her. 'Matilda, think...how can it be? I took your virginity, ruined you, and you tell me that it's fine? As if all we did was take a gentle stroll in the countryside, holding hands, not tumbled together like two rutting animals on the ground!'

His disparaging words stabbed at her, furious tears springing to her eyes. How dare he? How dare he belittle such a wonderful act, coarsen it? 'It wasn't like that!' she yelled at him.

'Then how was it, Matilda?' His burning eyes snapped over her, goading. 'Tell me.'

'It was the most amazing, thrilling experience that I've ever had in my whole life,' she blurted out, words stumbling out over each other. 'And if it never happens to me again, then it wouldn't matter because I will still have the memory of you.'

Her simple words smacked him straight in the chest. Hard. Temper died in his throat, snuffed out by her honesty. Awestruck, his heart turned over, contracting with emotion. He grabbed her hand, thumb unconsciously playing along the inner seam of her palm. 'Matilda, stop this.' He shook his head. 'I know what you're trying to do and it's your kind heart that's making you do it. Stop trying to absolve me of any guilt. What I did to you was unforgivable.'

'I forgive you, Gilan. Without you, I would never have known.'

'Without me, you would have found yourself a decent husband!' he flashed back. 'Stop trying to make me a better man than I am, Matilda. You constantly see the good in me, like you do with others…like you did with your sister's husband. But it's no good. I cannot be the person you want me to be. Things have happened in my life…things that I am not proud of.'

'I don't want you to be anyone else but the man that stands before me,' she said, her breath hitching at the risk she was taking. 'I have seen you, Gilan. I know you. You like to pretend that you don't care, but you do. You cared when my sister was in labour, you cared enough to protect me from my brother-in-law, so how can you say such things? Despite what you think, Gilan, you have a heart.'

'You're wrong, Matilda.' His hands dropped away.

'It doesn't really matter anyway,' she replied, her voice little, forlorn, her breath shrinking inwards on itself. She stifled a long shuddering breath. So be it. She had tried to reach him, tried to tell him. But he simply wouldn't listen, blinkered by whatever dark devils held his heart in thrall.

He watched as the rift of sadness crossed her face, as she hitched her gaze away with shadowed eyes and knew genuine, heartfelt shame. He had broken her and left her in pieces, shattered. There was nothing he could do to make it better. The situation was hopeless.

The next morning arrived far too soon, the thick air laden with the promise of a scorching day to follow. The birds had woken early, chirruping and trilling through the trees, calling to each other with incessant song. Golden light filtered down through the dancing green leaves, striking the wet grass around the sleeping soldiers, the heavy dew forming a sparkling net of droplets. Across the river's lustrous surface, a light mist veiled upwards, burning off slowly in the rising heat of the sun. A dazzling flash of a bird startled the gentle scene, colourful feathers skimming the limpid water, dipping, then soaring up, up, wings beating strongly.

Wrapped in the smelly blanket, the material sticky with grease and sweat, Matilda had no wish to move. All she wished was to become invisible, to hide away and lick her wounded pride in private. Her limbs ached; her eyes were scoured dry from lack of sleep. The walk back from the river last night had been uncomfortable, awkward. Arms crossed high against his chest, unspeaking, Gilan had waited until she had dressed and rebraided her hair, watching her crawl around the ground to pick up the silver hairpins, released, forgotten, from her fingers at the first touch of his lips. Mouth clamped in the agony of humiliation, she had scrabbled around for them in the river mud, forcing them savagely into her scalp to secure her hair.

Flesh tingling from the aftermath of his lovemaking, Matilda had followed his burly frame resentfully through the woodland. His long strides were brisk and she had tripped, stumbling to keep up with him. She wanted to hate him, but her heart stopped her, clouding with such misery that the temptation to fall on her knees in the dank earth and weep threatened to engulf her.

She was aware of the soldiers around her beginning to stir, to roll from their blankets, to straighten up with a myriad of groans and coughs. Harnesses jangled; the sound of creaking leather, of stoppers on drinking flagons being pulled, pervaded the air. How wonderful it would be to lie here until they had all vanished, Gilan included. Maybe they would even forget about her and leave her to brood on her own downfall. Her eyes popped open, long lashes scratching against the coarse weave of the blanket; no, that was not the way, she was a fighter, remember, not a quitter. And right now, especially after what had happened with Gilan, finding her brother was of paramount importance.

A boot jabbed violently into her side. 'Hey, boy, can you shoot?' a voice bellowed down at her. Henry.

Matilda twisted around, untangling the blanket from her arms, and sat up, eyes blearily adjusting to the stocky man looming over her.

'Yes, yes I can,' she managed to croak out. Her right flank ached, pain sifting through her muscles from the point where Henry had kicked her.

'Good, we need everyone today, in case we need

to fight. Here, have this.' He threw down a bow and a quiver of arrows. They hit the dense pile of leaf mould beside her with scarcely a whisper. Out of the corner of her eye, she saw Gilan, hefting his saddle up from the base of a tree as he watched her and Henry, then caught the slightest shake of his head.

Damn him! she thought. How could she possibly refuse Henry's order, without drawing attention to herself? How could she not shoot? Surely it would look far worse if she hung back fearfully, skulking around the corners of a fight. Scrambling to her feet, she shouldered the bow, slinging the cloth tube that held the arrows across her back and went down to the shoreline to help with the horses. Chucking the bow and arrows down onto the loose stones, she hoisted her unwieldy saddle into place, made more difficult as the horse's back was on a level with her eyebrows.

'Grow some legs, lad!' With a raucous chuckle, one of the soldiers clapped her smartly on the back as he passed. She ducked her head beneath the mare's belly, reaching around to fasten up the leather straps to hold the saddle in place, the horse's flank warm and smooth against her cheek. Once secured, she straightened up, careful not to bring her head up too fast so that her hood slipped out of place.

'Drink?' A leather bottle, the stitched seams rubbed pale with use, was shoved into her line of vision. She tilted her head, arching one ebony-coloured brow. Gilan towered above her, hefty shoulders blocking out the sun. Her heart jolted, knifed through with a renewed line of anguish. Her breathing quickened, raced. She wanted to shove the tanned hand away, to dash the bottle to the ground and watch the contents slosh out, sink away. But then everyone would see and question the apparent fury in a peasant lad towards a noble knight.

'Why, thank you,' she replied, her voice a mocking chant. Her fingers clasped around the neck of the bottle and she tipped some of the contents down her throat, wiping the stray droplets away from her chin with one sleeve. His eyes were upon her, frowning at the stark white of her face beneath the hood, fatigue creasing out from the corners of her eyes.

She caught the look in his eyes. 'Don't,' she muttered quietly beneath her breath. 'Don't you dare!'

He frowned, lower lashes fanning spikily over his high cheekbones. 'Dare…?'

The lifting sunlight touched the pale wheat of his hair, firing the tips into a haze of gold around his head. Her heart squeezed painfully, wrenching tight with emotion. Setting her mouth in a grim, severe line, she shoved the bottle back into his chest, hard. 'Don't you dare pity me!' she whispered fervently. 'Laugh at me, shun me, ride me over with your horse for all I care, but don't look at me like that. Don't...'

Her words dried in her throat as Henry strode towards them. 'Ah, good, we're all ready to go. Shoulder that bow, lad, and let's make tracks.'

Matilda snatched up the bow and arrows, then stuck her foot angrily into the stirrup and swept neatly into the saddle, wheeling her horse around so she could lead the way once more. A heaviness weighed down the muscles in her chest; Gilan had made it perfectly clear he wanted nothing more to do with her, so why make it harder by coming close to her, offering her a drink? It would clearly be far easier if he was out of her sight and she had nothing more to do with him. And after today, that wish would come true. She would never see him again.

By noon, they were working their way up a diagonal track through a dense pine forest. Columns of light shifted down through chinks in the thick canopy, hitting the spongy ground with bright circles of sun, highlighting the mounds of spent pine needles that muffled the horses' hooves. The air was resonant with the fresh, bracing smell of pine, the needles warmed by the heat of the day to release their scent. Above the trees, the sky was a cloudless blue, the sun blazing, scorching the countryside with an incessant, unrelenting light.

'The lad seems out of sorts today,' Henry remarked to Gilan, nodding significantly at Matilda's rigid, inflexible spine up ahead, her jerky, graceless movements with the reins.

'Perhaps you've scared him, by asking him to fight,' Gilan replied quietly, glancing at the pale curved wood arched against the ragged weave of her tunic. 'You've made him nervous by involving him. He's only supposed to be guiding us, after all.' From the moment he had seen Henry throw the bow at Matilda, he had determined to part her from the weapon before the meeting with King Richard. There was no way Matilda was going to fight.

She hated him, of course. As much as such a beautiful, kind creature was capable of hating another soul. After the way he had treated her last night, after the way his body had lost control at the sight of her, emerging, wet and dripping from the river, seized by a fiery, unstoppable desire, her behaviour was completely justified. Shame washed through him again at the memory, flooded his chest, his guts. He had seen the sadness in her eyes, the brilliant blue of her irises dulled, faded with despair, and knew he had done that to her. Why could she not see that he was no good for her, why did she persist in wanting to believe he was better than he really was?

Matilda fixed her gaze stonily ahead, battling to smother the stormy tears that threatened to blur her vision. Up front, no one could see her face or see the wretchedness that tore at her. If only she hadn't asked him to help her; if only she hadn't been forced to seek out her brother for protection. Then she would never have known. Never have known how wonderful it was to lay with a man, to feel the strength of his hard body against her own. She would have remained in blissful ignorance, living out her days as a dried-up old spinster. Alone. Would that have been preferable? Before she had met Gilan, this was the future she had mapped out for herself, but now, now she *knew*. She tried to tell herself that he wasn't worth all this, that he wasn't worth crying over, but it wasn't true. He was worth it. He was worth fighting for. But maybe she wasn't the woman to do it.

She took a deep shuddering breath, stifling the bubbling stutters that welled up in her lungs. No, this wouldn't do. This wallowing in self-pity—how could it help? What would Henry say, if he discovered her face awash with tears? He would send her packing, straight back to her brother-in-law, John, without a moment's hesitation. She was so near to finding Thomas that she couldn't allow her silly behaviour to jeopardise the whole escapade. She had to forget what had happened last night, banish the memory, folding it up neatly like a precious piece of fabric, tucked close to her heart, never to be looked at again.

Wound up in her thoughts, Matilda failed to see the arrow flying through the air, until it landed, thwacked into the soft ground in front of her horse. The brilliant steel stuck upright in the earth, shaft vibrating violently in the light. With a terrified squeal, her mare reared up, whinnying desperately, hooves clawing at the air. The sound rent the still air, shocking. Startled, birds flew up from the branches in a cacophony of shrill, hurried chirruping.

Instinctively, Matilda threw her slight weight forwards, clamping her arms around the animal's neck. She hung on grimly, the animal's hooves thrashing down relentlessly on to the spongy ground. 'Gilan!' she yelled out without thinking. 'Watch out!' Another arrow whizzed through the air, then another, this one inches from her ear. At her back, Henry bellowed out orders; she could hear the crash of bracken, of twigs, as the soldiers sought positions of safety. She sent a desperate wish heavenwards, praying that Gilan would be safe, and then realised her mistake. In her panic, she had called out his first name.

As the mare's hooves hit the ground, Matilda bounced down out of the saddle, landing squarely, her slim legs braced apart for balance. Immediately, she plunged into the undergrowth, forcing her way to the other side of a huge mound of brambles. She found herself surrounded by thick trunks, the light shadowed by the dense planting of pines. Perfect. No one would spot her here. Breathing heavily from exertion, from fright, she crouched down, tipping the quiver of arrows and the bow from her back. She fitted one arrow to the bow, pulling the drawstring back, ready to shoot. Her legs wobbled with nerves, her stomach churning, but she screwed up her eyes and scrutinised the boundary line at the top of the forest, the direction from which the first arrow had been shot. No one. Not a single soul. Her brow furrowed as she forced herself to concentrate. To focus. In all this mayhem, maybe Henry wouldn't have noticed her blunder, for how would a low-born guide know the Christian name of the man who had hired him?

A blood-curdling yell ripped the air, then another, and another. But the sound came from above, not from the top of the hill. Stunned, Matilda jerked her head up, searching through the high branches, fringed with dark green needles, drooping with clustered pine cones. And there they were. Men, dressed in ragged, dirty clothes, jumping from the trees, brandishing swords and arrows. Knife blades flashed between their teeth. Their faces were black, smeared with soil, and their teeth gleamed out from the darkness, leering with menace. They ran towards the soldiers in a straggling group, stretching out through the trunks in a jerky line.

Higher up on the slope, Matilda had the advantage, being able to look down on them. She pushed her hood back, raising herself on her knees and took aim. Her arrow flew through the air, struck one man in the shoulder. With a howl, he clutched at the quivering shaft, falling to his knees. Matilda armed the bow once more, shot again, and again, each time hitting with deadly accuracy. Henry's soldiers fought back with practised, seemingly effortless skill. As she shot, she could see the flashing blades through the trees and hear the scuffles, grunts and curses of hand-to-hand combat.

The clash of swords, the shouts echoed up to the swathes of dark green fronds above. But where was Gilan? Believing herself to be unseen, Matilda raised herself up gingerly into a crouching position to give herself a better view.

A rock smashed down on to the side of her skull.

Chapter Seventeen

Face slick with sweat, Henry watched the last of their attackers flee through the trees, the man scrambling down, down towards the river, knocking his shoulders against the gnarled trunks in his haste to escape. Sheathing his sword, Henry wiped his gauntlet across his brow, pushing back the damp hair from his forehead with stubby, leather-encased fingers.

'Leave him!' he bellowed out to one of his soldiers who seemed intent on pursuit. 'I think they've learned their lesson for today.' He swept a cursory glance on the fallen ruffians, lying face down with arrows in their shoulders, already beginning to groan from their wounds. 'Only two casualties, on their side. And both of them shot in the back, from up there.' He lifted his head, and nodded upwards along the track. 'We have your guide to thank for that, Gilan.' He twisted his head around, looking for the diminutive figure. 'Where is the lad, anyway?' He shrugged, the fine wool of his surcoat bunching around his thick shoulders.

Aye, where was she? Rivulets of fear twisted in Gilan's belly, icy threads. He raked his gaze across the scrub, scouring the trunks for a glimpse of her petite, lithe figure, a flash of her pale face.

Henry slapped him on the back, grinning. 'No need to look so worried, Gilan. He probably took this as an opportunity to run off. I suspect we made too many demands on him.'

'No, she wouldn't do that,' Gilan growled out. He sprang away from Henry, from the look of astonishment on Henry's face, moving up the track in great loping strides, his big, blond head shifting constantly from left to right as he peered beneath the trees. The whole ruse of keeping Matilda's identity secret faded to insignificance; all he wanted, all he prayed for, was to find her alive, unharmed.

'She...?' Henry spluttered out, shouting after him. 'What do you mean...she?' He shook his head, a look of consternation crossing his face. Had his friend taken leave of his senses?

Gilan reached the point on the track where her horse had reared, saw the huge gouges in the earth where the hooves had plunged down. Now the animal cropped a patch of spindly grass farther up, bridle dangling forlornly. He hoped she was hiding somewhere; in the frenzied heat of the attack, he hadn't been able to reach her, to make sure that she was safe.

'Matilda? Matilda, where are you?' he called out, swinging his body around so his voice boomed out across the forest in all directions.

'Have you completely lost your mind?' Henry powered up behind him, barrel chest flexing violently with the exertion. 'Who is this "she"? Who are you calling to?'

But Gilan failed to answer him. His keen eye spotted the broken brambles, the route that Matilda had taken away from the path. Henry grabbed Gilan's forearm, stubby fingers clawing at his sleeve, stalling him. 'What the hell is going on, Gilan? Perhaps you'd care to explain?'

'Not now!' With a short, sharp movement, Gilan wrenched his arm down, out of Henry's grip and plunged into the thicket of brambles, forcing his way through the inhospitable, scratching mass of thorns, cruel points that tore at his tunic, his chausses, hacked at his face, his hair.

And there she was. His sweet, kind Matilda. Flung on to her back, face stark white, a bloody gash marring the side of her forehead, skin purpling around the wound. Blood trickled down her cheek, staining her peerless cheek, running past the lobe of her ear and dripping on to the ground.

Sound sucked away from him. The twitter of birds above, the stiff breeze through the high branches, Henry's outraged questions booming out from the other side of the thicket.

For one tiny stunned moment, his whole body stilled, strung with a horrible tension, a fear, a terror of what he might discover when he dropped to his knees and placed a hand to her neck. Pierre. Pierre had lain like this, his arms thrown out, and Gilan had thought him to be alive. But he had been dead. With a sharp, jerky movement, he threw the image from his head. Matilda needed him now. He sank on his knees into the pile of spent pine needles beside her.

Moved his fingers against her neck.

Her blood pulsed against his trembling fingers, powerful and strong.

Joy, complete and utter joy, surged through him. 'Lord in Heaven,' he breathed shakily, relieved, pushing one arm beneath her slim shoulders and lifting her against him, against the sturdy ridges of his chest. He hadn't realised he'd been holding his breath. 'Thank God.' Her hood slipped back, revealing the glossy beauty of her hair, as he ran one thumb across the fine silk of her cheek, then pressed a kiss to her brow, frowning at the puckered edges of the wound.

Unconsciousness lifted away from her, pulling away like drifts of flimsy silk. The layers floated away into the bright, light air. Birds sang around her, sunlight dancing on her face. Someone held her, carefully, cradled against a broad, unyielding chest. She knew who it was. Who *he* was. His surcoat pressed against her left cheek, the soft wool tickling gently.

'Gilan,' she whispered.

'Aye, it's me.' His voice, deep and resonant, wrapped around her like a swaddling blanket. She was safe. Just for a moment, she would keep her eyes shut, and savour the muscled cloak of his arms around her shocked limbs.

'My head...?' She lifted one arm, touching her slender fingers tentatively to the patch of blood. She couldn't seem to stop trembling.

'Someone hit you,' Gilan replied softly. 'You were doing such a good job, taking those ruffians down. I should have taken the bow and arrows away from you—that way no one would have realised you were here.' Beneath the slick of blood on her forehead, he could see the edges of the wound gaping open and frowned. The cut would need stitches.

'But you couldn't do that,' she stuttered out, unable to keep her chattering teeth under control, 'because Henry would have asked too many questions.'

Behind them, someone was thrashing through the thicket of brambles, cursing heavily, mostly cursing Gilan. And then Henry himself burst out into the small clearing, followed by two of his soldiers, mouths agape at the scene before them.

'A maid!' Henry gasped as he struggled to extricate himself from the last of the trailing brambles, his face bright red, eyes flaring wildly. 'Our guide was a girl all along?' His outraged expression swiftly observed the details of the maid in Gilan's arms: slender legs encased in rough chausses, dark silky hair knotted to her head—how had he been so dense not to spot the deception earlier?

Panic flickered through Matilda's veins at Henry's furious appearance; she struggled to heave herself into a sitting position, intending to explain herself, but Gilan held her down, tucked securely in the circle of his arms. His fingers squeezed into her upper arm, sending her a silent message: let me deal with this.

'Yes, Henry, she was, and she is. This is Matilda, lady of—'

'I don't give a fig who she is, Gilan! The fact

is it's unheard of, it's preposterous, that a maid should travel into the company of men like this! And you knew! You knew all along—why didn't you tell me?'

'Because you wouldn't have allowed it,' Gilan replied. 'You know what a stickler you are for rules.' With one hand against Matilda's ribcage, he could feel the flutter of her heart against the flat of his palm.

Henry's eyes narrowed on his friend. 'She shouldn't be here, Gilan.' Fixing his hard gaze on Matilda, his mind worked rapidly. 'She needs to be taken to safety, a manor where someone can tend to that wound. Do you know of such a place hereabouts?' He directed the last question to Matilda, raising his voice as if she were hard of hearing.

'I know of a place,' Gilan said quietly. Keeping hold of her, he shifted his weight beneath Matilda to his knees, and then on to his feet. One arm swept firm beneath her hips and he swung her into the air, so that she landed with a faint squeak against his chest. 'My home, or rather, my parents' home. It's not far from here.'

'Excellent.' Henry rubbed his hands together at the seemingly easy solution. 'One of the soldiers can take her.'

'I'll take her.'

Henry scowled at him, petulance dragging at the harsh lines of his face. 'Out of the question. I need you with me when we tackle Richard.'

Gilan shook his head. 'You don't need me, Henry. You are quite capable of handling Richard on your own. But Matilda…' he swept sparkling granite eyes across the enchanting face cushioned against his chest '…Matilda needs me.'

No, Matilda wanted to protest. I don't need you. The words wavered through her aching brain as her head rolled against his shoulder. Why could she not speak them out loud? It was if a thick mist swirled in her brain, obscuring the power of speech, making her stupid, befuddled. Shivers rattled through her; she wound shaking fingers into the front lacing of Gilan's tunic, clutching frantically, thinking she might fall. Her eyelids fluttered down as she succumbed to another wave of sinking, black unconsciousness.

'I'm not sure I understand…' Henry said slowly, pushing stubby fingers through his rusty hair. But he did. He understood completely. His friend's tender glance towards the maid had explained everything. He folded his burly arms across his chest, creasing the gold fleur-de-lis embroidery on his tunic, frowning deeply.

Gilan raised his eyes towards Henry, the man

he had shared a lifetime with, and shook his head. 'I'm not asking you to understand what is going on here, Henry, for in truth I scarce understand it myself. All I know is that I must care for Matilda. She is vulnerable and needs my protection.'

'You're in love with her…' Henry breathed, so quietly that Gilan failed to hear. His expression lightened, a wide grin breaking across his face. He shook his head ruefully. 'I'm being selfish, Gilan. I'm become too accustomed to you fighting at my side. Go now, with my blessing. Take the maid to your home and look after her. I will meet you there after I have dealt with my wayward cousin.'

'But I will catch up with you,' Gilan said, 'once I am assured that Matilda is safe.'

'Out of the question!' Henry barked at him again. 'I forbid it! You stay by her side, or you'll have me to deal with. I will miss you, Gilan, but you're right, I can challenge Richard alone. Now take your precious burden and be gone.'

'Matilda, wake up! You need to drink some of this.' Gilan's rough voice barged into her wadded cocoon of sleep, a wallowing tide of comfort that she was reluctant to give up. The mouth of a leather bottle was pushed up against her lips and she jerked back as a fiery, unpleasant liquid poured down her throat.

She spluttered angrily. Her eyes sprang open; she batted the bottle away, hand flailing upwards. 'Stop it, Gilan! Are you trying to make me drunk?'

'I'm trying to keep you awake.' He scowled at her grey, pinched features. After leaving Henry, Gilan had pushed his destrier as fast as he possibly dared, Matilda wedged securely before him, her shoulder tucked into the angle of his arm. Throughout the journey, she had lapsed in and out of consciousness, and now the wound was bleeding afresh. He reined in his horse at the top of a ridge, at a point where the land fell away in gentle slopes to a huge, low-lying plain of fertile pastureland. Above them, a pair of buzzards soared and circled, rising higher and higher in the warm uplift of wind on the edge of the land.

'I need to bind it,' he muttered, the breeze riffling the blond strands of his hair. 'Matilda, hang on to the horse's mane and, for God's sake, don't fall off!'

'Why? What are you doing?' Following his terse instruction, she lurched forwards, clutching fuzzily at the frothing chestnut mane, trying to counter the rising tide of sickness in her stomach. She stared miserably at the shining brass on the bridle—how in Heaven's name had she ended up like this? The bash on her head had certainly complicated matters, for by now she had hoped to be far away from Gilan and licking her wounded pride in the company of her brother. But here she was, huddled in the sweet cradle of Gilan's arms, craving his touch, vulnerable, exposed and hurt. Her mind loped crazily, skittering this way and that. She frowned—why was she finding it so difficult to gather her thoughts, to think her way out of this situation? Her head swam, a rising tide of cloudy befuddlement threatening to engulf her. A sour, metallic taste coated her tongue and she swallowed hastily. God forbid that she was ill in front of him!

'I need to bind your wound.' She jumped as his voice jarred into her. Lifting the hem of his surcoat, Gilan exposed the sun-bleached linen of his shirt beneath. Grabbing the flimsy material, he tore at it with strong, tanned fingers, ripping off a long length from the hemline.

'Gilan, you've ruined your shirt,' Matilda gasped, as she turned to see what he'd done. Her hood had fallen back and wisps of her shining hair tangled with the breeze. Her face was deathly white.

It was worth it. He would give her all the clothes on his back if it meant he could heal her more quickly. Reaching up, he wound the strip of fabric across her forehead with infinite gentleness, his fingers grazing her forehead, the perfectly drawn uplift of her eyebrow. Ripping one end of the make-shift bandage, he tied the ragged tails of fabric into a knot above her ear.

'There,' he said, frowning critically at his handi-work. 'That should last you until we reach home.' Despite the heat of the day, he could see she was trembling. He pulled her hood forwards, hoping the gesture would warm her a little and stop her shivers. Against her will, her body sagged against him. She felt so frail, so feeble, and annoyingly, she couldn't explain it. She had a bump on the head, not a sword through her chest. Heaviness dragged at her limbs, sapping her strength, her blood moving slowly, thickly through her veins. She lifted one hand to touch the tight bandage on her head; already the ache had subsided a little. 'I...thank you, Gilan, I'm not sure what's wrong with me at the moment...' Her hands fluttered outwards, a gesture of consternation. A tiny frown puckered the space between her eyebrows.

'Not sure...?' He glared down at her. 'For God's sake, Matilda, someone nearly killed you! You have a gash the size of a horse's hoof on your head and it's a wonder that you're even managing to stay upright!'

'Is it really that bad?' she asked in a small voice.

'Yes!' he said, then caught her worried expression. 'No, not that bad,' he lied.

'I'm sure I could have ridden my own horse, saved your destrier this extra burden.'

He glanced down; the fringe of her eyelashes curved over her cheek, black velvet feathers. 'You need to stop this, Matilda. Stop thinking about me, or my horse. Think about yourself for a change. My horse is perfectly capable of carrying both of us,' he said. 'Let me take care of you.'

Matilda angled her head up, studied the determined line of his chin as he set his horse in motion once more. Her heart swelled with emotion at his words. How could she tell him there was nothing in the world that she craved more than for him to take her in his arms and care for her, love her? But he truly believed he was not capable of such a thing, not with her, anyway. In her vulnerable state, she would have to be careful, not allow herself to be drawn in by his compassionate manner. For if she did, her heart would surely break.

Chapter Eighteen

Isabelle of Chesterham reached out thin, bony fingers to cup a full-blown rose, the pink velvet petals hanging heavy with sparkling dots of dew, inclining her body to inhale the scent. She pulled her head back quickly, narrow mouth twisting with disgust. The sweet smell made her nauseous. Everything seemed to make her feel sick these days: the yeasty bread in the mornings, her mother-in-law's judgemental glances, the endless waiting. Above all, the endless waiting. She flattened one hand across her distended stomach. Waiting for this wretched baby to be born. Waiting for Gilan to return, to pick up the reins that Pierre, her husband, had dropped. Gilan would become her husband now, she would make certain of it. If only he would hurry up and come home.

She sighed, glancing at Berta, to see if the maid-servant had noticed any traitorous expression in her face, any hint of expectant excitement at the thought of being wedded to Gilan. But Berta continued to walk stolidly beside her, bovine half smile pinned to her round, flat face. Gilan was by far the more handsome brother, taller and broader than Pierre. He had inherited his mother's shining hair, his father's muscular physique but he was more formidable, too, less approachable than his brother. She would have some work to do, but ultimately, she was sure to win him over, and force him to bend to her will. She, Isabelle of Chesterham, could surely not be denied a little happiness after all the grief she had suffered.

Sweat prickled beneath her arms, began to trickle down her sides, gather beneath her breasts. She wished she had chosen a lighter gown to wear today; although the waist belt of her houppelande sat above her growing belly, the gold-threaded embroidery around the high, tightly buttoned neck itched her throat and she longed to pull the whole thing off and sit on the warm grass in her linen shift, legs outstretched and bare.

'Let's walk around to the bailey,' she barked at her maid. 'I can't stand much more of this heat—and the front of the castle casts a shadow. Then we will go inside.'

'As you wish, my lady.' Berta curtsied, then led

the way to an oak-planked door, set in the stone wall that circled the formal gardens, shoving it open with stumpy, calloused fingers.

At least there was more to see in the inner bailey, thought Isabelle, as she stepped around the east turret of the castle. Anything to relieve her long-suffering apathy. Soldiers paced along the curtain walls, marching stiffly between the fluttering flags that carried the earl's colours; younger knights practised their skills in one corner of the bailey, rushing one by one at a straw-stuffed sack that hung by a rope from a wooden scaffold, attempting to stab it with one fatal blow. Their shouts and roars of approval rose into the heavy, shimmering air. Isabelle watched covertly, her thin mouth curling with appreciation at the sight of all those honed masculine bodies clad only in flimsy shirts and buckskin trousers.

A rapid clatter of hooves, then a shout, almost a cry for help, made everyone stall in their duties and turn to stare towards the gatehouse. A tall man, head shimmering with golden strands, skidded to a stop in the middle of the bailey, a bundle of what looked like fabric, or clothes, gathered in front of him.

Gilan!

Isabelle clutched one hand to her throat. My God!

She recognised him immediately: that gleaming vitality, the strong, vigorous body and the generous upward tilt of his mouth that made her feel instantly weak with longing.

'How do I look?' she demanded, digging her fingers into her maid's doughy forearm.

'Beautiful, my lady, as always,' Berta replied.

'Hand me my cloak! I don't want him to see my awful stomach!' She snatched the fine silk from Berta's arms and swung the material around her shoulders, arranging the voluminous gathers across the front of her dress to disguise her pregnancy.

'There,' she declared, satisfied. 'Can you see anything?'

'Nothing, my lady,' answered her maidservant, glancing across the bailey. 'Oh, look, there's someone with him,' Berta said, watching as Gilan threw himself down to the dusty cobbles and reached up to lift the bundle down, slowly, carefully. Already he was shouting orders at the soldiers and they scurried off to do his bidding.

No, not a bundle of clothes. 'What is that?' Isabelle stuttered out.

'I think...I think it's a boy.' Berta narrowed her eyes, trying to see beyond the throngs of interested people in the bailey, and caught the white flash of a bandage. 'Looks like he's injured.'

Carrying Matilda, her head lolling back over his upper arm, Gilan strode grimly towards Isabelle and Berta, to the spot where they loitered on the steps leading up to the main door of the castle. Holding on to the iron rail for support, and keeping her cloak firmly across her bulging stomach, Isabelle managed a wavering curtsy. 'My lord Gilan, you're home at last. How good it is to see you.'

He nodded briefly at the noblewoman on the steps, his piercing eyes fixing on the maidservant. 'Run ahead and fetch my mother, as quick as you can, Berta.' By now he was at the top of the steps, carrying Matilda over the threshold.

Desolation crashed down around Isabelle as she stared up at Gilan's retreating figure. My God, he had practically ignored her. Her! His late brother's wife! Surely she deserved a little more respect than a cursory bow? She watched as Berta scuttled after him, keen to follow his orders. Why had he not asked her? She could have helped him, helped to offer comfort to the injured lad. Then he could have seen how caring she was, how kind she could be in difficult circumstances.

A soldier paced towards her, hefting saddlebags against his chest. No doubt they belonged to Gilan. He was the only person who had arrived at the castle that day.

'Stop,' Isabelle said imperiously. The suspended pearls quivered in her headdress.

The soldier halted before her, bowed as low as he was able.

'Tell me, what was the matter with that lad?' she asked. 'Has he been injured in a fight?'

'Lad, my lady?' The soldier's eyes observed her with surprise. 'No, you have it wrong. It was a maid who has been hurt. It was a maid who my lord Gilan was carrying.'

Following Gerta's bobbing figure, Gilan pushed through the thick, woven curtains that screened the great hall from the castle's main entrance. Adjusting his grip on Matilda, he hoisted her more securely against his chest; she groaned faintly at the movement, lifting one hand to the makeshift bandage on her head.

'Where are we?' she whispered, swallowing hastily, trying to relieve the parched state of her mouth. Her tongue moved woodenly.

'My home.' Gilan glanced down at her, appalled by the pallid greyness of her face. 'I can take care of you here.'

'You always take care of me, Gilan,' she murmured, her head rolling back against his shoulder, eyelashes fluttering down once more.

Anxiety pierced his heart. He couldn't, wouldn't lose her! A horrible vulnerability washed over him, a desperate powerlessness in the face of injury, of death. As he strode forwards across the vast flagstone floor, his piercing gaze switched towards the high dais, watching as Berta bustled up the wooden steps and over to a solitary figure, bent over some rolls of parchment. The white-gold hair flashed in the sunlight streaming down from the diamond-paned windows. His mother, Marie! He almost choked with relief at the sight of her. A rush of love washed through him, a powerful surge of family connection, of memory. Marie glanced up, her willowy frame half rising in her seat, mouth falling open in surprise. Tears spilled from her beautiful grey eyes, running freely down her cheeks, scattering droplets across the stretched parchment.

'Oh, my son, my son!' she called out, her smile shining through the tears. Her voice echoed up to the rafters of the hall. 'I never thought I would see this day! You have come home!'

His parents would want to know, of course. They would want to know all the details of Pierre's death. And he would tell them everything; how he had caused the whole sorry mess. Sadness puckered his heart. But there would be time to tell them later. Right now, Matilda needed him.

Marie saw immediately that Gilan's main concern was the injured maid in his arms. Now was not the time for celebrations, or questions, despite the dancing skip of her heart. Descending the wooden steps, she walked briskly towards her son, her brain rapidly absorbing all the wonderful familiar details of him: his bright head of hair, the pewter eyes that matched her own, his formidable breadth and height.

Standing before him, she reached up with the flat of her hand and laid it gently against his cheek, a gesture of welcome, of love, before dropping her gaze to the woman in his arms. 'I think we need to find this maid a bedchamber.' With narrowed, critical eyes, she assessed the girl swiftly, taking in her ashen skin, the fraying linen around her head. 'What happened to her?'

'Someone hit her with a rock,' Gilan spat out, surprised by the tremble in his voice. 'There's a nasty gash on her forehead.'

'Come this way.'

Moving through a low doorway in the corner of the great hall, Marie led him up a spiral staircase and into a chamber on the first floor. Berta was already in the room, lighting the charcoal brazier in the corner, tucking in clean linens around the mattress, throwing a huge fur across the top. Thank

God for his mother, he thought, with her calm foresight, her ability to see ahead.

'Lay her down, Gilan,' Marie ordered.

Bending easily, he placed Matilda down on the furs, crouching over her. His fingers flew to the bandage at her head and he plucked frantically, trying to release the tightened knot that he himself had fastened. His fingers wouldn't work! His mind skittered haphazardly, he couldn't think straight! In harried despair, he seized the knife from his belt, intending to slice the bandage away.

'Gilan, stop! Move away from her now. Much as I love you, you're in no fit state to deal with this.' Marie pushed him gently aside, sitting on the edge of the bed alongside Matilda. Her slender fingers worked deftly, expertly, at the white length of cloth, until she had unbound Gilan's handiwork to reveal the ugly, purpling gash. Her son stood over her, scuffed leather boots inches from his mother's embroidered silk slippers, burly arms crossed over his chest, watching closely.

'What do you think?' he demanded. 'Does it need stitches?'

Someone rapped at the door. 'Gilan, fetch that, would you?' Marie flicked her eyes up to the brooding figure of her son, frowning. 'I asked for a bowl of hot water, cloths, to be sent up.'

He held the bowl, as his mother dropped cloth after cloth into the steaming liquid, slowly cleaning the wound, dabbing away the clots of drying blood. 'She's not going to die, Gilan,' Marie reassured him, smiling gently. 'She'll have a pretty bruise for a week or two, but no untoward effects, as far as I can judge. Right now, she needs to sleep and rest.'

To his mother's complete surprise, Gilan sank to his knees by the bed, grabbing one of Matilda's pale, limp hands in his big, bearlike grip. 'Thank God,' he breathed, kissing the pale, frozen digits, 'I don't know what I would have…'

He stopped. *I don't know what I would have done without her.* The unspoken words hung in the air, mocking him. Was that what it had come to? That he couldn't live without her? That this vibrant, feisty girl, who had burst into his life with such energy and such self-possession, who had given herself so freely to him, had come to mean so much to him? He knew the answer. He felt his mother's eyes upon him, and Berta's, both watching him intently, closely.

'Who is this maid, Gilan?' Marie asked, pushing herself on to her feet, pressing her hands to the front of her gown.

'It's a long story.' He threw his mother a rueful smile.

'Then we had best summon your father,' Marie suggested, 'for it will save you telling the same story twice.'

At first, Matilda had no idea where she was. Her aching head was propped up against a soft pillow and a linen sheet covered her body, heaped with furs. A fire crackled away in the corner of the chamber; shifting her head against the pillow, she realised it was a charcoal brazier, the coals glowing merrily, despite the summer heat outside. The chamber was expensively furnished: elegant, colourful tapestries covered the plastered walls; intricate carving decorated the oak coffer beneath the window. The wood shone warmly. The low trajectory of light from outside suggesting that the day moved towards evening. A daddy longlegs skittered lazily along the ceiling, bouncing randomly along the wooden rafters.

Her head pounded; removing her hand from beneath the covers, she lifted her fingers tentatively to the throbbing patch on her temple. She remembered that attack in the forest, Gilan's frantic shouts. Then being carried against his muscular frame, on horse-back, and feeling ill, not wanting to be sick in front of him. Was this his home? Frowning, she screwed up her eyes, trying to remember. Was it he who had tended to her wound? There had been another voice, a gently accented voice delivering orders in a soft, calm manner and cool, deft fingers against her head. That hadn't been Gilan, surely?

'So, you're awake then.' A voice grated out beside Matilda. A shrill, clipped tone.

Surprise juddered through her. She had thought herself to be alone in the room. A woman sat in a low chair beside the bed, narrow lips curling into a lopsided smile, hands resting atop a huge, pregnant belly, fingers laced tightly together. Her knuckles gleamed white, as if the bone in her hands tried to escape the thin stretched skin. Hundreds of tiny pearl buttons secured the front of her gown from throat to waist, an exquisite gown, fashioned from a deep red satin. A jewelled headdress highlighted the brown curls of the woman's hair, gold-threaded net covering plaited coils over each ear.

Self-consciously, Matilda touched her own hair. Someone had released the glossy tendrils from the hairpins and now the full length of chestnut silk looped down across the sable bed furs. Tucking several strands hurriedly behind each ear, she shuffled her hips up against the pillow in a vague attempt to raise herself into a seated position.

'Who are you?' The woman was staring at her intently.

'I...I am Matilda of Lilleshall,' Matilda managed to stutter out. Where was Gilan? Maybe this wasn't his home after all, and he'd left her somewhere. A sense of wretchedness rushed through her and she recalled his words by the river: 'Stop trying to make me a better man than I really am.' Would he really leave her at a stranger's house, without saying goodbye?

'Never heard of you,' the woman remarked, her tone instantly dismissive. 'Are you one of the Marcher families? Who are your people?'

The woman's abrasive manner grated on her nerves. 'I told you, at Lilleshall, south of here.' Matilda sucked in her breath, propping herself up more securely on one elbow. Her head swirled dangerously with the bold, decisive movement. 'Er... is Gilan here?'

'Lord Gilan? What on earth would you want with him?' The woman's scant eyelashes flew upwards, her hazel eyes openly challenging, aggressive.

Matilda frowned. Why was this woman behaving in such an odd manner? Her fingers played nervously along the front of her chemise, the gauzy lace at the neckline ruffling against her wrist. 'He brought me here, didn't he? Is this his home?'

'Yes, it is. His parents live here and so do I.'

'Could you send one of the servants to fetch him for me, please?' Matilda asked quickly. She wanted to thank him, at least, for all he had done, and hopefully, release him from any responsibility he might feel towards her. He hadn't counted on her becoming injured; taking her to a place of safety was probably the last thing he had wanted to do. Still, if he hadn't picked her up, and looked after her, then Lord knew what Henry would have decided to do with her. Sickness rushed through her and she slumped back on the pillow, perspiration beading her hairline.

'Oh, he's very busy at the moment with preparations.'

'Preparations?' Matilda queried. The daddy longlegs now batted spindly legs against the stone arch of the window frame. The heat in the chamber seemed oppressive, leaden, pressing down on her thumping head. 'Oh, is he planning to leave?'

The woman laughed, a discordant, jangling sound. 'I should hope not! I mean...' she leaned forwards conspiratorially, lowering her voice '...that now he's home, he's making preparations for the wedding. Our wedding. I'm Isabelle, Pierre's widow. There's an agreement, you see, because Pierre died.' She crossed herself, raising her eyes heavenwards. 'God rest his soul.'

Marriage. The word tore into her with the force of a lightning storm, ripping into her heart. Matilda gripped her bare arms tight about her middle, trying to control the deluge of pain, of despair that coursed through her, trying to maintain some outward display of control. From the chair, the woman's eyes bore into her, assessing her reactions, the woman who was Gilan's sister-in-law, pregnant with his brother's child.

And Gilan was to marry her. Matilda collapsed back into the pillows, eyelashes shuttering down, black velvet fronds fanning across her heated cheeks. Waves of misery swung through her. Had Gilan known this all along? Known that, eventually, he would return home to marry his brother's widow? Had he known as their two bodies joined with shivering delight, rolling with utter pleasure at the river's edge, or when his lips touched hers in the dim glow of the cave, the rain crashing down outside? She had told him that nothing mattered but the memory of his body against hers. But now, she realised she had lied. It did matter. However much she tried to stifle the love she felt for him, to patch up the heartache of his rejection, the pain continued to surface, again and again. The pain of loving him, and knowing that he would never be with her. Tears crept silently from beneath her lashes, silvery trails across the peerless skin.

'I need to get out of here.' Matilda switched her gaze to the woman in the chair. 'Will you help me?'

'It would be my pleasure,' Isabelle replied, tracking Matilda's tears with secret glee. She rose from the chair with a sense of victory, of triumph. She had effectively snuffed out whatever fledging relationship had existed between this girl and her future husband, like a shot of air against a guttering candle. The maid might be sad, heartbroken even, but Gilan was hers, and there was not a thing this chit could do about it.

Despite the prominent size of her pregnant belly, Isabelle jumped up with surprising speed, approaching the bed and plucking the furs from Matilda, tossing them to the floor. 'Come on, then!' she chivvied, clapping her hands. 'If you want my help, then it has to be now. I have far more important things to be dealing with.'

Head swimming, Matilda inched tentatively towards the edge of the bed. A headache clustered on her brow, drumming relentlessly. A thousand chaotic thoughts ran through her mind: where could she go now? Could she continue north, alone, to find her brother? But the light was fading, which meant leaving at dusk. She would have to find a place to rest for the night. A few days ago, such an idea had been utterly achievable in her mind, but now, now she felt vulnerable, frightened. Was this what Gilan had turned her into? A nervous, pathetic shadow of a woman, with no mind, or self-confidence of her own? Her heart pleated with sadness and she bit down, hard, on her bottom lip to prevent a fresh wash of tears marring her face. She had come to rely on him, had become used to his dynamic, vital presence at her side. She missed him. She loved him.

'Now, where are the clothes that you arrived in?' Isabelle asked breathlessly, a terse smile pinned across her narrow mouth. She whirled about, trying to spot them. 'They were ideal, you looked so much like a boy when I first saw you.' She marched about, flipping open the lids on a couple of oak coffers, ducking her head to check behind an embroidered screen, then sighed. 'No, not here. She must have taken them away to be washed. They were in a fearful state. Horrendous.'

'She…?' Matilda asked, bare feet skimming the elm floorboards. She shivered in the diaphanous material of her shift.

'Marie. Gilan's mother. She was the one who

tended to your wound. Gilan was beside himself. I've never seen him like that before. It was quite amusing, actually. He was insanely worried about you.' She cackled gleefully, then covered her mouth hurriedly with her hand, as if embarrassed by the high-pitched sound.

'I'm sure he wasn't that worried,' Matilda replied dully, trying to summon the energy to stand upright. She felt as if she were distanced from her own body, floating, drifting.

'No, you're right,' Isabelle agreed vigorously, realising her mistake. 'He wasn't that worried. I expect he was exhausted from having to carry you all that way.' Isabelle's hazel gaze fixed on to Matilda like a crab's pincers. 'You were probably becoming a bit of a burden.'

Matilda nodded, swaying from the bed. The chamber reeled and she clutched out to the bedpost, grabbing the carved wood and a handful of curtain for support. A burden. Of course, that was all she was to him.

'There are no clothes here,' Isabelle announced. 'I will go and fetch a gown of my own for you. Wait here and don't go anywhere.' Lifting the iron latch on the door, she slipped through, the voluminous red-satin hem trailing after her like a serpent's tail.

No chance of that, thought Matilda, her whole

body shuddering with the effort of staying upright. Short of running away clad only in a chemise and bed fur, she had little choice but to stay put. She reached down to pull the pelt from the bed and up around her shoulders, wriggling her chilly feet against the floor. Maybe if she stood next to the brazier she would warm up a little? Staggering across the chamber, she reached the spot between the bed and the window, where the black coals glowed snug inside their metal casing. Her body cleaved to the heat gratefully and she pressed one hand against the stone windowsill to balance herself.

Panes of uneven, handblown glass formed the narrow, arched windows. The small glass diamonds were fixed into a grid of lead work; through them, she could see down into formal gardens laid out to the south of the castle. Rows of yew hedging divided the flat area into several areas of planting and paths: a herb garden, a rose arbour and a vast vegetable plot. Rounded heads of globe artichokes undulated in the breeze, grey and stiff, segmented. The gardens were surrounded by the towering curtain wall, turreted at intervals, protecting the castle within. Beyond the wall, acres of forest stretched towards the western horizon, where glowering clouds gathered, collecting ominously.

Three figures walked slowly together along the central path, heads bent towards each other in earnest conversation, arms interlinked. Her heart lurched as she recognised Gilan's immense shoulders, the gilt of his hair matching that of the elderly couple walking with him. The older man pulled himself along heavily with the aid of a stick, his step rolling sideways, marred by a significant limp. The lady was almost as tall as Gilan, hair shining out like a coin in the dimming light. She had to be Gilan's mother, Marie.

Matilda bit her lip, betrayal coursing through her. Despite everything that had happened between her and Gilan, he had helped her and brought her to his home. His mother had tended to her wounds. Was she really going to slink away without a word of thanks, like a fox in the night, head held low? Closing her eyes, she pressed her heated forehead against the cool glass of the windowpane. Of course that was what she would do. For to face Gilan now, knowing that he would never be with her, and skim her eyes across the beautiful carved lines of his face, inhale his heady scent of leather and horseflesh, was too much to bear. Her cobbled-together heart would surely shatter and she would never, ever, be able to piece it back together.

She had to leave now. Alone.

Chapter Nineteen

As the light faded into dusky evening, servants scurried about the great hall, setting flaming tapers against the thick wax candles set into hollowed stone niches, or stuck on to unwieldy wrought-iron candlesticks. A massive fire burned in the fireplace, dispelling the constant feeling of damp in the chamber, even in summer. The jacquard-weave curtains were pulled back from the main entrance, and the labourers and soldiers tied to the Earl of Chesterham's extensive estates filed in, tired, hot and dirty from their day's work, settling themselves at the trestle tables in keen anticipation of food. Wine sloshed out from the pewter jugs set upon the tables and goblets were lifted aloft. The noise of chattering rose steadily to a pleasant hubbub as people began to relax, watching with glee as laden platters, steam ascending in veiled drifts, were brought out from the kitchens.

Turning to his son beside him, Ranulf raised his silver goblet, brimming with rich French wine. The deep red liquid swirled in the candlelight, almost spilling. 'It's so good to have you home, Gilan.' He touched the cup to his lips, swallowed deeply. 'And thank you,' he murmured. 'Thank you for telling us...how it truly happened.'

Seated between his mother and father, Gilan inclined his head tersely, staring grimly across the crowds of people thronging the hall. Telling his parents about Pierre's death had been the most difficult thing he had ever had to do, but somehow, the telling of it had not been as difficult as he had anticipated.

He knew why. Against the white damask tablecloth, a pair of twinkling, forget-me-not eyes flashed before him. With her generosity of spirit, her beautiful kindness, Matilda had never given up on him, chipping away at the hard shell around his heart, gradually exposing the grief, the loss and the guilt that churned within him since his brother's death. She had softened the hurt, diluted it, peeling the solid layers away with her generous smile, the lightest touch of her fingers against his arm, the fragrant press of her naked limbs against his own. She was his salvation, an angel shining through the shadowed storm of his grief.

So when his mother and he had left Matilda in the upstairs bedchamber to recover and sleep, and the time came that he must speak of Pierre to his parents, he had been able to tell them everything, about how he had caused the accident and how he blamed himself. He told them how he teased Pierre on that fateful morning, calling him a slug-a-bed for lolling about in his tent, not realising his brother was ill and burning up with a fever; told them how he wished, time and time, again, that it should have been him who had climbed the scaling ladder.

But they didn't blame him. With tears in their eyes, his mother had turned him in her arms and hugged him; his father Ranulf had squeezed his hand. In silence, they had walked together along the garden paths, listening to the furious scream of swallows diving in the air above, and remembered Pierre. Their son. His brother.

Abruptly, Gilan threw his napkin down on to his plate and pushed his chair back, the wooden legs scraping violently against the polished elm floor-boards. He had changed into a tunic of grey velvet for the evening's feasting, the expensive material pulling taut across the magnificent breadth of his shoulders.

'Where are you going?' His mother glanced up

at him in surprise. Her white-blond hair had been fashioned into an elaborate twist at the back of her head, secured with emerald pins. The jewels winked in the juddering candlelight, green fire.

'Matilda, I must see how she is,' he said. And he wanted to talk to her.

Marie laughed, glancing pointedly at Gilan's empty plate. 'Sit down, my son, and eat. She'll be sleeping for a good while yet. And I left Berta with her. She'll come down and tell us when she wakes up.'

'I must say, I can't wait to meet this young woman,' Ranulf said, his hand hovering above a platter of floury bread rolls. 'Disguised as a boy and acting as a guide for none other than Henry of Lancaster himself—she sounds a complete tearaway!' He bit down into the bread, loose white flour dusting his top lip.

'I thought so, too, when I first met her,' Gilan said, failing to spot the swift knowing glance between his parents. 'I was so wrong.' He threw himself down into the chair once more. A flicker of colour snared his attention and he looked up to see Isabelle walking alongside the trestles towards the dais. The front of her dress bulged outwards, declaring the advanced stage of her pregnancy.

He whipped his head around to his mother, brows

drawn together in question. 'She's pregnant!' he hissed, his mind rapidly calculating the months and days that he and Pierre had been out of the country. 'But how can that be?'

His mother raised her eyebrows, a tight smile playing across her lips. 'Precisely. How can that be? She swears blind that the child is Pierre's, but we all know it's not the truth—Pierre was away for the whole year, like you.'

'But she wants Pierre's inheritance and she'll claim it through the child,' Gilan replied grimly.

'Not now, my son, not now that you're home. You're witness to the fact that you were with your brother all this last year,' his mother said calmly. 'And besides, a certain Lord Robert of Havering is paying a great deal of interest towards her. I suspect the child is his.' Her tone was dry, scathing. 'Although I'm sure that won't stop her angling for you to be her next husband. She always had an eye for you.'

Gilan shrugged his shoulders. He wasn't especially interested in Isabelle's schemes. Before he had left on crusade she had been a flighty, unsteady maid, quick to drop into a melancholy, brooding mood. Pierre had despaired of her inconstant manner on several occasions, unsure how to deal with his wife's volatile behaviour.

'On second thoughts, I will go and see Matilda,' Gilan said, pushing back his chair, 'even if she is still sleeping.'

'Running away, my son?' Ranulf murmured, smiling ruefully, rubbing one hand across his sore leg. The wound he had sustained in France plagued him continually. 'I wish I could do the same.'

Gilan approached the wooden steps at the side of the dais as Isabelle placed one slippered foot on the bottom step. Her vast stomach pushed out her skirts, gathered with tiny pleats from an embroidered seam beneath her bosom. The pale pink silk rippled like water, the bodice sewn with sparkling seed beads in the shape of flowers.

'Isabelle, greetings. I trust you're faring well?' Gilan asked courteously, extending one hand down the three steps in order to help her up. 'Need a hand up, my lady?'

'Oh, Gilan, I didn't see you there!' Isabelle gasped out, twisting her mouth into what she hoped was a winning smile, fluttering her sparse eyelashes in his direction. 'I'm not moving very fast these days!' She indicated her belly with a significant glance.

His tanned fingers clasped around her hand; she clung on to him with a surprisingly strong grip as he hoisted her up. Standing on the level beside him, still holding on to his hand, Isabelle swept him with her hazel gaze, a smug, self-satisfied smile playing across her bloodless lips.

'Still a handsome devil, Gilan,' she murmured coyly, savouring the stunning shock of his bright hair, the metallic sparkle of his eyes. She raised one hand to touch the lean, tanned line of his jaw, but he pulled back, abruptly, before her fingers made contact, frowning at her over-familiarity.

'Behave yourself, Isabelle. My mother is waiting for you.'

'Oh, Gilan, don't be like this. I'm pleased to see you, that's all.' She peeked at him from under lowered lashes, smiling coquettishly. 'Can't I greet my brother-in-law in the proper manner?'

'This is hardly the proper manner, Isabelle.' He raised one gilt eyebrow in her direction. 'And well you know it.' Prising her fingers easily from his hand, he moved down the steps. 'You'll have to excuse me, Isabelle, but I am needed elsewhere.'

'Oh, can't you stay?' Isabelle whined, patting at the coils of her wispy, brown hair. Her mouth turned down at the corners, a sour expression. 'I have to endure your parents day in and day out. It would be a delight to talk to someone different.'

'No, I'm going up to see Matilda—the girl I brought back this afternoon,' he explained. 'She had a nasty bump on the head.'

'I know,' said Isabelle, stretching out her hand down to him, 'I heard all about it. But I'm sure the best thing for her at the moment is to sleep, without interruption.'

Gilan shrugged his shoulders. 'I will sit with her while she sleeps. I wouldn't want her to wake up and think we've all abandoned her.'

'Berta is sitting with her, so there's no need for you to go,' Isabelle remonstrated. A hot wash of colour swept across her thin face.

'She doesn't know Berta,' Gilan countered in a calm tone.

Isabelle placed her hands on her hips, a dangerous gleam entering her eyes. 'And she knows you, I suppose?'

Gilan frowned. 'Yes, of course she knows me. I brought her here, remember?'

Isabelle snorted. 'How could I forget? You practically ignored me when you carried her up the steps.'

He inclined his head in apology. 'Forgive me. But you will have to excuse me now, Isabelle, for I must go to her.'

A hardness dragged at Isabelle's mouth, compressing her lips into a grim, clenched line. 'Haven't you done enough for her?' Jealousy tore at her voice, a raw, bitter hatred. 'I want you to sit with me!' She dug her fingers into the hard muscles of his forearm, pointed nails scratching his flesh beneath his tunic.

Gilan raised his eyebrows at the change in Isabelle's tone, the shrewish questioning. Here was the true Isabelle, the one his brother had found so difficult to deal with. Across the white expanse of tablecloth, across the glowing pewter ware and glistening movement of eating knives, he could see his mother looking over, frowning, then rising from her chair.

'And I told you, Isabelle,' he replied, steel reinforcing his voice, 'that I am going to sit with Matilda.'

A triumphant glint entered Isabelle's eyes, and she folded her arms across her bosom, shaking her head. 'Well, I suppose I'll have to tell you then, Gilan.'

'Tell me…what?' he rapped out. His eyes narrowed dangerously, glimmering dark pewter.

'That she's gone.' Isabelle's words emerged with deadly clarity. 'Yes, that's right, Gilan, she couldn't bear to stay a moment longer once I told her the truth.'

'What…what truth?' he exploded, a harsh red colour streaking his taut cheekbones.

'That, my love…' Isabelle's voice subsided to a

teasing seductiveness, faintly gloating '...we are to be married, of course! Surely it makes sense.... Gilan! Come back here!'

But he had turned away from her, sprinting across the hall towards the stairs.

Tears pouring down her cheeks, Matilda stumbled up the forest path, tripping once again on the enormous hemline of Isabelle's gown. Her toes sank continuously into the fallen debris of leaves and twigs, a smell of rotting fungus assailing her nostrils. She gasped for breath, scrubbing angrily at her eyes. She couldn't seem to stop crying. Bracing one hand against the scratchy bark of a tree, her lungs compacted, fighting for air, pain slicing across her brow.

Her progress was slow, too slow! Her legs shook with the effort of moving, her muscles puny, uncooperative. All she wanted was to be away from Gilan's home as quickly as possible, so why was her body so unwilling to move? What was the matter with her? This godforsaken dress didn't help, the trailing hem catching at her toes with every step. Her heart had dropped in dismay when she viewed the clothes Isabelle had brought back for her; for a start, they seemed more suited to the winter months: a gown of pale green velvet, high-necked, and a hooded mantle of lilac wool, lined with grey silk. There had been no time to do her hair; she had bound it into a rough plait that snaked down her back and hoped it would suffice.

A drop of rain hit her face, trickled down her cheek. Then another, and another. She had to move, find shelter. Above her head, through the criss-crossing grid of branches, fat grey clouds obscured the limpid blue of the sky, bulging ominously. Black crows wheeled and circled above their nests in the lofty branches, their harried calls echoing like an alarm.

She laid her head against the trunk, hot tears trickling down her face. Why did this have to be so hard? What she had planned to do was not insurmountable: find her brother, go home. It was what she had planned to do all along, before she had met Gilan. Before. It was all so different now. *She* was different. Pushing her palms against the tree, her heart shuddered with grief, at the loss of a man who had become so dear to her. A man whom she loved. And now, this man, this man who said he was not worthy of her, would go to another. Had he been lying to her the whole time? Had he always known about the marriage to his sister-in-law? Of course, it made sense, for one brother to marry the dead brother's wife, to take care of her. Why had she not questioned him more, instead of blithely succumbing to his charms, to his beauty? Why had she been unable to resist? She shook her head in disbelief at her own stupidity. Foolish, foolish girl! She had to go on, to force herself to put one foot in front of the other, to kick out at the awkward skirts and clear a path. She must keep going. She had to.

Gilan ran like a man possessed, muscular legs covering the ground in graceful, loping strides, heavy rain striking the shadowed angles of his face. As soon as he had seen the empty bed, the linen on the mattress imprinted with the sweet outline of Matilda's body, he had raced from the chamber and down to the gatehouse, seizing a flaming torch from an iron bracket on the way out.

There was only one way she could have gone.

He followed the track into the forest, his eyes sweeping across the twilight, searching frantically, for the slightest clue, the smallest movement. Sparks radiated around his head, spitting out from the flaring torch, sizzling as the rain hit the flames. He would find her. Her mattress had still been warm from her body, fragrant with lavender scent.

'Matilda!' he yelled. 'Matilda, where are you?'

Perplexed, she heard the hoarse shout, then shook

her head, thinking she had imagined his voice. Gilan? Why on earth would he come after her? Surely he would be pleased that she had taken it upon herself to leave now that he was with Isabelle again?

'Matilda!' The voice was closer now, yards from her back.

She stumbled again, finally succumbing to the frailty in her legs. Sank to the ground in a puddle of skirts, knees embedding in a sticky patch of mud. So be it. Let him find her. She didn't care any more.

'Matilda!' He crouched down beside her, tipping up her chin with one finger, scrutinising her pale, wan face in the light of the flickering torch. Her voluminous hood fell back, silk rumpling in plush folds behind her slender neck, the lilac colour highlighting the startling blue of her eyes. Water sluiced down her face, dripping off her chin. 'Why did you leave?'

Raindrops sparkled on her eyelashes, fringing her eyes with diamonds. 'Because…because I have to find Thomas!' The words ripped out of her, jagged, uneven. 'I will lose my home unless my brother takes his rightful place as Lord of Lilleshall. John will take it all and try to take me, too.' She hoped he couldn't see her tears, the reddened skin around her eyes. Not that it mattered, of course.

'But that was no reason to leave. I told you, I will help you find Thomas…when you are recovered,' Gilan said softly.

'Yes, but that was before…before…' Her speech trailed away miserably, cold hands pillowing in damp skirts.

'Before…?' he probed gently, his hand reaching out to brush her forearm.

'Before that woman told me you were going to marry her!' she blurted out.

A rueful smile lifted the corners of his mouth. 'Isabelle isn't going to marry me.'

Matilda hunched her shoulders forwards. Sniffed, then looked away. 'Why would she say such a thing, then?'

He smiled. 'Because she's mad, Matilda. She sits up in her chambers, dreaming up these barmy schemes, working out what would be best for her. The baby isn't even my brother's, yet she makes out that it is. She's always been unstable, unpredictable. My poor brother had a devil of a time dealing with her. But all that matters is that it's not true.'

'Well, it doesn't matter to me anyway, whether you marry her or not.' Pushing her chin in the air, she attempted to inject an air of confidence into her tone.

'Doesn't it?' he said quietly. His husky voice

sifted around her, nudged up against her heart. In the jittery flame of the torch, his hair shone like knife blades. Above their heads, the breeze picked up and stirred the tops of the trees, rustling the leaves.

Her breath wobbled in her throat and she stared deep into the shimmering grey of his eyes. The words hung on her lips, the words she wanted to say. The truth. Dare she risk it? She plucked at the jewelled belt that Isabelle had insisted that she wore, her manner hesitant, uncertain.

His hand covered hers, warm and strong, stilling her nervous movement. 'There's only one person I want to marry, Matilda, and she's sitting right here in front of me.'

'W-what?' she stuttered out, jerking her head up, stunned.

'I've been an ignorant pig,' he said. 'A stupid, blockheaded, ignorant pig.'

'Oh, I wouldn't—' she began.

'Don't you dare tell me that my behaviour was fine, that you understand,' he interrupted her, grinning. 'Because it wasn't fine and you have a perfect right to hate me, after the way I treated you. God forbid that I ever treat you like that again!'

She shook her head dumbly, a sense of wonderment flooding through her. The smallest trickle of hope seeped through the hard-packed earth of her resolve, gathering strength, knocking at her heart. 'I don't understand...' Her voice quavered. 'I left because I didn't want to be a burden to you. I didn't want you to feel any responsibility for me... after...after what happened between us. And then when Isabelle said you were going to marry her...' her voice drifted to such a subdued pitch, he had to lean forwards to catch her words '...I couldn't stay and watch all that. I thought that was the end.' Her tone trod carefully, muted, not daring to hope.

The calloused pad of his thumb caressed the delicate line of her jaw, ran over the rosebud push of her mouth; her flesh shivered beneath the delicious sensation. 'I've been a fool, Matilda. From the moment I first saw you, drawing back your bow at the top of the ruined turret, you began to change me, but I refused to admit it. I thought that after Pierre died, my heart would never recover, would never know again how to love another.'

His fingers tangled with hers, tightened.

'Love?' she whispered. Emotion rocked her, her tears of misery turning to those of joy. 'Are you saying what I think you are saying?'

'Yes,' he said. 'I love you, my sweet darling Matilda, I love you with all my heart.' The flaming torch dropped to the ground, hissing and spitting against the wet ground, as Gilan wound his arms about her slight frame, drawing her closer, upwards so the thud of his heart matched the race of her own. He touched his lips to hers, then groaned, covering her mouth with his in a kiss that would bind them together, for ever.

Epilogue

Summer flowers trailed from the hefty wooden rafters of the great hall at Chesterham: huge garlands of pink roses, entwined with glossy ivy, honeysuckle, and lavender. The fragrance filled the hall, the scent thick and heavy. A makeshift band played, lively fiddle music accompanied by pipes and drums. The trestle tables had been pushed back and couples danced, faces happy and flushed with wine, linking hands and arms as they skipped across the uneven flagstone floor.

'Oh, Gilan, I cannot believe this is truly happening,' Matilda leaned over and whispered in her husband's ear, her heart swelling with love for the man at her side. Tiny white rosebuds had been woven through her beautiful silky hair, complementing the cream silk of her wedding gown. 'Are we actually married? Is this real?' She stared down at the simple gold band shining on her left hand.

'If it's not, then I'm having the same amazing dream as you,' Gilan replied, planting a delicate kiss on the end of her pert little nose. A roar of appreciation rose from the throng of people dancing below the high dais.

'And Thomas…Thomas is here,' she breathed, following the tall, dark-haired man weaving in and out of the dancers. 'Thank you Gilan, thank you for finding him, for bringing him here.'

'It wasn't difficult. Once Henry had challenged King Richard, his knights were happy to return to their homes. Sick of all the fruitless fighting.'

Matilda covered Gilan's hand with her own. 'Now Thomas can return to Lilleshall and claim his home once more.'

'And appreciate his little sister for all her hard work,' Gilan added, flexing strong fingers beneath her warm palm, 'as well as all the sacrifices she has made to keep the estate running.'

Matilda shrugged her shoulders. 'He does appreciate what I have done, Gilan. Besides I enjoyed it—' she caught her husband's wry expression '—well, most of it, anyway.'

'I'll have to make sure I find some heavy farm work for you to do when we return to Cormeilles,' he teased. 'And a few outlaws for you to shoot.'

'Oh, Matilda's never happy unless she's scavenging around in the fields somewhere,' Katherine chipped in, her tiny daughter sleeping contentedly in her arms. With John pleading illness, she had come to the wedding alone with only her ladies-in-waiting in attendance. 'You'll have to remember to rein her in, Gilan. She's a regular hoyden.'

Gilan laughed. 'I will do no such thing, Katherine. I love Matilda of Lilleshall exactly the way she is. Beautiful. Kind. The sweetest person I have ever had the luck to meet. I love her with all my heart.'

Along the table, he caught his father's eye and grinned. With one arm tight around Gilan's mother, Ranulph lifted his pewter goblet, inclining his head in silent congratulation towards his son. At his father's quiet gesture, a soaring happiness rose in Gilan's chest, an overwhelming joy, brimming with possibility and hope, but above all with love—love for his family, and love for the darling wife at his side.

* * * * *

MILLS & BOON®

Why shop at millsandboon.co.uk?

Each year, thousands of romance readers find their perfect read at millsandboon.co.uk. That's because we're passionate about bringing you the very best romantic fiction. Here are some of the advantages of shopping at www.millsandboon.co.uk:

* **Get new books first**—you'll be able to buy your favourite books one month before they hit the shops

* **Get exclusive discounts**—you'll also be able to buy our specially created monthly collections, with up to 50% off the RRP

* **Find your favourite authors**—latest news, interviews and new releases for all your favourite authors and series on our website, plus ideas for what to try next

* **Join in**—once you've bought your favourite books, don't forget to register with us to rate, review and join in the discussions

Visit **www.millsandboon.co.uk**
for all this and more today!